Dear Stephanie

by Mandi Castle

All the best

Warm wishes

Prologue

I look across the kitchen at the granite bar and see my seven oxy pills lined up in a perfect row. I can hardly believe it's here.

The last day of my life.

I walk into the kitchen and make a dry Ketel One martini, cut a twist of lemon, and drop it in my drink.

"Plunk," it says to me.

I carry the martini back to the bar, stand next to it, and place one of the pills on the tip of my tongue.

"One," I say aloud and take a drink. It burns a little going down but warms quickly in my belly.

I think about my morning, the steps I took to get here. The sun spills through the floor-to-ceiling windows and bounces off the white walls to illuminate the room. I spent the morning cleaning my apartment. The smell of bleach mixed with lemon furniture polish fills the room, the smell of clean. The books align perfectly with the edge on the bookshelf. On the dining table, my pearl white blown glass vase houses a crisp bouquet of pink tulips. Perfect V's left behind by the vacuum cleaner adorn the plush white rug. The morning was well spent, perfecting the perfection.

I take another pill, place it on my tongue, and swallow a big drink of the martini. "Two," I utter for nobody's ears but my own.

I can't stop thinking about him. And more than him, her. The two of them. It's painful, and it hurts too much. I have to do this.

"Three," I say as I swallow the third pill.

I walk into my bathroom to take one last look at myself. I chose an outfit perfect for the occasion, something I won't mind being found in, something beautiful like me. A purple silk blouse and black pencil skirt paired with my favorite peacock feathered Manolo Blahniks and two carat princess cut emerald stud earrings. I can see my outer beauty, full lips, flawless skin, big round brown eyes, large breasts, long blonde hair. Outside, transcendence. Inside, emptiness. A wide gaping hole of sorrow.

I grab my phone and make two calls. I leave a voicemail for each. I knew they wouldn't answer, which was part of my plan.

With a sigh, I turn and walk back to the bar.

"Four," I say as I swallow another pill. I grab my phone and tap play on the suicide playlist that I made specifically for today. The slow guitar intro of "The Funeral" by Band of Horses sadly strums through the speakers. I close my eyes and let the music hold me for a minute.

"Five," another pill.

My head begins to feel heavy, and my body starts to tingle.

"Six," I say to the empty room. My heart races a little as I swallow this one. I remind myself that I'm doing what's best. For everyone.

I look at my last pill, take a deep breath, and place it on my tongue. "Seven," I say and smile as I drain the rest of my martini.

Stephanie

Dear Diary—no too cliché.

Dear Journal—no too formal.

Dear mystery person who will never read this—no, no.

Dear Stephanie ... hmmm. Dear Stephanie, I had a shit day. Dear Stephanie, I just had the most amazing sex. Dear Stephanie, I want to drown in my bathtub. Okay, Dear Stephanie it is. Here goes nothing.

Dear Stephanie,

It all started with a suicide, or an attempt rather. Because I'm here on a sunny day, running my fingers over the letters of my keyboard, telling you my story.

I tend to be successful in most of my endeavors. When I want something, I get it. It's simple, but for some reason, I haven't quite found the right combination to make it work. I've tested lots of concoctions. One day, I'll figure it out. Until then, I've been given an assignment. Let's just call it a detailed suicide letter. To you.

Apparently, I need to journal. I'm told this by my therapist. Yes, I'm in therapy. That's kind of apropos. It went something like this: Swallow six Xanax. Don't die. End up in therapy. You're not surprised, are you? Typical for a crazy. A big trail of baggage follows me everywhere I go.

Luckily, my new therapist just happens to be one of the most beautiful male specimens on the face of the Earth. Thank God for that. Otherwise, I might just throw myself off a bridge. Actually, a violent death scares me. When I envision myself ending my own life, I can't imagine a gunshot or a noose, or even a tall building. There will be no slit wrists in bathtubs. That might leave a scar. I'll go out sleeping, thank you very much. As soon as I figure out what pills will work. Lord knows I've tried several times.

I'm depressed. I know. I know. How can someone like me be depressed, right? I'm witty. I'm beautiful, and charming to boot. From the outside looking in, I look like I have it all. A twenty-nine-year-old trust fund baby living alone in a luxury apartment in the heart of downtown Dallas who doesn't work because it's unnecessary, has no family that she cares to speak to, and enjoys the occasional company of a pool of people she calls friends. Yeah, daddy took care of his baby, and now I get to live on his hard-earned money. Not a bad life ... most of the time. But apathy eats at my soul, and melancholy chews on my heart because well, sometimes life gives you lemons, and sometimes life gives you a huge heaping pile of shit.

Too much too soon, Steph? Then let's talk about Dr. Love aka the therapist. No, that's not his real name, but I'm a nickname sort of girl, and Dr. Love fits him. When I was assigned my therapist, I was told I would be seeing the utmost respected psychiatrist in the state upon my release from asylum. I refuse to see psychologists anymore because, come on, it's a waste of time. Trust me, I've walked this road a thousand times, at least. I need someone with a prescription pad for that one beautiful side effect of therapy—the drugs. Then she, my nurse in the loony bin, said she'd get an appointment set up with Dr. Morea right away. I rolled my eyes picturing an overweight oaf with a mustache sitting in a big brown leather chair with his greasy comb-over smelling of cheap aftershave. Dread understated my feelings of our first meeting.

Well, how surprised was I when I walked into Dr. Love's office to find the most amazingly perfect man sitting not in a brown leather chair, but in a nice plush chair the color of an eggplant? He sat in his purple chair reading something, probably my file detailing my past, expecting Lindsay Lohan on a bender to come through the door. Trust me, it's all in there: drugs, sex, rape, depression, multiple suicide attempts, and probably more than I really want to know. He looked up from the file but not all the way up, just sort of halfway so he was glancing at me from below his thick, black eyebrows with these beautiful coffee colored eyes. The shock on his face was priceless. I know. Where's my iPhone when I need it, right?

He clearly was not expecting me. I am above average in the looks category. Seriously, I'm not vain or arrogant, okay maybe I am, but God blessed me with the beauty gene. I inherited it from my mother who, in her prime, made people gasp when she walked into the room, and my father, well, his long line of mistresses would tell you that he is quite the looker. I am five feet nine with thick natural blonde hair (that I'm not above highlighting), dark brown eyes, and flawless skin. My mother is Cherokee Indian, so I got her high angular cheek bones, her rich dark eyes, and her beautiful tan skin. Thanks, Mom. My dad's family immigrated to America from Sweden, so basically think St. Pauli Girl meets Pocahontas. Also, I'm not an idiot. In fact, I'm quite the opposite, and when you mix brains and beauty, it can be lethal.

Dr. Love looked up from my emotionally shocking file and saw me enter the room. I know the look, and he wore it. I confidently walked over to the couch, also eggplant, and sat down and looked around the room. Pretty empty, a desk in the corner with nothing on top, no pictures of a wife/lover/family, a wall of floor-to-ceiling bookshelves lined with encyclopedias and typical psych books, a lamp on each end table, and of course a box of tissues for when I lose my shit over ... you name it. Pfft, as if.

I wore a short tan skirt and a white button up silk blouse unbuttoned just enough so that my perfect (surgically enhanced) breasts would be noticed but not the center of attention. I like that to be my face. I wore minimal make-up that day with my hair down.

I sat on the purple couch, resting my elbow on the arm of one end, and put my feet up on the dark mahogany table, crossed my ankles, then ran my left foot up and down my smooth shin, trying to get a rise. Wink. He looked at my feet but said nothing. I smirked and took inventory of the beautiful creature sitting in front of me.

Now, Dr. Love was not the only shocked person. Imagine my surprise when I saw this god sitting there expecting me to divulge all of my life's secrets. I mean, I never tell guys the truth about me. Never. What guy is going to fuck me if he knows I have to take a little blue pill every morning so that I don't stick a gun in my mouth and blow my brains out? Exactly. Zero. So, they all think I'm everything but a depressed suicidal lunatic, which is fine. They don't stick around long enough to hear the truth. I don't let them.

When I learned my new therapist was male, my heart danced a little. I always divorce my female therapists immediately. They, like most of my shared gender, sort of hate me, and frankly, the feeling is mutual. Male therapists, though. I can play this game. With expectations of a mustached perv, I purposely dressed the way I did. You see, I had a plan. I wanted to give the impression that I had it all together but also look sexy. Pervs are easy. I planned to seduce him. Flirt with him during our first few meetings, occasionally letting him get a peek at my cleavage and watching him get a semi while I hike my skirt up to scratch my upper thigh as I toss my hair over my shoulder and arch my back, parting my lips ever so slightly. It's a science, the subject where I excel the most. I can control men, the easiest thing in my world. They are puppets waiting for a puppet master. I just dangle the strings of my marionettes and watch them dance my choreographed routine.

Not my first rodeo, Steph.

The plan: He would fall in love with me and give me everything I wanted. Mostly drugs, but also, I needed him to let my mental hospital where I recently spent thirty-plus days know that I graduated therapy and would no longer need to waste my time on bi-weekly meetings with said specialist. Well, hell. That's out the door. Seduction yes, but when I saw this coal-eyed angel in the room, therapy would have to last for, well forever. So, that blew my plan. I had to come up with a new one, one that hopefully would result in my blowing Dr. Love.

I'm sort of a planner but not the kind who writes down lists and has sticky notes scattered as reminders around her apartment. Actually, I do make lists but funny ones, not the typical, "Get through therapy. Take your pill. Don't kill yourself." I write lists like, "Top Five Reasons Why I Should Break up with (insert douchebag's name)." I like to write lists and send them to my best friend. Then I make her call me and read them out loud over the phone saying, "Number One:" (She can't just say *one*. I also make her say *number*). "Number Five: His penis is curved downward, downward, not upward, which we all know is the wrong direction. No G-spot pleasure with a downward facing dick. Number Four: He refuses to manscape. Not gonna put my mouth anywhere near a nub in a shrub. Right, that's why he's "Danny Dumped." And so on until she gets to number one and we both have a good laugh at my current lover's expense. She loves my wit.

I have one girl friend, Janie. She's also beautiful, striking actually, the kind of beautiful that's not stereotypical but breathtakingly gorgeous. She's only five one with fiery auburn hair and iridescent white skin. Bone white, the girl glows in the dark, and it's porcelain. She's a true ginger, fire crotch and all. Her piercing blue eyes can cut through steel, and her body. Her body is magnificent, so amazing it should be sculpted and put in the Vatican. It's so perfect, not super thin, curvy actually, but in all the right places, giant natural breasts and booty for days. She's the kind of beauty that inspires artists to dedicate their entire lives attempting to duplicate her.

She stumbled into my life when we were eight years old. I met her riding the bus home from a field trip one day during third grade. Twin girls with curly black hair and over-sized foreheads were sitting behind her calling her carrot top. I saw that she had started to cry, not actual tears but a lip quivering cry, and I felt bad for her, so I walked over and sat next to her. I turned to one of the twins, I'm not sure which one because they were completely identical and said, "Hey, five-head, shut it."

Janie immediately went from quivering to ballsy, pushed herself past me and took the other twin into a full-on choke hold. I kicked Tweedle-Dee in the shins, made her fall down, and then punched her in the face.

The bus driver quickly realized what was going on, stopped the bus, and separated all of us. The next day, our motley foursome had to go see the headmaster of our school. The twins went in first, together of course with their pinched-face mother. They both came out red-faced and sniffling. Janie and her mom went in second, and when she came out, she was crying, actual tears this time. She made eye contact and gave me a "thanks for saving my ass" look, and since then we've been best friends. I went in last, alone, which was typical. We had to stay in after school detention for two weeks. During which time, we passed notes making fun of the teacher and the rest of the troglodytes in the room. Janie is by far the coolest person on this Earth, next to me of course. Without Janie, I would not be alive.

She's seen me at my worst and at my best. She may as well have ridden into my life on a white horse, all armored in kindness because she's the one person who I know without a doubt, I can count on, have always counted on. She was the first person to convince me to go to therapy back when we lived together in college and she saw the dark monster I call depression. She set up an appointment with this woman who wore her hair in a lumpy ponytail who conde-scendingly cocked her head to one side every time she asked me a question. I fired her after one session, which will not be happening now, thanks to Dr. Love.

Not gonna lie, Steph. I'm not unthrilled about *this* ther-apist.

I sat on his purple couch, and we did the introductory doctor-patient tango.

"Hi, I'm Paige Preston. I was sent here."

"I know, Ms. Preston," he interrupted me. "I've read your file. You don't have to say any more."

What the what? I've never been to a therapist where I don't have to say more. I'm in love. What? Too soon? Well, you haven't seen him.

"I understand you have battled with depression for quite some time. You don't have to go into it right now. I know it's been a rough couple of months for you."

To which I replied, "Well let's see ... I overdosed, had to stay in a crazy ass loony bin, have daily, I mean daily, group therapy sessions where I met a plethora of crazies like me. Group therapy, by the way, is a complete waste of time. The specialists finally allowed me to sleep in a bed with a blan-ket, which was scratchy, thin, and terribly cheap, after weeks of suicide watch and being monitored even in the most private, I mean personal, moments. And the best part was every time I was given a pill, the mad bitch in the pharma-cy made me show her my empty pill-less mouth." I looked up, making eye contact, and raised one eyebrow. "Oh, or were you talking about the rape? Yeah, pretty fucking rough, Doc." I know. I'm sort of a bitch. Don't judge.

"Yeah, like I said, we don't have to get into that right now. Why don't I tell you about me?"

Oh, yeah, doc, I thought to myself. Tell me what you look like with that pin-striped custom fit dress shirt unbut-toned and un-tucked. Let's discuss the shape of your hips when you remove those wonderfully snug brown trousers. Professional look, hot. Now, let's drop these clothes on the floor and let me straddle you and show you how to get totally and organically fucked. My number one subject. I am dynamite in the sack. Think explosive, slutty enough to do the things that guys fantasize about and dirty enough to enjoy them at the same time. Throw in my killer body and my mother's genes, and men can't get enough of me. I'm pretty fucking hot, and I like to fuck, so you know, win-win.

I also have an uncontrollable libido. It's kind of an anomaly actually. Often people who take my daily blue pill experience low sex drives and some even suffer the terrible side effect of the inability to orgasm. But not I. I can't imagine. I'd rather live with the monster of depression than not have orgasms. They make the world go round. I'm sure Dr. Love will have some theories on this, but for now, let's just imagine him naked on top of me.

While Dr. Love talked about himself for the rest of our session, I imagined his mouth between my legs. I found it terribly hard to concentrate on what he was saying. I kept getting distracted by his lips, his soft, pink, full lips and his stubble, black sprinkled with occasional silver specks. I'm a sucker for stubble. I love the way it feels on my skin, so when I wasn't staring at his utterly kissable lips, I was focused on how it would feel if his stubble brushed up against my thigh, my breast, oh my god, my neck. I practically came right there in his office. He finished saying whatever it was he was saying and escorted me to the door.

"Ms. Preston, thank you for meeting with me today. It was a pleasure getting to know you," he said as he leaned casually against the door jam. It was almost like he didn't want me to leave.

"Oh, Doc, the pleasure was all mine." I squeezed his bicep, earning a look of surprise from him with my forwardness, and turned away. I glanced over my shoulder at him standing in the doorway as I took the first step down the stairs. A sly smile reached the corner of his mouth.

As far as therapy sessions go, and I've had plenty, this one was by far my favorite.

Parnevik

Dear Stephanie,

Today is Saturday, and I have no plans. That's unusual for me, as my social calendar usually keeps me occupied on the weekends, but today, nothing. It's 12:30 p.m. I'm in bed, having one of those days. I can't seem to force myself from my warm cocoon, so I figure, why not? Let's talk to Steph.

I had a great session with Dr. Love yesterday. For the past six weeks, I've seen him twice a week, or more if I have a breakdown (which I sometimes feign when I need my dose of Dr. Love). He asked me how the journaling is going. I didn't really know how to respond. He only told me that I needed to do it last week, and I've made one, *just one*, entry. He gave me no parameters. He didn't tell me to write daily or weekly or whenever I want, just said to write down my thoughts and emotions.

The session went something like this: I walked in, sat on the purple couch, and started playing with a strand of hair, twirling it between my fingers then pulling straight. It's kind of my nervous habit. I wore a total fuck me outfit, which I always wear on Fridays so I can ensure the doc will jerk himself off with images of me over the weekend. I chose one of my favorites—short black dress shorts with a two-inch cuff at the thigh paired with a black and white striped fitted V neck short sleeved top (it's August in Texas) that hugs tight at the waist and stretches perfectly across my chest offering not only a view of my amazing cleavage but perfectly enhancing the girls in all the right places. I put this tease of an outfit on, and I want to fuck myself. I've never waited this long. I figured I'd show doc that I'm a sure thing and, if he didn't take the bait, I'd run through his imagination throughout the weekend. I also wore one my favorite perfumes. Gucci Envy. Guys want to lick it off, it smells so good.

He actually gasped when he sat down in his chair, sucked in his breath through is teeth. I love that sound, but instead of climbing on top of me and ripping off my shorts, he did the psychiatrist thing and started in on asking me questions.

"Ms. Preston," he started.

"Please, doc, please call me Paige." I mean six weeks and he still uses my last name, six weeks of sitting on his couch, looking perfect, and he hasn't made a move. Six weeks of surveys, meditation techniques, hammering questions about suicide, triggers, and asking the same goddamned questions about my family, my tendency to do drugs when I'm depressed, my personality. I evade these questions as well as I can. I think I'm annoying Dr. Love a little. I could help him relieve some of that tension, but he has to get naked first and, for the love of all that's holy, call me by my first name. Good grief.

"I'm not ready to call you Paige yet, Ms. Preston. I hardly know anything about you. Let's talk more about your drug addiction, Ms. Preston." Emphasis on *Ms. Preston.*

Dr. Love was growing frustrated. Maybe he should have taken five deep breaths and thought of his happy place.

"I don't have a drug addiction, *Jeremiah?*"

"Ms. Preston, call me Dr. Morea. Why don't we start with some relaxation techniques to calm you before we get into anything heavy."

I closed my eyes and listened to his velvet voice. I couldn't help but think about his calling me Ms. Preston, which made me drift back a few years.

Let me tell you, Stephanie, about Paige Preston. See, Preston isn't even my real last name. My given name was or is Parnevik. Thanks for that one, dad. My whole life people said stuff like, "Parnevik will suck your dick." When your last name kind of rhymes with dick, and you're known as a slut around school ... well, kids can be cruel and frankly not clever. I also hate my dad and all things that tie me to him, other than his money, so it was an easy decision. I legally changed my name the day after my twenty-fifth birthday when I was granted access to my entire trust fund. "Preston" has its own story. It's sort of a tribute, really.

When I was in the eleventh grade, a handsome anatomy teacher strolled into my world. Mr. Preston was one of the young teachers, the ones who blend right in with the students, smooth and unscathed by years of enduring low pay and obnoxious entitled teenagers.

He was the picture of perfection, a piece of delectable chocolate eye candy, the kind you put in your mouth and hold to savor the taste and let it melt just enough before you chew. Delicious. He stood at least six four, a former college basketball player turned high school basketball coach.

They usually have to teach a class, too, so he taught anatomy, and as soon as he walked into my high school, I went straight into research mode. I found out what he taught and immediately changed my courses and placed myself in his eighth period anatomy class, the last class of the day, that way, on Fridays, I would be the last girl he saw before the weekend, and just like Dr. Love, he'd picture me. I was always able to get the office staff to do whatever I wanted, namely because my father donated an exuberant amount of funds to my private all-girls school.

Being placed in his class began a thrilling infatuation. I waited all day for anatomy. Seventh period literature, my former favorite subject, started to drag. I sat watching the clock, half-heartedly contributing to the discussions of some of my favorite novels, waiting for the bell so that I could jump from my desk, fumbling my books in time to make it to the girls' room to reapply lip gloss and brush my hair. I would run from the restroom to the science hall and stand two doors down to compose myself before I entered his class. I always slipped into my desk just before the bell rang, and there he would stand. Dark and statuesque, with a gentle confidence, shoulders squared, chin held high, a quiet smile playing on his lips, and I would wrap myself in the electric bolt of heat that he shot through my skin, watching every slight move he made with teenage admiration. I fell in love. Yearning, irrational, heart-swelling-in-my-chest love. You know, teenage love. Full of imagination and fantasy. Thoughts filled with holding hands and kissing, lying in bed, enveloped in heat and lust. And it grew. A tiny delicate seed developed into a monstrous weed, and I could no longer contain an imaginary relationship. I needed more.

I turned on my charm. We had to wear uniforms, blue and green plaid skirts and white button up shirts that were required to be tucked in, and black shoes. Other than that, we could be individuals. Pfft. So since I couldn't wear the kind of clothes to get his attention, I played the girl who needed help so she wouldn't fail this class, which would seriously piss off my super-rich dad who contributed probably more money in a semester than Mr. Preston made in an entire year.

I deliberately made poor grades. Do you know how hard it is to take a test when you know all of the answers and purposely miss just enough so that you'll make a sixty-nine? Yes, that pun was fully intended. Pretty difficult, a task only one with stellar intelligence can complete.

I'll wait for your applause.

About five weeks into the semester I managed to get my grade low enough that I would be able to get it back up before the end of the semester and also not so low that I would actually get an F on my report card. Daddy didn't like his baby girl to get failing grades, which is why one Friday after class, I walked up to his desk and asked if he offered any tutoring. I knew the answer was yes, but in my most pouty, sweet school girl voice, I said, "Mr. Preston. Do you have a minute?" as I twirled a strand of blonde hair between my fingers.

"Of course, Paige. Is something wrong?"

"Well, kind of. I'm not doing very well in your class. I'm sort of ... failing," I said and looked at the floor and pressed my black Mary Jane into the linoleum squishing an imaginary spider.

"Yes, Paige. You are failing, no sort of about it," he replied all baritone and sexy, sending shivers down my neck.

He suggested that I join a group of other students over the weekend who were working on an extra credit project.

"Geez, I can't this weekend. My parents are flying me to Barbados to meet them at their beach house. I was sort of thinking of maybe tutoring? You do have tutoring sessions, right?" I said in my "please Mr. Preston" voice.

Marionette strings, Steph, remember?

"Yes, I do offer tutoring after school on Tuesdays and Thursdays from 4:00–5:00. Would you like to join the group?"

Group? No, we can't have sex in front of a group, Mr. Preston.

I explained that I work better one-on-one and that I didn't think I would benefit from group tutoring all while biting my lower lip and looking at him through fluttering eyelashes. "I'll pay you for the time. I mean, I know you have a life, and I don't want you to feel like you're not getting anything out of this." Money always gets the teachers. Our poor messed up society pays teachers pennies considering what they have to deal with, even at my prestigious private school, so I played the money card on more than one occasion when I needed it.

"Why don't we meet on Monday then, after class? Will that work with your schedule? Will you be back from Barbados?" he said, with a little disdain really.

"I will." I wasn't really going to Barbados. I just made that up so that I wouldn't have to spend my weekend with a bunch of idiots who needed extra credit to pass anatomy. I mean it's anatomy. The foot bone's connected to the leg bone. The leg bone's connected to the thigh bone. You know the song, only Mr. Preston made us use the scientific terms. The phalanges connected to the metacarpals, and so on ... ha. I actually missed that one on one of the quizzes.

He also said that he would need a consent form filled out by my parents as well as Dr. Walker (the headmaster of the school.) Easy enough.

"I really appreciate it, Mr. Preston. Is there any extra credit work I can do over the weekend while I'm on the plane? It's like a three-hour flight."

"Sure, just let me get you some worksheets you can complete." He bent over into the filing cabinet he kept behind his desk while I measured up his scrumptious gluteus maximus, a constant practice of mine when he turned to write on the whiteboard. Mr. Preston had an award winning ass. He wore a suit almost every day, a requirement at my school, but he never left the jacket on, always draping it over the back of his chair. Anytime I walked past his desk, I would purposely drop something just so I could get a whiff of his scent. He wore a spicy sort of woodsy cologne, masculine and musky, and it suited him perfectly.

His pants fit him perfectly, like a glove made for a golden ass. He didn't keep his wallet in his pants pocket, so there was never a barrier between his ass and my eyes, just fifty-five minutes of pure admiration. Obviously, anatomy was my favorite subject. I manipulated myself into a front row seat by suggesting one of the girls in the front row trade seats. We all drooled over Mr. Preston, so she did not welcome the suggestion. She consistently threw me the eat-shit-and-die look throughout the rest of the year. Whatever, one more reason for her to hate me.

The next Monday rolled around, and we had a pretty good tutoring session, just Mr. Preston and me. I played the "Oh, I see" game when Mr. Preston taught me some cutesy way to remember the bones of the hand. I knew the bones of the hand, but a girl's gotta do, right? We continued to have our sessions every Monday for a couple of weeks, and what? Yeah, yeah, I made a C on my first report card. I thanked and thanked Mr. Preston for his time and cheered with him as we celebrated my mediocrity. I even jumped up and down and clapped.

He slowly began to turn. I noticed that occasionally, when he lectured, he would let his hand linger on my desk or the back of my chair. He made eye contact with me regularly, and on some occasions when I faked amazement at the endocrine system or something like that, he would shoot me a brief smile and a wink. I knew that if we kept meeting at the school, he'd never end up between my legs, so I had to come up with a plan. I decided that I needed to convince him to come to my house for tutoring.

I went home one night and sat on my bed half pouting, half venting, but mostly planning. What would be my next move? He loved basketball. He talked about it all the time. He was a huge Mavericks fan, so I decided to go with that angle. I called my brother, Patrick, and had him tell me everything he knew about the team. I took notes and studied. I even watched a couple of games. It was actually kind of fun, a breathtaking sport where big, beautiful dark-skinned men run back and forth across a court, pouring sweat all over their giant tattooed biceps. Why hadn't I watched this before?

The next week during tutoring I casually mentioned Tuesday night's game and how we (the Dallas Mavericks because now they were my team) almost lost it to the Heat if not for so and so's (I don't remember the name anymore) last minute three pointer.

"You watch basketball, Paige? I had no idea. Well, except for the school's games." (Girls basketball ... snore, but I went to almost every game to watch him in his glory. I even cheered in the stands.)

"Mr. Preston, I have twin brothers who eat, sleep, and breathe sports. It's practically in my DNA."

"DNA, huh? You've been paying attention. I didn't think any of the girls at this school cared about sports, even most of the girls on our team. I'm surprised."

"Yeah, I'm a fan. Go Mavericks. I watch all the games."

"Really? That's kind of impressive, Paige."

"Thanks Mr. Preston. Have a good night." I should have added, "Thinking about me in nothing but your Mavericks jersey."

I can't remember how long it took for him to come around, but I remember the day vividly. In a weird way, we were becoming friends. I got the feeling that he didn't really have many friends, kind of like me. Sometimes we would sit after our sessions and talk, mostly about sports, but sometimes about life. He couldn't get over the fact that I had a nanny and a maid who cooked all of my meals. I just thought that was normal. Most of the girls at my school had nannies and maids.

Their mothers couldn't be bothered to drop off and pick up children from school, to clean their own piss from their bathrooms. There was too much gossip waiting to be had at the country club where they would all sit around a table, sizing each other up over white wine spritzers while discussing the latest tennis pro and which one of them was going to be next in my dad's bed. All except for Janie's mom. Janie's mom stayed home where she organized volunteer groups that fed the homeless around Dallas, or found homes for neglected mutts, or somehow turned rain into sunshine. Janie's mom should have taught them all a lesson in motherhood.

Mr. Preston found my lifestyle fascinating, and the more we talked, he slowly began telling me more about himself. He loved to talk about playing college basketball. I pretended to care but truly just sat half listening so I could calculate my next move. Then he said, "Well, Paige, I'm starving. Do you want to grab a bite to eat at Joey's? I know a bunch of the girls from the team will be there."

Bingo! Cha-ching cha-ching cha-ching.

"Oh, Mr. Preston, I would love to, but Willa won't be happy if I do. She always has my food ready for me when I get home, so I'd hate to upset her. Plus, she doesn't like to eat alone."

"Oh, well okay," he started to say.

"Mr. Preston, I have a great idea. Why don't you join us for dinner? Willa's an amazing cook, and I'm sure whatever she's prepared for tonight will be delicious. Seriously, she still cooks enough for my brothers, even though they've been in college for three years, so there will be plenty. Plus, you'll love her. She tells the best stories. Come on. I insist."

"Willa will be there?"

"Of course, she'd never leave me home alone to eat by myself. It's kind of an understanding we have since my brothers left for school."

"Paige, thanks, but it's probably not appropriate if your parents aren't home."

"Mr. Preston, my parents are never home. Willa is practically my second mom. She's worked for us since I was ten. She would love another grown-up to talk to over a meal. Seriously. It's fine."

I watched the wheels turn in his mind as he thought for a minute.

"It's fine. I promise," I reaffirmed.

"Well, if you're sure she won't mind. Okay, what the hell? I mean heck, sorry."

"Geez Mr. Preston, watch your language," I said, and we both laughed. I gave him my address and told him to meet me there in thirty. I had to get home and do some damage control.

See, Steph, Willa and I never ate together. She and I had a hate-hate relationship. The truth is, Willa never stood a chance. Growing up with maids and nannies, one gets used to a sort of revolving door, and we certainly had our share of maids cycle through, but I had one nanny for most of my childhood.

Lucy was our nanny before I was even born. She was all things soft and warm with chubby arms that always welcomed me into a warm hug. I loved to lay my head on her chest and listen to her sing songs in Spanish. I learned Spanish along with English and was bilingual from the time I could speak. She always wrote me notes in Spanish and tucked them into my lunch box, signing them, *Te amo, Lucy.*

She loved me. I never had any doubt. She used to lay in my bed with me at night when I was scared and shush me to sleep. She always made me blueberry pancakes for breakfast even though my father told her they were going to make me fat. She introduced me to books and showed me the splendor of wrapping myself in someone else's words. I've been addicted to books since, reading one after the next before even coming up for air.

Lucy talked to me, not at me like adults tend to do children. I cherished that woman, adored her in a way that I've never cared for anyone else.

Then one day, she was gone. My brothers told me that she left us, that she didn't want to be with us anymore, which I refused to believe. I asked relentlessly about her, even tried to find her family, but I never got anywhere with it. At eight years old, my resources were limited. I later learned one night after my mother had finished a bottle of Cabernet that my father fired her because she caught him with a woman, and she had threatened to tell my mother. As if that was any news to my mother. I hated him for firing her, still do actually. Lucy was the only adult who I ever truly trusted as a child. A string of nannies followed, but nobody ever stuck until he hired Willa. Like I said, she didn't stand a chance. Lucy's shoes were impossible to fill, so I never let myself get attached.

She and I had an understanding. I wouldn't tell my dad that she kept a bottle of rum in the pantry from which she sipped every thirty minutes, and she wouldn't hang around after I got home from school—another win-win. Dad and mom would continue to think I was safe at home with my babysitter while they were wherever they were, and Willa would go out to the maid's quarters right after the final bell rang for school.

Tricking Mr. Preston was a piece of cake. I rushed home and carefully orchestrated the lie. Willa left a note saying that her aunt was ill and in the hospital. She hated to leave before I got home from school, but she was her aunt's only family in town, and since she was so sick, Willa didn't want her to be alone. I even wrote the note and left it on the island so that if Mr. Preston wanted to, he could see it existed, and before you worry that he would obviously know my handwriting since he was my teacher and all, I planned for that. I wrote it in a fake handwriting, with precise and perfect penmanship. I checked the maid's quarters to make sure that Willa was in for the night. She had already passed out in her recliner, watching *Wheel of Fortune*, empty bottle on her end table, so I was home free. She typically fell asleep right after I got home from school. Must have been all that rum she drank during the day.

I ran upstairs and changed into my *real* clothes, dark blue jeans and a red cardigan sweater with a white camisole underneath, no bra.

Twenty minutes later, the doorbell rang. I ran downstairs, my tiny breasts jumping with each step then realized that would seem too eager, so I slowed my breath and counted "one, two, three" on each step. By the time I got to the door, I was no longer breathless ... until I opened it.

Mr. Preston had changed, too. He stood, all six foot four of himself wearing jeans and a white fitted thermal with three brown buttons at the collar, unbuttoned, showing all of the sculptured perfectness of his chest muscles. Just under his shirt, I caught a glimpse of necklace made of white sea rocks, and resting just at the apex of his collarbone was Jesus Christ himself in tarnished silver, staring down at me from the cross. Holy ... something. I needed a new pair of underwear at the sight of him.

I showed him into the house while he complimented the place and its gorgeousness. Then we walked into the kitchen to begin our meal. As we entered the room, Mr. Preston asked if Willa might need any help with dinner. To which I responded with the perfectly innocent made-up story. I even made a casual hand gesture toward the note to make sure Mr. Preston noticed it. He nodded along with me and bought every word. He tried to leave, but I can be very convincing.

It also helped that Willa had prepared one of her best meals, completely coincidental, a roasted pork shoulder with scalloped potatoes, green bean casserole, and a small mixed salad with her homemade poppy seed dressing. If the way to a man's heart was his stomach, which way to his dick? His stomach, apparently as well. We ate the meal at the island sitting side by side, exchanging surprisingly easy conversation. I didn't even fake anything. I was totally myself.

We talked about Jen whose chair I stole in class and how she constantly looked like she had just smelled something gross. We talked about Ms. Stevens and the rumor that she was so crazy she kept cats in her classroom closet. He laughed enjoying my witty gossip. Once when he laughed, he grabbed my upper arm and sort of shook me as he chuckled. That was the first time that he ever actually touched me.

When we finished dinner, I invited him into our theater to watch the game (another awesome coincidence). We walked up the stairs to the second floor and down the hall. I flipped the light switch and then dimmed the lights to create a movie theater setting. We turned on the game and started watching from the velvet maroon theater seats. My dad had furnished the room. He wanted to feel exactly like he was at the movies every time he turned on the television. Mission accomplished.

Mr. Preston and I were on our first date. We jumped up and cheered and cursed the refs and all of the customary sports fan bullshit. When the Mavs won, I jumped up and hugged Mr. Preston. He caught me, and before he put me down, I placed my lips right on his. He set me down on the floor and grabbed both of my shoulders and said, "What are you doing?"

Then he grabbed me around the waist, pulled me into him. And then ... he kissed me. A kiss worthy of fireworks, symbols bursting in the background, violins stringing a love song. A sensual kiss, starting at the lips where he gently pressed his firm lips against mine, brushing my bottom lip with his top while long wanting fingers traced up and down the side of my sweater. Then he pulled me into him with both hands, chests colliding, causing fire to ignite in my belly and shivers to run up and down my spine and the backs of my legs. He shoved his tongue between my parted lips and covered my mouth with his. I could feel him growing and throbbing against my belly through his jeans. We quickly pulled off each other's clothes. I stepped back to see the picture my imagination had drawn a thousand times. Beneath his shirt was another side of heaven. His dark brown skin practically shimmered as it stretched over his chiseled chest and abs. I reached out and touched his stomach. I mean, I had to feel it. It was a masterpiece. He had me down to my white cotton boy shorts and cami before he took a break for air.

"What are we doing, Paige?" he breathed as he nibbled on my earlobe.

"Well, I think they call it sex, Mr. Preston, but you're the teacher," I replied.

"Oh God, Paige, please don't call me Mr. Preston, and please don't call me teacher right now," he panted as he slid my panties down my legs and dropped them on the floor. He pulled a condom over himself, and then I took him, or we took each other. Pounding, loud, and hungry.

That night I had my first legitimate orgasm, leg shaking, heart stuttering, body trembling orgasm. I had never actually had one during sex before. I was only sixteen, and my experience was limited with boys my age who had no idea what they were doing, so until that encounter, my only orgasms had come from yours truly. Holy Mary, Mother of God ... nothing had ever felt so good.

When he finally climaxed, he pulled me to him so that our chests were touching, my head resting on his shoulder. We sat there panting, sweating, and savoring. Then he sort of tapped out. That's the best way I can describe it. He tapped me three times on the thigh and then picked me up and set me in the chair next to him. He got up, grabbed his clothes, and went to the bathroom right outside. No holding, no basking in the light of this amazing experience. He just left the room. I started to panic a little. I got up from the chair and walked into the hallway. I knocked twice on the bathroom door. "You okay, Mr. Preston?" He didn't answer. I waited a few minutes and then decided to get dressed. While I was pulling up my jeans, he walked back into the room.

"Paige, I'm sorry. I shouldn't have let that happen."

"Mr. Preston, please stop. I wanted that. You and I both know I have wanted that for a long time."

"You what?"

"Mr. Preston ..."

"Paige, I think after what," he took a deep breath and then continued, "after what we just did, maybe you should call me by my name, Michael, unless we're at school. Oh God, what have we done?"

He couldn't, wouldn't meet my eyes.

"Well, *Michael*, please wipe that guilty look off of your face. I've never had anyone regret having sex with me, and you are not going to be the first."

He walked up to me and took my hand in his. He stared down at me and then gently brushed his lips over mine. "Paige, I have a lot going on in my mind. You're my student. I'm your teacher. You're sixteen, for crying out loud. What we just did is not only immoral, it's illegal. I need to wrap my brain around it is all."

"Why don't I wrap my legs around you instead until you get it all figured out?"

He let go of me and took a step back. "Not tonight, kiddo." I hated that he called me that. I rolled my eyes and pouted myself out of the room.

The next day in class, I strolled to my desk, chin held high. Most girls would blush in this position, but I sat in my front row seat, and stared him down for fifty-five minutes while imagining the way his hands felt as they held my ass the night before. He barely glanced in my direction. I expected him to ask me to stay after class, to offer some sort of explanation or an invitation for a second round, but nothing. He never came back to my house. Mr. Preston and I only had sex that one time. I set out to catch my prey, and

I did. I captured him and caged him for one blissful night, but he realized he was too noble to do it again, so he started ignoring me. He even had the nerve to transfer to the all-boys private school. He claimed the opportunity to coach boys would look better on his resume.

When I could no longer see him daily in class, I found out where he lived and followed him home after school almost every day. I watched him through his window sitting in his La-Z-Boy reading the paper, or watching his tiny little television. Then one night, I was hunkered down in my Beamer when a sedan pulled into his driveway and a woman stepped out. He came out of his house to greet her, and a smile spread across his entire face. He didn't just hug her. He caressed her. His hands never left her. He laughed and brushed his cheek against hers. Then they kissed. This was obviously not a new thing. He lifted her up and carried her inside. She was tall. She was blonde. She was beautiful. She was the older version of me. I threw up in my car.

I raced home and ran straight to my mother's bathroom where I found a bottle of Percocet. The bottle said to take one as needed for pain (although, to my knowledge, my mother had never experienced actual physical pain, she always had a bottle of Percocet.) I was alone in the house. My parents were god knows where, and Willa was in her room. I quickly called Janie. She could tell I was crying. I never cried, never cry, so she was shocked. She tried to comfort me. She had no idea what was going on, just that I saw my "boyfriend" (I told her I was seeing someone from college because she would have never approved of a teacher-student tango) with another girl. She said the typical, "that stupid asshole. Has he even seen you? What was he thinking?" bullshit, and then I let her go.

I grabbed the bottle of pills, went to the bar and grabbed a bottle of Ketel One Vodka and took both to my room. I rolled around on my Mr. Preston smelling sheets until I couldn't take it any longer. I put a handful of pills in my mouth and chased them down with a big gulp of vodka straight from the bottle. I don't know how long I laid there before I fell asleep. I just kept drinking the vodka. It couldn't have been long, but it was long enough to numb the pain, the aching in the pit of my lonely core.

I woke up to bright, eye stinging light and the vilest taste in my mouth, looking into the big blue eyes of my best friend's mom. "Oh, Paige. What were you thinking?" she said in a hushed voice. I didn't answer, just turned my head away and went back to sleep. Apparently after talking to me, sweet Janie got worried and came to my house to check on me and found me lying on my bed in a pool of my own vomit. That was my very first suicide attempt, the first of many.

A week later, I was sitting in the back seat of my dad's Cadillac Escalade driving back home with Mom in the passenger seat and Dad in the front seat, his hand resting gently on her knee as he drove, a picture of cookie-cutter suburbia. My parents flew straight home upon hearing of my overdose. My mother stayed by my bedside until I was released. My father visited every day. He even brought me a bouquet of my favorite flowers, pink tulips. Every time he looked at me, he furrowed his blonde brow and said things like, "oh Paigey girl" (my childhood nickname) and "my sweet babycakes." He even kissed me on the forehead when he left. Every time. My mother didn't travel with my dad when he left again. She *actually* stayed home and took care of me.

She was home when I got home from school and would sit and talk to me about my day and my classes. We would eat dinner together every night. She took me shopping. We got pedicures, manicures, and facials at her favorite spa one day. We stayed up late watching chick flicks that made my mother cry. We held hands during the really sad parts and laughed aloud at the funny parts in the very theater where I experienced my first Big O. She let me sleep in her king-size canopy bed where she drank wine and offered me a sip here and there. It was like a scene out of a movie, not anything like my life. When I was younger, she spent more time at home, but she and my father still always traveled, and I was left to be cared for by a nanny. This was different, though.

She was home. She was present, and she was worried about me.

Then one day I came bouncing into the kitchen expecting to see my beautiful mom sitting in her favorite spot at the end of the island and found Willa cooking away at the stove. She didn't turn around and greet me, just said, "Your mother had to join your father overseas. She left this morning." And that was it. My short lived peachy existence lasted one month. Then they were gone. Again.

So I figured it out. My parents cared when I really *needed* them. As long as I was partially sane, they were off on some business trip doing whatever it was that they did without me.

Thus began the suicide saga of Paige.

I didn't turn Mr. Preston into the authorities. I couldn't make myself believe that it would never happen again with him. Turning him in would ruin him, ruin our tainted affair, and out me to my parents, which was clearly out of the question, so I let it go. That blonde bitch, however, got a taste of Paige's dark side. I didn't do the battered teenage revenge either. I'm way above slashing tires and keying her pathetic Toyota Camry. Remember, I'm clever.

I watched her for weeks, learned her routine. Then I slivered myself into her life. I joined her gym. When she went to happy hour with work colleagues, I used my fake ID and sat two stools down from her. I even followed her into church one day, but I couldn't sit through the whole thing.

Slowly, over the course of a couple months, I maintained a close distance to Sheila. I know, Sheila, the bland older version of me. What could he see in her? I got to know her through conversations she had at all of her favorite spots. Sheila worked as an office manager at a pediatrician's office, volunteered at the animal shelter on Sundays, had lots of friends, was always with someone, never alone, lived with a roommate, a gay man named Cliff. She was practically a saint, aside from the fact that she was fucking my boyfriend, which I watched her do on too many occasions.

I decided to introduce myself and become "friends" with the saint. I followed her into a spin class one night and took the bike next to her. I had never been to such a class before and had no idea what I was getting myself into. Loud bass tones thumped in my ears as a tiny black woman with sculptured legs climbed onto the only bike facing the five rows of opposite facing bikes. She suggested that we warm up while we waited for others to join the class. "Anybody new?" she asked.

Like hell if I was going to admit that in front of my competition who pedaled her bike in perfect step with the beat of the music. I followed her lead and did exactly what she did. As the class started, the instructor yelled for us to increase our resistance. Sheila moved hers to fifteen. I did the same. Thirty-four seconds later, I was out of breath, sweat spilling down my back.

"Increase your resistance, people," the tiny black devil yelled. Sheila took hers to thirty. Fucking thirty? Are you kidding me? Again, I followed her lead. I looked at the clock. Forty-five minutes left to go. There was no way I was making it through the whole thing. Then the tiny devil said we could rest. I stopped pedaling. "DON'T STOP PEDAL-ING." Shit. I watched Sheila take her resistance down to five. I did the same. The rest of the class was hell, a very fast dance between me and my nemesis going from shrill hell to tiny bouts of bliss, all the while pedaling like I was being chased by a vicious fucking dog.

During cooldown, as I wiped my soaking chest with a towel, Sheila turned to me and said, "I've never seen you in class before. Do you take spin somewhere else?" I looked behind me to make sure I was the target of this question.

"Um, I usually come to the morning class."

"Oh, with Tony?"

"Sure, with Tony." I agreed, trying to hold in the vomit creeping up my throat.

"I've never met anyone who could keep up with me in spin before. I figured I should shake your hand. I'm Shelia."

Are you kidding me with this bitch? I thought to myself.

"Pam." My mom's name came out of my mouth before I could even think.

"Nice to meet you, Pam. I'm going to head over to the juice bar. Want to join me?"

Visioning an opportunity to infiltrate, I accepted without question. An hour later, my new best friend and I made a date to have coffee later that week. Over coffee, Sheila and I exchanged typical getting to know you conversation. She told me all about her job, etcetera, etcetera, etcetera, and I told her about my classes at the local university and my sorority, etcetera, etcetera, etcetera. I asked Sheila if she was seeing anyone.

"Yeah, I've been dating the same guy for over a year." Really? Over a year. Funny how Mr. Preston never mentioned her while he was fucking me, but bygones, right?

"Oh, wow. That's a long time. Are you serious?"

"Well yes, of course. We're in love."

"Love? That's exciting. So are you talking about marriage?" I asked, trying to untwist the jealousy knots in my stomach.

"We've talked about it, but my Michael. Sorry, Michael ... that's his name ... has a lot on his plate right now. He just recently started coaching at a new school. He's a high school basketball coach, so I'm not pressing for anything," she sighed. "I have wondered what he's waiting for, though."

It took every ounce of willpower not to kick the bitch when she called him *my Michael*. I mean she might as well have hiked her leg and peed on him with that territorial mark.

"Fucking men, Sheila. He sounds like an enigma." I watched her flinch at the word, "fucking."

"A beautiful enigma," she said with a smile. "And he's such a great guy. I'm not in that big of a hurry. I'm only twenty-five. I have plenty of time for marriage."

"Yeah, I guess so," I replied looking up from my mocha, "Still, you have to wonder why if everything is so great, he's not making an honest woman out of you." She looked at me annoyed. "I'm only kidding, Sheila. I don't even believe in marriage, so you don't need to justify anything to me."

"I'm not justifying," she said defensively, "God, sometimes when I talk about him, I do start to wonder, you know?"

"Totally," I replied in an I'm-your-best-girlfriend voice. "Listen, Sheila. You're only twenty-five. You are a catch. If he doesn't decide to marry you, he's an idiot. Just be glad he doesn't cheat on you, like all of the men I've ever known."

"Oh, no. Michael isn't a cheater. He's just not that kind of guy."

"Of course he's not," I said rolling my eyes.

"What does that mean?" I watched as she traced her thumb around the handle of her coffee mug. Under the table, I could see her left foot. She had the ball of her foot on the ground without her heel touching, and her leg nervously began to twitch.

I had her.

"Sheila, you're very sweet. I'm sure *your* Michael is different than all of the men I know, or maybe I just attract the cheaters. I just don't trust men at all. But that's just me. Until he gives you a reason to not trust him, you shouldn't worry."

"What do you mean?"

Seriously, this woman was older and should have been wiser than I was, and she asked me for advice on her relationship with a man who fucked me behind her back. What the hell? But wait, I did plant the seed, and apparently I was an excellent gardener.

"I mean, I always know when a guy is cheating. You have to look for the signs. Follow your gut," I leaned in, "female intuition."

"Like for example?" She was hooked.

"Does he always take his phone into the other room when he gets a call? Does he have frequent guy nights? Does he stay at work later than necessary?" I added the last part because I knew that Mr. Preston, or *her* Michael, was notorious for staying late, like with me, on many occasions.

"I don't think Michael is a cheater. He's too good of a guy," she practically barked.

That pretty much ended the conversation. She decided she had to skedaddle. I paid for our coffees and grabbed my bag already planning my next move.

Over the course of the next few months, I courted Sheila while planting ideas all around her of "her Michael's" infidelity. Like I said, Steph, I'm a planner, and I can show excellent restraint when necessary, unless of course it comes to sex. I became obsessed. I needed to end them, and to do it dramatically.

Because Sheila had begun to tread water in the sea of doubt, I had to keep the momentum going, which would require staging. I jimmied the lock to Mr. Preston's back door, something I learned from a boyfriend who liked to steal for the rush of it, when I knew he was out of town for a basketball tournament to stash a little evidence for Sheila to later uncover. I placed an earring on the floor next to his bed, and my favorite, which I think was both brilliant and possibly just good timing, I watched this terribly gaudy woman apply her lipstick in the bathroom of a restaurant and use a tissue to blot her lips. She tossed the tissue in the trash, so I carefully used another tissue, confiscated hers, and placed it in my purse to be later thrown into Mr. Preston's bathroom trash can, a little kiss good-bye from me to Sheila.

I made it a point to meet with Sheila the day before Mr. Preston was scheduled to return home and convinced her that she should surprise him and wait for him to get home as a "welcome home, let's make love" kind of gesture. During this conversation, while I was saying to wait on his front porch, she informed me that she had a key, (information which would have been good to know earlier) so instead we planned for her to be waiting in his place when he arrived home. She decided sappy and romantic was their style and chose to get a bottle of wine and bubble bath. I told her she should get a wig and handcuffs, but whatever. Tomato, tom-ah-to.

Right on schedule, Sheila arrived at Mr. Preston's house to have the night of her life, and I pretended to go home to study, in keeping up with my college student disguise, but instead, I went home, traded my red Beamer for my dad's silver Benz, and strolled over to Mr. Preston's neighborhood just about the time I knew he'd be arriving home. I sat in the car and waited for my creative apocalypse to occur, and just as most of my plans do, it all unfolded perfectly.

Sheila's car was parked in his driveway when he got home. When he got out of his car, I could tell he was happy to see hers. Made me want to fucking shoot someone, but I sat, grinding my teeth, waiting. Then it happened.

She stormed out screaming, "I knew it. I knew it." She thrust something at his face, I was thinking probably the earring. It was small.

"Sheila, that has to be yours. I swear to Christ, Sheila. I am not cheating on you."

"Screw you, Michael," she screamed as she slammed her door. He looked baffled and dumbfounded as he watched her drive away. I was shocked that even in anger, she didn't swear. Good grief.

I saw Sheila at spin class the next night, and she told me everything. It was the earring. She saw it before he even got home. She never mentioned the lipstick tissue, and I so badly wanted to ask. I had to keep telling myself to think of dead puppies to keep my grin at bay, but I sat there comforting her speaking of other fish in the sea and bad seeds and girl power while silently giving myself imaginary high fives. And then I quit going to spin and slowly removed myself from Sheila's life. I watched to see if she and Mr. Preston ever rekindled. They did not.

Paige 1, Mr. Preston 0.

And that is why, Stephanie, nobody fucks with Paige *Preston*. Because I will fuck you harder.

Closer

Dear Stephanie,

Sometimes I go out with a mission. Sometimes things just fall in my lap. Friday night, that's what happened. Janie got us tickets to Kings of Leon at the House of Blues, which is one of my favorite venues to see a show. Decent acoustics, intimate setting, fully stocked bar, what's not to love?
We got there just as the opening band was finishing. The energy was contagious, standing room only. Janie was exhausted and not really feeling it. In her defense, she had just returned home from a week-long trip to Africa where she probably fed an entire village or something. She complained more than a little bit about jet lag in the cab on the way, so I told her to go take a seat, that I would get us some drinks, and what a fantastic twist of fate that turned out to be.
I saw him immediately. Tallish, but not too tall. Not short either. He had his back to the bar leaning against it, was facing the stage and sort of just bobbing his head to the music. He wore dark jeans and a black V neck T-shirt that hugged him in all the right places, particularly his biceps. Our eyes met, his framed in black plastic glasses, dark obsidian beautiful eyes. He gave me a half smile and then turned his gaze back to the stage. I walked over to where he stood

and sidled into the space between him and another person at the bar, gently brushing his arm with mine.

"Oh, excuse me," he said.

I smiled.

The bartender came over and took my drink order. I ordered myself the usual, a Ketel One martini with a twist and Janie a vodka soda.

"You shouldn't have to make the drink run," he said, without looking at me.

I smiled again and said, "Are you flirting with me?"

"That depends." He turned to face me and offered me a full wide smile. I wanted to lick him immediately.

"Oh? On what?"

"Which drink is yours?"

I raised my glass. "The martini," I said, and took a sip.

"Well, I don't really like vodka sodas, but I'll drink it if it means I can keep talking to you." He grabbed Janie's drink out of my hand and took a big sip.

I let out a ridiculous girlish giggle. Gotta love a confident guy who can make you laugh.

"Thanks," he said and clinked my glass, raising an eyebrow, "Next round's on me."

"You're welcome."

"What's your name?"

"Paige Preston." I reached my hand out to shake his, but instead of shaking my hand, he held it for a second, looking into my eyes, and then he brought it to his mouth and kissed the top. I almost melted, and I don't even do romance. This guy was good.

"Nice to meet you, Paige. I'm Leo Torres. The show's about to start. You better get to your seat." He motioned with his head toward the stage.

"I only like men to tell me what to do in the bedroom."

"Oh yeah?" His eyes softened at that. He leaned in, brushed my hair off my shoulder and whispered into my ear, "Then don't leave here without me."

And just like that, I was toast.

I stayed with him at the bar for the entire concert, neither of us ever going to our seats. Janie texted me halfway through the show and said she was going to get a cab home, that she was too tired to watch a concert alone. I could hear her annoyance through the type, but if anyone understands me, it's Janie.

The more music we heard, the nearer our bodies came to each other. When they played "Closer," he placed me in front of him and put his hands on my hips. We swayed to the music together, my hips grinding into him, and I felt the reaction his body had to mine. When the song ended, I turned around and brushed my lips against his. He grabbed the back of my neck and pulled me into a short, sweet kiss. By the time the show ended, all I could think about was getting into his bed, wherever it was. Apparently, he felt it too because just as the crowd erupted in applause, he looked at me and said five of my favorite words, "Let's get out of here."

We grabbed a cab. When we got into the backseat, the driver asked where we were going. He looked at me. I shook my head. "We aren't going to my place," I said. Nobody ever gets to go to my place.

"Oh, okay. I'm just in town until tomorrow, so I'm staying at a hotel. You're cool going back there with me?"

"I'm cool."

He gave the driver the name and then turned his attention to me, and before I could even take a breath, his mouth was on mine, hot and needy. Sexy and sweet, kissing me like it was the last time he was ever going to kiss a woman. He wrapped his arm around my shoulders and pulled me into him, nibbling on my bottom lip then sucking, gently parting my lips with his tongue. The perfect kind of kiss. The kind of kiss that makes you want to never stop, and we didn't. We kissed until the cab came to a stop in front of his hotel. He paid the driver and then helped me out of the car.

We made it into the elevator before his mouth was on mine again. He pressed me up against the wall and held me there while his mouth continued to explore mine. This man made kissing an art form, and I resigned myself to the fact that if all he did was kiss me for the rest of the night, that would be enough, but judging from the firmness pressing into me, he wanted more.

The elevator announced our arrival at his floor. He took my hand and guided me to his room, not saying a word. When he opened the door, he pulled me in behind him and then shoved me up against the wall. He fumbled for my shirt, and pulled it over my head.

"Mmmmmmm," he moaned when he saw me without my shirt. He pulled each strap of my bra down and kissed my shoulders. I reached back and unclasped the hook, letting it fall to the floor. He put his hand down the gap in the back of my jeans and brushed the top of my panties with his fingers. My skin responded with chills. "Get out of these jeans," he said as he pulled his shirt over his head revealing a body that begged to be bitten. His chest, his arms, his beautifully cut abs. I wanted my mouth on him. All of him. I'm pretty sure I growled.

He watched me as I unbuttoned and unzipped my jeans, and when I pulled them down and kicked them off, he was on me immediately again with his mouth. Kissing me, touching me through the outside of my panties. He picked me up and carried me to the bed, dropped me down and then fell on top of me. I told him to get out of his jeans, too, which he quickly obliged, and then he kissed me through my panties. I wanted them off, but every time I tried to get rid of them, he stopped me and shook his head. I let him lead. This man's mouth was award winning. So much so that he made me come through my panties, pressing his mouth into me without even touching my skin.

When my waves finally ended, he climbed on top of me. He somehow finished undressing without my noticing but left his glasses on. Score one for me. I heard the familiar rip of a condom package and watched him as he slid it on. Sexy, delicious, irresistible. He looped his fingers on either side of my panties and pulled them down.

"Jesus you're beautiful," he said as he slipped them off of each foot. He ran his hand up the side of my leg, parting my thighs with his body, and then I felt him hard and hot against me. He looked into my eyes, inches from my face and said, "I'm going to fuck the life out of you." Then he entered me. I arched my back and gasped for air. He was perfect, and his mouth had nothing on this. He knew what he was doing, an expert in bed. He aimed to please, and he did. Over and over and over again.

When he finally finished, we were sweaty and out of breath. He tried to pull me into him, assuming that I was going to sleep there, but I rolled away and got up to get dressed, which seemed to surprise him. He said, "You're not staying?"

I shook my head, "No, I better go." I don't spend the night.

"What if I tell you to stay?" he said casually, sitting up against the headboard, his naked chest glistening with his and my sweat.

"Well, it depends," I said with a smile.

"Oh yeah? On what?"

"On whether or not you can repeat what we just did."

He smiled and patted the bed next to him.

"Put down your clothes, and get back over here. I told you, I was going to fuck the life out of you, and if you can still walk, we aren't finished."

Needless to say, I stayed the night. We didn't sleep.

Pamuy

Dear Stephanie,

I had a session today. I don't know where to begin. First Dr. Love asked me how the journaling was going. Again, I wanted to say, "Hey, doc. I have a life, you know?" but I couldn't hurt Handsome's feelings, so I told him that I basically start typing and have diarrhea of the fingers. He laughed at the metaphor and asked me what sort of things I've been writing about. I froze, I mean froze. I sat there with my mouth open looking at him with wide brown eyes, and he caught it.

He said, "Ms. Preston, what is it? Why are you shocked? Part of the reason I want you to journal is so that you can express some of your emotions on paper and then feel comfortable enough to share them with me. I'm not asking to read it, nor will I ever. Your journal is yours, but we need to start talking about some deeper stuff. Have you written about anything specific? A major event in your life?"

I had to think fast. So far, I've written about illegal sex with a teacher and an amazing one-night stand with a stranger. I'm fairly sure this isn't what he has in mind as far as journaling goes, so I inventoried my mind for something to share with him. I'm totally screwed up, and I could have told him a number of things, so I decided it would be best if I just dove right into why I ended up in his office in the first place.

"Well, I've basically been writing about the rape," I said through semi pursed lips.

"Okay, would you like to talk about it?" he asked, grabbing his clipboard and silver ballpoint pen.

"Should I lie down and close my eyes, Dr. Freud?"

"If you would be more comfortable."

I sighed, rolled my eyes, and began, "So, I was walking home from the night club where my girlfriend, Janie, and I had just spent the night dancing and downing Patrón shots. I was completely shitfaced, so Janie wouldn't let me drive home. She tried to get me into a cab, but I refused and told her that it wasn't far to walk. After arguing with me for what seemed like four hours, Janie got into a cab with the guy who had been dry humping her ass all night. It was like 3:00 in the morning, and the street was mostly empty, just a few of my fellow drunks and me.

"I walked, mostly staggered, singing "Kodachrome" to myself. I didn't notice that there was a guy behind me until he was right next to me. I recognized him. He and I had danced a few times during the night, and he viciously tried to get my number. I kept teasing him and telling him that I would by the end of the night, but he really wasn't my type, too short and too pale, so I just basically let him buy me drinks all night. I don't know why I do that. I can afford my own drinks, but I love to waste these douchebags' hard-earned money.

"So he looked at me and asked me why I was such a cock tease. I told him that I'm not a cock tease, that I never intended to do anything with his cock, and if he wasn't such a twerp, he would just keep walking and leave me alone, or something like that."

I stopped and looked at Dr. Love. He had his clipboard on his lap and was holding his pen between his thumb and his index finger, resting the tip on his chin. He looked sexy and professional at the same time. I could see him picturing my story in his head. He sort of paused in thought and then looked at me.

"Kodachrome?" he asked, "by Paul Simon?"

I nodded.

"You're kind of young for that song, aren't you?"

"Maybe, but my mother loved Paul Simon. I've listened to him since I was a little girl. 'Kodachrome' is my favorite song of his. You know, it makes me think all the world's a sunny day."

Dr. Love started writing on his yellow pad.

"Okay, Ms. Preston, tell me more about that night."

I wanted to talk more about music, but I could tell Dr. Love thought he was getting somewhere with me, so I continued.

"Apparently this guy still thought he had a chance. He said something like, c'mon gorgeous, let me see you naked, a come-on line dripping with charm. I told him to fuck off, but he kept walking with me, half stumbling into me.

"By then, I was getting kind of nervous because I couldn't quite shake him, and there was no one else around. I couldn't run in my Louboutin four-inch heels, so I didn't really know what to do. I should have pulled out my phone and called 911 or something, but I was hammered and not thinking straight." I rolled my eyes.

Dr. Love nodded for me to continue, gesturing with his pen to go on.

"He kept trying to get me to stop walking and finally grabbed my upper arm. He pushed me into an alley between two buildings and pressed me up against the outside wall of one of them. I was wearing a short dress, so he basically stuck his hand between my legs and tried to get me to have sex with him still thinking he had some sort of chance.

"I told him to get lost, looked down at his crotch and made a remark about gherkin pickles, which pissed him off. He grabbed me, wrapped his hand around my neck, and shoved me hard against the wall."

I mindlessly fingered the little scar on the back of my head.

"Then he ripped off my panties and did what he set out to do, shoving his tiny semi-hard dick into me, panting his sweet whiskey breath into my face. It lasted about three minutes." I will never drink Jack Daniels again.

"Then what happened?"

"I picked my panties up off the ground, put them in my purse, and walked home." I left out the part where I wiped his jizz from my inner thigh with my underwear, too much for Dr. Love to know.

"What did you do when you got home?" He set his pad and pen down.

"I did a line of cocaine, which was all I had," I said with a sigh.

"How did you end up in the hospital, Paige?" That's right, Steph, he called me by my first name. We are making progress.

"I saw the sun coming up and decided I should sleep, so I took some pills."

"What kind of pills?" He leaned in, making eye contact.

"Listen, doc, you have my file there, and you know what kind of pills I took. Why are you asking me questions that you can answer yourself?"

"Because it's important for you to tell *me* the truth, or you'll never get better." His voice was firm, authoritative. I watched his Adam's Apple drop as he spoke.

"Xanax." I twisted my hair around my finger, not making eye contact, eyes still lingering on his neck.

"Were you trying to kill yourself?"

"No, doc. I was having a very bad anxiety attack."

"Were you trying to kill yourself?"

I turned toward him, looked straight at him and nodded, "Yes."

"Because of the rape?"

I shook my head. "No."

"Why?"

"You don't have enough time."

"I have all the time in the world, Paige."

43

"Because, sometimes I just want to sleep and never wake up."

He picked up his pen and wrote something on his yellow pad. I knew that phrase was a red flag and hoped he wouldn't recommend another stay in a treatment center. I could smell him, rich and intoxicating, and for the first time since meeting him, instead of wanting to rip off his clothes, I wanted to bury my head in his chest and sob.

"I don't want to talk about this anymore, Doc." I blurted out. I was already on the edge of composure, and I knew talking anymore about killing myself would push me over that cliff.

He paused for a second, looked down at his pad, and then back up at me. "Tell me more about your mom."

"There's nothing to tell."

"When you mentioned her earlier, your voice changed. You softened a bit."

"And?"

"So, I'd like you to share more about her," he said looking at me, confusion in his dark eyes.

I blew the air out of mouth. "My mother was beautiful, breath-taking actually, and self-centered."

"Was?" He unconsciously clicked his pen. Click, click, click, click, as I battled in my mind what more I should say to him.

"She's dead," I finally managed, sinking my fingernails into my palms.

"Do you want to talk about her death?"

"Not really."

"Were you close?"

I didn't answer right away. I silently sat on the purple couch thinking about my beautiful mother, her graceful walk, the way her long black hair always swayed side to side as she moved around a room, her soft false confidence that she carried everywhere she went, the sound of her voice when she sang along with the song on the radio, her smell, always soft lavender with a hint of vanilla, her laugh, joyful and loud, so unlike everything else about her. Then I thought about the end. The pit of my stomach ached. "She fell down the stairs," I said through gritted teeth. "She *fell* down the stairs. She lived in the same house for twenty-two years and never even slipped. Then one day, she and my dad were surprisingly there together and alone. My dad had given all of the staff the day off, conveniently. I had already moved out and was in college. They were alone, and my mother fell down the stairs." I paused. I never cry in front of people.

"She's not actually dead. She hasn't spoken since the fall, something the doctors can't explain. She's trapped inside of her body. A body that still works but has no desire to, so basically dead. My dad immediately put her in a home and left her there. I don't even know if she recognizes me."

"That must be tough. Do you visit her often?"

"Nope."

"You speak of your father rather harshly."

"Yep."

"Paige, I'm sorry your mother is ..." he drifted off.

"Don't. Please." I raised my hand, gesturing for him to stop. "Thanks, but there's nothing you or anyone else can say about the situation with my mother. It is ..." I paused for a second, "I'm done talking about it with you, with everyone." And with that, I grabbed my bag and left his office.

He called after me, but I had to get out of there before he saw me cry. Like I said, no one ever sees me cry. Period. I keep my thoughts opaque to the naked eye, always a purposeful expression unyielding my true emotion. A mask, so to speak.

My mother and I were never close, except for when I was a little doe-eyed girl. I spent countless hours in her bathroom watching her get ready for events where she accompanied my father. That was where I learned about beauty and its sanctity. She showed me how to apply makeup, often letting me have her powder puff when she finished so that I could apply imaginary powder to my chubby pink cheeks.

She always listened to music as she got ready. We would sing along dancing around on the marble floors. I remember laughing as she held both of my hands and twirled me around the bathroom, squealing with delight, saying, "Again, mommy! Again!" She would giggle and lift me up on her hip and kiss my temple through my hair. My fondest memories of her, so happy, so beautiful, a genuine smile on her crimson lips.

When I got older, no longer a cute little puppy, she started spending most of her time chasing after my father trying to keep him away from the countless women he kept in waiting. They did a poor job of hiding his infidelity from me. A child shouldn't know her parents' struggles, but I knew. I heard my mother's crying, I saw the dark circles under her eyes. I waited for her to get out of bed on mornings when I knew she drank herself to sleep. I saw her chase pills with wine. She wore her unhappiness like a cloak. She knew the monster, too. She may have even been closer to him than I ever have been.

One day, when I was a teenager, I was terminally bored, so I decided to snoop through my mother's closet looking for pills. She kept the really good ones hidden. I found a locked box on the top shelf of her closet. I sat on her bed and ran my finger along the edge of the pale pink wooden mystery, tracing the little delicately painted vines on its edge.

I had to see what was in it. I ran to my father's office and got his letter opener. I jiggled the tiny gold lock every which way until it finally clicked in my hand. I pulled open the top and stared into the green velvet lined box. Inside was a tiny revolver, bullets, and a vial of what I determined later to be cocaine. Thanks for that little treat, mom, even better than pills.

I held the revolver in my hand, mocking a cowboy from TV twirling it on my index finger. I held it to my temple, then in my mouth looking at myself in the mirror over my mother's dresser. I tried to imagine my mother sitting on the very bed where I sat holding this beautifully crafted dainty little pistol in her hand, holding it in her own mouth, wrapping her red stained lips around the barrel. I realized then that my mother and I had more in common than either of us would ever admit.

After her accident, I went back into her closet and retrieved her secret little box. The revolver was still there, along with the bullets. On a piece of her personalized stationary marked with a "P" for Pamuy, my mother had handwritten a letter in her tiny jagged script. To me.

Dear Paige,

Please don't end up like me. Find someone who really loves you for who you are, not just your beauty. For that, sweet child, is only temporary. Yigaquu osaniyu adanvto adadoligi nigohilvi nasquv utloyasdi nihi. (May the Great Spirit's blessings always be with you.)

~Mom

I'm pretty sure this was her suicide letter. She just never had the balls to actually do it. I still have her revolver. Maybe I will one day.

B-Large

Dear Stephanie,

D-Love: I'm concerned

That was one of many texts I received from Dr. Love. I haven't seen him since the day of the last entry over a week ago. After telling him all about my family's drama, I had to unwind. I called Janie, and she and I went for dinner and drinks, which turned out to be just drinks ... lots of drinks. She and I have a tendency to do that. We set out to have a nice "grown-up" night, and once the vodka starts flowing, we forget all about the food. I'm well aware that drinking and drugs are probably not the best crutches, but a girl has to lean on something.

Over drinks, Janie told me about her little sexcapade with the dry humper from the cab. We laughed and discussed her inability to not fall in love. She tossed her martini back, and then decided she had to leave, probably to see him because she's terminally monogamous, but she blamed it on work.

See, even though it's painfully unnecessary, Janie works. She has her hopes set on changing the world and has developed a charity organization that digs wells for thirsty kids in third world countries or something philanthropic like that. I'm bored to tears when she tells me about it, but I donate a healthy sum of my inheritance every year to help with my taxes. Janie has always felt guilty about all of the money she has. I don't feel guilty at all. I'd roll around naked in it.

Janie left me at the bar to go get laid. I ordered another martini, and as I was sipping it, I vigorously scrolled through my iPhone trying to find someone to hang with me. I had an aching to get utterly pissed. Finally, I decided to text my neighbor, Blake aka B-Large.

Me: *Meet me at the dive in five ;-)*
B-Large: *Be there in four if you promise I'll score ...*
Me: *I'm timing you ...*

Enter B-Large, another one of my puppets. I can always count on him to come running when I call. It's kind of fun. Blake is a tall, lean, beautiful Greek God, with dark loosely curly hair that he constantly has to tuck behind his ear and piercing green eyes, a hedge fund manager who makes ridiculous dough, so we get along quite well. He lives in the apartment next to me, and we often hang when there's nothing else to do. Since I was feeling a little "lonely," I knew he would be good company.

The thing about B-Large that I find particularly attractive is his ever generous supply of cocaine hence the nickname. He thinks it's because he has a big dick, but it's really that he always has a large supply.

Three and a half minutes later, B-Large met me at the bar. We drank a few more drinks. Then we headed back to his place, holding hands, stumbling with drunken grace. Once we got there, I told him that I was dying to get high. He pulled out his magic little box, cocked his head to the side, and shot me his sexy smile.

Then we went to town. Between bumps, we had sex. That's sort of our M.O. We do cocaine, have sex, do a little more cocaine, have sex, do a little more cocaine, etc. until I get sick of him and decide to track back to my own place, take a sleeping pill or five, and sleep until my hangover wears off.

This time was different though. Once our high wore off, I wasn't ready to leave. B only had a little blow, and we depleted it pretty quickly, so getting higher wasn't an option. I really didn't want to be alone. Thinking about my mom and all of the stuff that I told Dr. Love, I couldn't go back to my apartment.

By this time, it was Saturday morning, so B-Large didn't have to work, which is why he did coke with me. He never does it during the week, or it affects his ability to focus on hedge funding, whatever that means. He has tremendous willpower. I also recently learned that he reserves this recreational activity for yours truly. Part of me knows I should bolt with that knowledge, but the other part of me is drawn to him. I can't quite put my finger on it, and that's probably why I keep coming back for more.

I think Blake was surprised that I had not done my typical retreat. He asked me if it would be okay if he showered. To which I said, "It's your house. Do what you want."

While he showered, I sat on his sofa, his soft, luxurious white leather sofa, put my bare feet up on the ottoman and turned on the TV. I channel surfed, old-fashioned style, listening to the first syllable of each word from a half a dozen infomercials, intent on selling me on pajama jeans or something called a Bump It. Five a.m. Saturday television ... snore. I hit power on the remote and pushed myself off the couch.

I walked over to his floor-to-ceiling bookshelf and took inventory. "He reads," I thought to myself. The idea surprised me more than you'd think, Steph. See, B-Large, is just this fun loving goofy guy who loves to drink and dance and have fun.

He's terminally good-looking with straight, perfectly white teeth that fit beautifully beneath his pretty pink lips, which open to a smile that will make a nun drop her panties. He is forever the life of the party, the only white guy ever dancing with an actual sense of rhythm. We fit well together in that way, so when I saw that he has a collection of classics, I was shocked ... in a good way.

I trailed my fingers along the worn spines noting the names of Ernest Hemingway, F. Scott Fitzgerald, Thomas

Hardy, Truman Capote, J. D. Salinger, and many, many more, reflecting on the times in my life when I found solace in these exact stories. After Lucy left, I drowned myself in literature. The more I read, the more I wanted, and even though some of the books were way above my maturity level, I read with intensity, completely diverging into the story, escaping the world that seemed hell-bent on breaking my spirit. A new respect for B-Large brewed in my heart.

Then I heard him come in the room. When I turned around, I almost had to pick my jaw up from the floor. He came in wearing nothing but a white towel wrapped around his waist. His curly dark hair dripped onto his shoulder, chest hair gleaming with dampness. I followed a drop of water as it swam down his tan skin into his belly button. He looked at me with his succulent apple green eyes and smiled. "What?" he asked.

"Um, nothing," I mumbled biting my lip.

"I half hoped you were going to join me in there."

"I think maybe I should have," I said with a grin.

"Well, nothing says I can't shower again."

"Listen, B, I better go. I need to shower and sleep and if I stay here, you know what will happen."

"What?" He bit his lip, walking toward me and let his towel drop.

"Yeah, that," I said as I backed toward the door.

We were in his bed fifteen seconds later and didn't leave for the rest of the day. For the first time, it was just sex, no blow, and frankly, it was fabulous.

Between romps, he invited me to go to San Diego with him for the week. He had to go for business but didn't have to be there until Tuesday. Since Monday was Labor Day, he suggested that we take a flight out the next morning and play on the beach all day Sunday and Monday. Tuesday, he would have to work but would only be in meetings part of the time, so the rest of the time, he said we could just hang, take it easy.

Still reeling from therapy and desperately wanting company, it sounded like a good idea to me, so I said, "Sure, why not?" I knew I could always leave early if I changed my mind. We booked our first class trip right then, celebrated with some sex, and fell into an amazingly peaceful sleep, something that I never, ever do.

I awoke very early the next day with B-Large sprawled across me, his arm heavy on my waist. I slipped out from beneath him. For a minute, I just stood there naked in the dark next to his bed, admiring him, parted lips, chest gently moving up and down, long beautiful fingers relaxed on his pillow, unruly black curls everywhere. I sighed, debating whether or not to climb back in and jump him but thought better of it and headed to my place. I had to get ready and pack, and I'm a little meticulous with both processes.

Two hours later, we were in a car headed to DFW airport. B-Large fed me enough champagne on the airplane to talk me into joining the mile high club. We tried to both fit into the bathroom, but the flight attendant put the kibosh on that one, so he settled for light fondling under the blanket. Good enough.

We were half drunk and positively horny when we arrived at noon, gotta love the two-hour time difference. We took a car with a guy outside holding a sign marked "Demopoulos" (B-Large's last name) and headed to our five-star beach hotel where we quickly checked in, had a quick boink, and changed to our swimsuits.

We didn't want to waste any fun-in-the-sun time, so we skipped lunch and headed straight for the beach. B-Large donned a pair of bright orange board shorts with a broad white stripe down each side of his legs. He set his wide mouth in a crooked grin as he slipped a white T-shirt over his head. Smoking hot doesn't even begin to describe this guy. I wore one of my faves, a teeny tiny white (to accent my bronze skin) triangle top bikini with Brazilian cut bottoms. B-Large practically foamed at the mouth when I took off my shorts.

We played on the beach, sipping mai tai's from the beach bar, basking in the California sun. We splashed and frolicked in the ocean. B tried a little surfing, only to come back to our beach blanket with a nose full of salt water and a big bruise on his thigh. He was awfully cute though, acting like the boy who needs his mom to take care of his boo-boo. I played along and kissed it all better.

By sunset, we were hammered. We wanted to ride bikes, but the guy at the bike stand wouldn't let us take them stating that he wasn't allowed to rent bikes to people who had been drinking. Considering we were holding our drinks at that very moment, we didn't quite have a leg to stand on, so B handed the guy a hundred-dollar bill. Apparently, Ben Franklin had more clout than we did, rules schmules.

We took one of the double-bikes and rode along the streetlamp-lined boardwalk singing, "double your pleasure, double your fun," passing other bikers, families walking, and several people out for their daily run. We turned heads with our childish glee. We laughed, genuine, unforced, belly laughs. It was awesome and fun and immature. And real.

I know it's strange, but I don't typically have fun, even though I pretend to most of the time. I fake it. My mind doesn't usually calm enough for me to enjoy the moment, another reason why I like drugs. This was different though. Nothing was forced, not the laughter, not the fun, the joy, none of that. B almost succeeded in making me forget about reality ... for a little while anyway.

We stopped at a tiny shack of a bar where we nicknamed the bartender "the Beer Nazi." They had rules written over the bar:

#1 Know what you want to order, or go to the end of the line.

#2 Know what your friends want to order, or go to the end of the line.

#3 Have your money ready, or go to the end of the line.

#4 Order immediately when asked, or go to the end of the line, etc."

B and I laughed every time some poor schmuck walked up to the bar and took a breath before talking. We said, "no beer for you" in our best "Soup Nazi" impression from *Seinfeld*. Finally, after far too many beers of our own, they cut us off, so we had to drunk ride back to the hotel. I don't know how far it was, but is seemed to take forever, partly because riding a two-person bike is more difficult than it looks, especially after a day of drinking in the sun.

We stopped on the beach and parked our bike against a light pole to take a walk in the sand. I kicked off my sandals and jogged behind Blake who just walked right out of his flip flops. I know it sounds like a picture of romance, but it's never been like that with me and B. He's always been just a friend with benefits. I know B is more into me than he lets on, but he doesn't push it. He just hangs out with me and makes me laugh.

One of the things I find so charming about B-Large is that he's totally into himself, so he rarely asks questions about me. He used to when we first met. He constantly asked about my family, why I didn't work, my childhood, but he realized soon that I was a closed book and has since stopped any inquisition.

I find it refreshing not to have to lie to him. He knows very little about me other than I like to drink, have sex, and do cocaine, so when he suggested a walk on the beach, I just figured it was to play some more, and I was right. He had magically scored some blow from a dude at the bar, so we took it down to the beach and each did a quick bump. We played in the water for a while, made out in the sand, then decided to head back to our room. I have no idea what time it was at this point, but the moon shone high in the sky surrounded by a pincushion of stars.

When we got back to our room, neither of us was ready for bed. I mean, we'd just done cocaine, so we were going to be up for a while. B turned on the TV and asked me to "snuggle" with him.

Listen, I don't snuggle or cuddle or share space. I learned a long time ago what happens when you get let someone into your zone, and there's no more room in my life for that kind of heartache, but B was all disheveled and sun-kissed and cute, so I climbed up on the big king-size bed and awkwardly sat next to him.

He lay down on his side and pulled me into him curling himself against my back. He ran his fingers through my hair and rubbed my shoulders a little. Then he lifted my hair up and kissed the back of my neck, his lips igniting my skin. I pushed my hips into him wanting more.

But that night, B did his snuggle thing and before I knew it, he started talking. He tends to talk a lot when he's high, so it's not a big deal, but this time he seemed ... emotional. He asked, "Yesterday in my apartment, you didn't leave like you normally do. What's up with that?"

Oh no. First mistake.

"I don't know. I guess I was having too much fun."

"You've never slept with me before."

"No, we're always too high to sleep," I nonchalantly replied.

"I know, Paige, but did something change?"

I rolled over and faced him at this point resting my head in my hand.

"B, are we having a relationship talk because if that's what you think this is, stop. You know I'm not into it," I said looking him directly in the eyes.

"No, Paige. Sorry. It was nice though, sleeping next to you." He reached up and playfully ruffled my already tangled hair.

"Well, geez, Blake. Why the hell did you just give me a mini heart attack?"

"I'm sorry, gorgeous. I didn't mean to surprise you. I was just wondering."

"Well since we're talking about surprises, what's up with all of your books?"

"What do you mean?" he asked as his sideways grin formed across his lips.

"A. You read? B. You're into the classics?"

"What the hell do you know about books, Paige? I don't read anything by Candace Bushnell or that chick who writes about vampires, no. I read the good stuff."

He really knows so little about me. I read. In fact, I read everything I can get my hands on from Emily Brontë to

Candace Bushnell to Leo Tolstoy. I don't limit myself to any genre or any time period. I read written words, period. Reading offers me an escape from reality that even drugs can't give me. I don't work, so I have a lot of free time. Books help me get from morning to happy hour without getting lonely.

"So you've actually read them?" I asked.

"Yes, of course."

"What's your favorite?"

"I don't know. I like them all."

"Not good enough."

"I'm not going there with you so that you can use it against me later. Take off your swimsuit and get over here."

"Stop trying to distract me with sex. Tell me. Maybe I've read it."

He rested his head back on his pillow, looking up at the ceiling.

"Mary Shelly's *Frankenstein* is up there, and I love *In Cold Blood*, and crime mysteries, I've read about a billion of those. I'm not sure I have a favorite."

"You're a reader. You have a favorite."

"Promise not to laugh?"

"Why would I laugh?" I asked as I played with the curly dark hair that ran across the top of his shorts.

"I don't know. What's your favorite book?"

"I'll tell you if you tell me."

"Okay, say it at the same time."

"Fine. If that will make it easier, weirdo."

"On three. One, two, three."

"*To Kill a Mockingbird,*" he said. I remained silent.

"Are you serious, B?"

"Yeah, my favorite book of all time is about a ten-year-old girl. It's lame. Stop looking at me like that."

"I actually find that incredibly ..." I thought for a second, trying to find the right word, "chimerical." I said untying my bikini top from my neck.

"Did you get that off a Word of the Day calendar?" I punched him in the arm then laid back on my side of the bed leaving a little space between us.

"No, ass. I'm just impressed a little."

"You're impressed?" I nodded. He coaxed me toward him summoning me with his index finger.

I crawled over to him on the bed.

He grabbed my face and pulled it into his and kissed me.

"Mmmm," he moaned.

Then he untied the ties on the side of my bikini bottoms and laid me on my back. He kissed my neck then the side of my breast. He tickled tiny little kisses that sent chills down my stomach all the way to my inner thigh. Then he started teasing me with his fingers, tracing me with the tip of his finger in and out until my hips were raised in invitation begging for more. I laid there quivering, my body betraying every bit of control that it had. Who was this guy with these moves, and why the hell had we not met?

He put his mouth on me and began an oral assault that made parts of me more tender and sensitive than I ever realized was possible. I moaned and jerked and tightened around his tongue trying to hold back the impending breakdown of my release when all of a sudden, he stopped. I picked my head up and looked down at him with asking eyes. He just smiled as he pulled off the orange shorts and slid inside of me, warm and hard. He held my gaze, while slowly moving himself in me. Then he did something he never does during sex. He kissed me.

Oh my god. This was epic B-Large sex. He was slow and deliberate taking me to levels of ecstasy that I didn't know existed making me cry out and beg for more. I must have said don't stop a thousand times. I've had some really good sex, lots of really good sex. I've had really good sex with Blake, but, Steph, this one experience makes everything else I've ever felt look like amateur hour at open mic night, and it wasn't just because of the leg trembling orgasms.

I felt it in my chest.

When we were finished, I went into the bathroom, weak and quivering, to shower and pull myself together. I looked into the mirror and saw a pink-skinned flushed Paige staring back at me. He left little red bumps all along my neck and chest from where he rubbed his face against my skin. B-Large gets the best kind of stubble, the kind that develops just after lunch and lasts until the next day when he shaves again. My lips were puffy and red from all of the biting and kissing. My hair was tangled and ratty, which I'm certain had as much to do with the sand and saltwater as the sex.

I jumped in the shower and cleaned the day off of me. When I finished, I toweled off and wrapped the towel around my body tucking it in under my arm. I ran my comb through my hair, getting all of the tangles out then walked into our room where B sat waiting for me, still naked (he's terminally naked, a borderline exhibitionist) with a glass of water in one hand and a pill in the other.

"I thought we should try to get some sleep," he said as he handed me the pill.

I didn't ask him what he was giving me. I never do, actually, just take whatever it is. In a way, we're highly trusting of each other for two people who claim to be just bed buddies. We don't even use condoms, which goes against all of my rules. I use birth control, Mirena, so I'm not worried about getting pregnant.

He and I both get tested for STD's regularly. We actually have dinner parties at his apartment together so that we can read each other's results. I know, sweet, isn't it? When we're both clear, we celebrate with champagne and sex. We've never not been clear, so I'm not sure how we would handle that.

I started over to my suitcase to pull out my nightgown, but he stopped me. "No. Don't get dressed. Sleep naked with me." I love it when a guy gives me commands in the bedroom, so I just dropped my towel and crawled into bed with him. B kissed the top of my head and whispered, "You never told me what your favorite book was." I pushed my body against his and ran my finger across his chest.

"You won't believe me if I tell you."

"Sure I will. I believe everything you tell me."

"It's actually *To Kill a Mockingbird*, too. I've probably read it a thousand times."

"You don't have to lie to make me feel better, you know? I'd admit to just about anything for a replay of the last half hour," he said, running his fingers along my arm.

"It really is my all-time favorite book, B. It has been forever."

"Really? What makes it your favorite?"

I took a deep breath as we lay there in the dark with just the quiet television lighting the room. This would be a moment of truth or lie with Blake. I chose truth, but only a small glimpse of it.

"Cal always reminded, reminds me actually of my childhood nanny."

He laid there for a second not saying anything. I dared not even look at him until he broke the silence and said, "Who wouldn't want a Calpurnia?"

Relief washed over me that he didn't try to probe further. I made the decision to one day tell him about Lucy. It took a while for the pill to take effect, so we watched a movie until we fell asleep. B held me close to him. And I liked it.

The next day we slept in until neither of us could spend another minute in bed. We got up, dressed, and went down to the restaurant for brunch. We were both famished, considering we had nothing to eat the previous day. Thankfully, neither of us talked about the night before. It was strangely a very quiet meal, and not at all awkward.

Since Blake had to work downtown, we transferred to an upscale hotel in the Gas Lamp District. During the day, while B-large worked, I walked the streets of downtown San Diego, shopping, having lunch, wasting time, a little sailor watching, basically waiting for a text to meet him for happy hour when he finished his day. I was giddy with anticipation every time I heard the ding on my phone. Several times that ding was a message from Dr. Love asking why I missed my session on Tuesday, then another asking why he hadn't heard from me. On Friday, he sounded even more frantic.

D-Love: MS. PRESTON, YOU NEED TO CALL ME BACK–ASAP!!!!!

I purposely ignored his calls and texts, teasing him a little, letting him wonder where I might be or what I might be doing, showing him who's in control of my time.

Once I finally heard from B, we would meet up, have a nice dinner, go out for a drink or two and head back to the hotel. We did this almost every day. This type of monotony would typically make me crazy, but strangely, I sort of enjoyed it.

We walked holding hands, laughing with each other. He's always been very affectionate, but normally I push him away. On this trip, however, he frequently leaned in and kissed my neck or my cheek as we strolled down the street. I wondered if this was what Janie's boyfriend fuss was all about.

On our last night, we got to the hotel a little early and had a few drinks in the hotel bar. Then we ventured into a dark room filled with big leather chairs, small coffee tables, and an overwhelming smell of incense. In the middle of the room, stood a large chess table, so B-Large challenged me to a game. He had no idea that I was a closet chess junkie until I schooled him three times. I went to state twice in high school, but that I don't tell anyone.

We sipped on martinis playing chess, laughing, talking, doing what I'd seen so many of the couples around me do when I realized that's sort of what we were pretending to be, a couple. I've never had a boyfriend before. I tried to allow myself to get used to the idea. Could Paige Preston be girlfriend material?

The other thing I realized in this dark smoky room was that I was having a really good time without drugs. Aside from the one night on the beach, our noses stayed clean during this little trip which is out of the ordinary because B-Large and I spend a lot of time together, time that usually revolves around snorting cocaine, having sex, and partying.

Like I said, I like that he doesn't try to figure me out, that he doesn't seem to care about my past or about my family or really about anything other than my body, but during this little trip, I learned things about *him*. I never realized how smart he was or how charming and funny he can be. I never saw him through clear eyes. He's kind of amazing. I sat across from this precious man who deep down I've counted on to always keep me company when no one else was around, who has been consistently there to put his arm around me or open a door for me, or fuck me three sides of Sunday, and yet, I'd never actually noticed him. B-Large was real.

We flew home the next day with dry mouths and puffy eyes. We didn't sleep much the night before, spending most of it naked in the big soft bed. He held my hand on the plane, and instead of making out and drinking, I laid my head on his shoulder and fell asleep. Something changed between us this week, something remarkable.

I guess tomorrow I'll call Dr. Love and let him know that things are looking up for Paige.

Daddy

Dear Stephanie,

I saw Dr. Love today. Depressed Paige disappeared, and content-to-her-heart's-desire Paige sat happily on the purple couch with a smile and a half surprised look Botoxed onto her forehead. He couldn't have missed it. After a fifteen-minute lecture on why I should never go a week or more without contacting him, missing my sessions, etc., to which I mechanically nodded in agreement, we got down to business.

I wanted to dive right into my new boyfriend and all of the exciting things I learned in the last week, but Doc had other ideas. He apologized for being all tongue-tied over my mother and that whole situation and said that he thought we should talk more about her and him.

Him ... aka my father.

I never talk about my father. I try not to even think about him. My father is an egotistical, self-praising, arrogant, pompous, deceptive, manipulative, dishonest, distrustful, heartless, cold pervert.

I could go on.

Where would I even start in telling Dr. Love about my father? I could tell him about the "dad" everyone else sees, the dad who always dresses in expensive designer suits who wears a million-dollar smile and holds a firm handshake, the man everybody loves, everybody admires, everybody wants to be deep down inside.

Peter Parnevik, a man of many words, pretty colorful rainbow words that burst from his mouth in his smooth, velvet voice, always the center of attention, the kind of man who when he walks into a room, everyone takes notice. Handsome Peter Parnevik, tall and lithe, with dark blonde straight hair always parted perfectly on the left side, always, large white flat teeth, his only flaw being the tiny two slightly crooked teeth on the bottom row, only noticeable when he speaks passionately about politics, money, or God forbid religion, two little teeth that make me want to punch him in the cleft of his perfectly chiseled pink-skinned chin. Men respect him. Women desire him. People love my father. Because he excels at manipulation.

Even I did at one time. Once I was a vulnerable, naïve girl, and he was the center of my universe. He bounced me on his knee singing, "Trot trot to London, trot trot to Lynn. Watch out pretty Paigey or you might fall in" at which point, he would let me fall between his legs as I laughed so hard my plump little belly ached.

When he was not traveling for work, he tucked me into my bed and told me stories of little girls riding on unicorns through castles with whimsical towers and long-haired princesses in his soft smooth voice. He would always finish his story, "and they lived happily ever after." Then he would lean in, pull my pink and white checkered quilt up to my chin tucking it around my tiny little body, plant a soft kiss on my forehead and whisper, "sweet dreams, babycakes."

I would listen to the soles of his shoes tap tap tap on the hardwood floors all the way to my door. He always left it open a crack to let the hall light filter into my room.

On too many nights to count, I lied awake in my bed listening to him and my mother argue in hushed voices with an occasional, "Goddammit, Pamuy," or "You fucking liar, Peter" shouted but then immediately the whispers would begin again. Eventually, the quiet voices would stop, and I would creep out of my bed and tiptoe to their room, listening outside of their closed door to hear my mother giggle.

Then I would hear the rustling of their bed, tiny creaks here and there, my mother's voice oohing, my father's grunting. The never ending cycle of my father's constant infidelity, my mother's insecurity, neither actually having the nerve to end the relationship, two co-dependent and selfish fools believing that love could mend it all.

My mother could go from enraged lunatic to pathetic puppy loved school girl with a flash of my father's smile. In a word, he is charming. He oozes charm from everywhere, from his teal eyes to his poetic vocabulary. He charms in a way that could even melt my ice cold heart. All he ever had to do was call me his "Paigey girl" or "pretty pretty Paige" to nuke the iceberg that he personally planted between my ribs.

Like I said, I didn't always hate him. I think I mentioned that he was a pervert, a cunt seeking snake always sniffing around for a new hole where he could find shelter. He never had sex with me or anything, thank God, but he never hid his countless mistresses. I caught him one night. It was my tenth birthday.

We spent the day celebrating me and the day I was born. We had brunch at my parents' country club. I ordered my favorite breakfast, crispy edged Belgium waffles made soggy in the middle by melted real butter, dripping in warmed maple syrup served with a side of fatty bacon that I dipped in my syrup.

It was our tradition. On mine and my twin brothers' birthdays, we always had brunch at the country club where we could look like the model family. My brothers, Paul and Patrick, would wear matching Polo shirts and pleated pants with braided leather belts and shiny brown loafers.

My mother always dressed me in some puffy dress with a full skirt, ruffles on the collar and the sleeves, a pretty ribbon tied perfectly around my waist, white tights and black dress shoes that clicked on the floors when I walked but left little red marks on my tender heels when I took them off.

My dad would sit with us briefly, sipping his black coffee, eating his Eggs Benedict, scanning the room for someone more interesting, more enticing until his eyes would finally catch his prey, and he would ever so politely excuse himself from the table, place his napkin next to his plate, and saunter over to some other person, the sound of his pathetic phony chuckle gradually fading as he finally reached his target. He would look toward the table at various times raising his cleft chin flashing a fake smile in acknowledgment of my mother as if saying, "This guy has much more to offer me as we discuss the tantalizing subject of the latest treatment they did on the greens of the golf course. Sit there and look pretty, Pammy."

At this point, Pam would order her third mimosa or fourth bloody mary and sit nervously wiping the corners of her mouth a hundred thousand times between drinks, picking at the pieces left of her dry whole wheat toast and plain egg white omelet. A bland breakfast she always suffered through in order to stay trim.

On my tenth birthday, we did the brunch thing and then went back to our house where my parents invited some friends over to continue the celebration. Janie was there with her parents along with several of my other schoolmates, but Janie and I never associated with the other girls, so once we scarfed down some pink birthday cake and some sherbet punch, we headed up to my room and played in my Barbie house making Ken and Barbie do very inappropriate things with their anatomically incorrect plastic parts.

Sometime just before dark, Janie's mother came into my room and told us that it was time for them to go. After many protests from Janie which were followed with threats that she would be grounded for the week, she and her parents made their way home. I walked her out to her car and watched as her dad maneuvered their Bentley around the rows of other identical cars. Janie waved to me from the back window as if we were never going to see each other again. Our good-byes are always dramatic, even to this day.

Once her car was out of sight, I walked back into the house. I watched the caterers scurry around trying to manage all of the empty wine glasses. The room was noisy and crowded, full of people I hardly knew. My dad always networked when he was home, said it was necessary to maintain a good relationship with our neighbors and our community, so if they met the minimum income requirement and had shaken my dad's hand, they were invited. I loathed them, all of them. I looked around for my mother or my father and didn't see them anywhere. I've never been a fan of crowds, so I decided to stroll around our property and get some air.

We had a beautiful garden filled with fragrant pansies and big pink and yellow roses that filled the June evening air with the rich smell of the beginning of summer. I made my way down the flagstone path trailing my hand along the tall thick shrubs that lined the walkway, thinking about all of the new things I received for my birthday when I heard my father's whispering. I crept slowly toward his voice secretly thanking my mom for putting me into the too tight shoes which were now sitting in my bedroom closet next to a pair of ridiculous tights.

As I got closer, I heard a female voice. I hid myself behind a potted mini palm tree and glanced into the grotto. Inside was a naked Peter sitting on the wet rock straddled by a beautiful auburn haired girl with glow-in-the-dark white skin. He ran his fingers up and down her back as she squirmed and giggled.

"Daddy!" I yelled before realizing it and quickly cupped my hand over my mouth trying to retreat again behind the tree, but they saw me. She turned and looked at me, the piercing blue eyes of my best friend's older sister gazed into mine. My disgusting horny pervert dad was fucking my best friend's seventeen-year-old sister in my swimming pool. My mother and countless of their friends were just feet away drinking champagne and red wine laughing about something irrelevant while my heart shattered like crystal, throwing shards of glass across the damp stone where I stood bare-foot and suddenly very cold.

I ran inside and locked myself in my room. I sat on my bed holding myself rocking back and forth while salty tears poured down my cheeks, pooled into my lips, and dripped onto my ruffled collar. I practically kicked myself. I wondered how long it had been going, if it was something new or if she was the reason my mother had been drinking herself to sleep every night, and if my mother knew, why would she stay with him?

Then I realized it was all my fault. Melody knew my dad because I knew Janie. Janie's parents knew my parents through our friendship. I practically fed Melody to my father. I hated myself for it, but I hated him more. I decided to end my friendship with Janie. Fortunately, if Janie is anything, she's persistent, and she didn't allow it. I did, however, refuse to ever speak to Melody again. To this day, I have not said a single word to that fire-crotched whore.

I waited for my dad to come in and explain it to me, to tell me it was a mistake, to tell me he was sorry. I wanted so badly to bury my head in his chest and let him comfort me. He didn't tuck me in that night or ever again. There were no more princess stories that ended happily ever after.

Yeah, happily ever after, fuck you.

I grew further and further away from my father, inches to miles to continents apart. I don't speak to him. He makes his attempts, but I refuse.

And here I was in therapy, trying to decide what to tell the good doctor about this man, this man I reverently called "daddy." "What would you like to know about my parents, doctor?"

"What was your relationship with them like?"

"Pretty much non-existent."

"Elaborate, please." He was beginning to match my short answers with short questions. Ping-pong, his serve.

"Non-existent, meaning it ceased to exist."

"I don't need the definition, Paige. I do have an MD." That's right, *Paige*. I heard it, too.

"I didn't have a relationship with either of my parents. They were basically gone my entire life, only here for birthdays and holidays and fundraisers."

"Who took care of you while they were away?"

"I did."

"Even when you were young?"

"I was never young."

"What does that mean?"

"I came out of my mother's womb red-faced and mature, an old soul, she used to say. I didn't even cry when I was born, at least that's what she said. She said a lot of things that were not true."

"Like what?"

"Like, 'see you later'. Then days would turn into weeks that turned into a month, then two, and so on." Once I didn't see my parents for three months. No holidays or birthdays between February and May. I actually used to mark the calendar with red x's for the days that they were gone. That year, it looked like my calendar started her period.

"What were they doing when they were away?"

"Business, always business, for my dad at least. My mother had nothing to do with his business other than to be the pretty little trophy that stood by his side. She rarely let him go without her."

"Let him?"

"Let him." He wrote something on his yellow pad.

"What sort of business?"

"Jewelry. Emeralds." Being the only child, he inherited his family's emerald mines in both Switzerland and Australia. He traveled to the mines frequently. When he wasn't "manning the mines" as he would say, he would spend a lot of time in other countries negotiating with jewelry merchants, making money. His first love. I always found it funny how emeralds and dollars were both green and both equally important to my father. I also find it strangely ironic that my birthday is just seven days from having an emerald as my birthstone. Stubborn Paige, born two weeks late. I can imagine the stupid jewelry he would have wrapped in pink little ribbons and handed to me with smiling eyes awaiting my astonishment at the shock of another green gem in a velvet box.

I purposely wore any of the jewelry he bought for me on days that I knew he and my mom were scheduled to come home, hoping that maybe he would notice. I remember too many times sitting at the top of the stairs, caressing an emerald pendant around my neck, waiting for my dad to come through the door from a long trip on his expected day of return, only to sit there, sore and tired for hours, disappointed that yet another trip got extended. Aching with loneliness through another meal eaten on a TV tray instead of the dining room table. Another meal eaten without them.

"They traveled a lot for work?" asked Dr. Love.

"They traveled a lot and said it was for work. My grandfather never traveled that much. He lived in the states for the later part of his life and managed to run things quite successfully from his office in Manhattan."

"Tell me about your parents. How did they meet?"

I told him their story. My mother grew up in Oklahoma, on a reservation riddled with stereotypical alcoholism and drug abuse. Because of it, her parents were strict, refused to let her out of their sight. As a teenager, she became rebellious and got in with the wrong crowd, drinking, doing drugs, having sex. Her father was respected and prominent within the community, and once he realized the path she was taking, he kicked her out of the house. At seventeen, my mother was on her own. Like my father, my mother was an only child, had no family she could turn to, so she started waitressing. She wanted to get out of Oklahoma, so she worked for a couple of years, living in a ratty apartment until she saved up enough money to move to Dallas. She got a job at the airport. That's where she met my father. He was flying home from Dallas to New York and sat at her bar. He says he fell in love immediately, that the moment she looked at him with her big brown eyes, he was done. Every time he told this story, he always said, "The hardest thing I ever did was leave that bar thinking I would never see her again."

They exchanged phone numbers, and the next time my dad came to Dallas, he took her on their first date. Three weeks later, they eloped. My mother always said that my father married her so quickly so that his parents wouldn't have a chance to disapprove. They did at first, but they grew to tolerate my mother as she struggled to fit in with their lifestyle. They lived in New York for a while, but the winters were too much for my mother and sent her into a terrible depression, so my father compromised, and they moved to Dallas.

He had to travel anyway, so where he had his home office wasn't that important, or at least that's what he said to convince his father not to take the business away from him. I think that's one of the reasons my father always worked so hard, to prove to my grandfather that he hadn't made a mistake. They had my brothers shortly after their move, which won my mother's approval in my grandparents' eyes. Twin boys to groom to take over the business. What could be better?

I told Dr. Love the short version of the story and then he asked, "Do you love your parents, Paige?"

I pondered that question. Do I love my parents?

"What is there to love, Doc?"

"You aren't Jesus, Paige." I looked at him confused. "Jesus always answered questions with questions ..." He cleared his throat. "In the Bible."

"I'm not very religious."

"I'm sorry. That was unnecessary. Do you, though ... love your parents?"

"I don't know."

"Do you hate them?"

"Yes." It came out of my mouth before I could pull it back in. I didn't think, just spoke, very unlike me.

"Why?"

Inhale. Sigh. Eye roll. "They had other things to do than to love me."

"Like travel for work?"

"Yeah. Like travel for work. And for pleasure." You know, most parents take their kids on family vacations in the summer, watch their little girls squeal and splash in the waves, take pictures of lopsided sandcastles just before the tide takes them back to the ocean, rub ridiculous amounts of sunscreen on peachy white skin. My parents went on extravagant vacations. Sometimes my mother would show us pictures of the places they had been, an excluded beach in Thailand, skiing the Swiss Alps, wine tasting in Italy. We were never in those pictures. "We were never included in their fun. In their life."

I said *fun* as I made quotation signs in the air. They never made it to open house at school, or even Christmas programs. I never played any kind of sport because I didn't want to be the girl who didn't have anybody cheering in the stands. On prom night, Janie's mom insisted that I come to her house to get ready. I know now it's because she knew nobody would be there to tell me how beautiful I looked in my prom dress, to take my picture next to the mantel, to give me a curfew and tell me not to drink.

"You feel abandoned." A statement, not a question.

"I was abandoned." We sat in silence for a minute. Dr. Love wrote on his pad. I looked around for an ashtray wondering how inappropriate it would be to pull a Parliament from my bag in his office and light it up.

"Go on, Paige," he said in a warm butter voice.

"I never had to worry if my mom was going to come into my room and catch me smoking pot or letting some schmuck feel me up. I was actually jealous of the kids who got grounded because at least their parents noticed they did something wrong. I never sneaked out of the house because no one was listening. I actually envied a friend of mine in college whose mother did coke with us. How fucked up is that? But at least her mom knew her, knew what she liked. My mother just didn't care, about me anyway," I finished in a whisper. Great. What was happening here? He's getting me to tell him stuff.

"When did this start? When did you start to feel like you were alone?"

"On my tenth birthday." The day the earth shook beneath me.

"That's very specific, Paige. What happened?" I told him the story, every detail. I've never told anyone about that night. I never even told Janie. I wanted to protect her from that. I held it in and watched the man formerly known as my daddy turn into a stranger. The traveling increased, the hugs decreased. He disappeared that night, faded into the dark June sky and never returned.

After my elaborate confession, Dr. Love leaned forward in his chair, placing his notepad on the table between us. He paused for a minute, took a deep breath, and then looked straight into my eyes. "He was ashamed, Paige."

"What?" My father knows a lot of things. Shame is not one of them.

"Don't you see, Paige. He obviously held you in a special light, his only daughter, the one female who he genuinely loved, truly loved. You caught him doing something ugly, something vile, really, and he couldn't face you. Did he handle it poorly? Yes. Cowardly? Obviously, but you feel abandoned because he felt ashamed."

"Ashamed." I repeated the word in a whisper while it screamed in my ear. "I did love him." I quietly said as a single tear slid down my cheek.

"Thank you, Paige." Dr. Love said as he walked me to the door.

"For what, sharing my fucked up family with you?"

"No, for being honest."

"You're welcome."

He walked me to the door, then smiled, dark eyes staring into dark eyes. I turned on my heel and walked away. By the time I got to my car, I was sobbing.

I sat holding my steering wheel hunched over shaking violently, mascara mixed with tears and snot running down my cheeks. I looked at the clock. I gave myself ten minutes to pull myself together. When I was no longer ugly crying, I took three deep breaths and called my person.

That night I had a true and sober girl's night with Janie. Janie knew my relationship with my dad was at best tangled, so when I called her, I told her that my therapist was insisting on hearing about my parents. She immediately sympathized with my state of mind and insisted that she would come to my house as soon as she finished working. She brought over our favorite childhood slumber party movies, *Adventures in Babysitting* and *Dirty Dancing*, and we lounged in my bed eating pizza from the box and laughing, quoting our favorite lines to each other. "Nobody puts baby in the corner," we said, cheese dangling from Janie's lip, making us laugh like children. She left a little after midnight, and instead of taking a pill or nine, I actually went to bed clear headed accepting my reality.

Maybe therapy isn't so bad after all.

Boyfriend

Dear Stephanie,

I have a boyfriend. I know, what? I have a boyfriend. I can't get used to saying it, but it's true. There's no other description. B-Large somehow managed to become my boyfriend. Boy. Friend. As in, I don't want to have sex with anyone else. Who am I?

Since we came home from San Diego, we've seen each other almost every day. He cooks me dinner most nights that we're together, and surprisingly, he's actually a good cook. I'm not a very big eater. I prefer alcohol to food, but since B started cooking for me, I've learned to love all sorts of new things. He's ridiculously adorable in the kitchen, too. He wears this hideous apron that says "Kiss the Cook" and hums to himself as he whisks or stirs or sautés, or whatever it is that he's doing. It takes every ounce of this girl's self-control not to take him on the kitchen counter. I mean, the boy is a god. He's rich, he's smart, he's amazing in bed, and he cooks. I think I've won the lottery.

Last weekend he took me camping. First of all, this city girl would never willingly agree to camping, but he surprised me. He told me he wanted to get away and to pack warm clothes and comfortable shoes for two days, so of course, I packed three pairs of skinny jeans, one cream off the shoulder cashmere sweater, one red cowl neck wool sweater, a couple more backup sweaters, my brown leather riding boots, and a handful of naughty lingerie. I didn't even pack a jacket. I'm not a huge fan of surprises, particularly when they involve travel because it makes my packing ritual so challenging. Blake said to pack light, so I probably packed and repacked twenty-seven times. I finally popped a Xanax and decided I'd go shopping if I needed anything else.

Right on schedule, we rolled out of the parking garage. Then we drove for hours, but it felt like days up Highway 35. I watched Dallas disappear from my window. Tract homes replaced tall buildings as we drove through the northern suburbs, and before I knew it, we were driving over the bridge for Lake Lewisville, also commonly referred to as "Lake Death." In the summer, you can't turn on the news without hearing about some search team looking for a body of someone who decided to hop off the boat and just go for a swim. I'm pretty sure the Loch Ness Monster has a cousin who lives at the bottom of this lake and pulls people under at random.

And then, as is typical for the suburbs, traffic stopped. I took a deep breath.

"You okay, Paige?"

"I don't like bridges."

"It's just a short bridge."

Blake put his hand on my thigh and squeezed.

I have a huge fear of bridges, particularly driving off of one and drowning, so I held my breath until we made it across. It's ironic really that I'm scared of dying, yet I want to kill myself.

We made it over the bridge, and as we crossed the Oklahoma state line, B changed his satellite radio from our typical alternative station to terrible country music, which was purposeful in order to get us into the spirit, or so he said with a crooked smile.

I always pictured my mom's home state as brown, dead, and dirty. She talked of Oklahoma with complete disgust, but what we passed could only be described as beautiful.

Tall evergreen pines lined the highway as if purposely creating a barrier between man and nature. Everything looked crisp and clean. I had to wonder why my mother hated this place so much. Blake turned off of the highway and down a country road lined on both sides with thick rows of trees shading our path. I envisioned a spa at the end of the road where we would sit in hot mud baths sipping cucumber water. The anticipation was killing me, and Blake refused to even acknowledge my inquiries.

He turned down a dusty gravel road that dead-ended to a patch of soft green grass lined with you guessed it, more trees. Then he stopped, put the car in park.

B grabbed my knee and said with contagious boyish delight, "We're here."

"Where?" I asked.

"Here. For our weekend getaway." I looked around. No cabin. Anywhere.

"Not to piss on your parade, but seriously, where are we?"

"We're going camping, baby."

"As in, pitch a tent, build a fire without a gas log and a switch, camping?"

"You got it, sweet cheeks. I'm thinking we can put the tent over here." Did he say tent? He pointed between two trees. "And the fire will go here."

"Seriously, Blake. Dude, are you fucking with me right now?" In what world did he think I would ever consider and agree to sleeping outdoors?

"No, Paige. This will be fun. You'll see. Now help me unload the truck."

And with that, he ended the conversation. I stood there in the middle of a no exaggeration forest with my mouth permanently unhinged, watching with wide eyes as my city-boy boy-toy got up close and personal with nature. He popped the trunk and started unloading things as I took in our surroundings.

Birds squawked and sang back and forth to each other, probably announcing the arrival of intruders and plotting how they were going to seek their revenge. I took a deep breath. The air was crisp and fresh and clean.

"Don't just stand there, Paige. I've got a ton of stuff here that we have to set up. It will be dark soon, and we're going to need to get the fire started."

So I picked my jaw up from the ground, the dirty, bug infested ground and helped. What else was I supposed to do?

After several attempts, the tent finally went up, and we shoved our sleeping bags and pillows inside.

"Did you bring an air mattress?" I asked Paul Bunyan.

"No, baby, we're going to rough it this weekend. Don't you ever get sick of the city?"

"No, how can you get sick of the city? I love our city."

"Come here." I walked over to him, and he stood behind me, wrapping his arms around my waist. "I'm going to make you love it here. Trust me. There's nothing more romantic than sex under the stars." Then he pulled my hair up and kissed his favorite spot on the back of my neck.

Point taken. Another win for B. I eventually stopped pouting and relished in his charming excitement. He really was like a little boy so eager to show me all of his unknown world. Once we had everything set up and enough firewood for the night, we walked along a slow moving creek that wound through more dense trees. He held my hand and told me about his first time camping.

He chose this spot because it was the first place his dad ever brought him to camp. This was where he learned to fish and build a fire, and every September his dad would bring him and his brothers (which I didn't know he had) to this exact spot to give their mom a break, and they would sleep in a big tent, fish, swim if it wasn't too cold, play UNO when they were little and poker once they were old enough to understand the game. He told me about his dad and how he was his hero as he stared off into the distance, and I listened and enjoyed hearing what a "normal" family does.

Then he said, "If we ever have kids, I'll bring them here to camp any time you need a break."

I stopped and stood in silence, swallowed the lump in my throat, and replayed our conversation in my head. He seriously did just say something about having kids with me. I didn't know what to say, so I said, "Well, let's head back to the tent and get started."

"Get started?"

"Making you some company for your camping adventures because this girl doesn't camp."

He pulled me into him and then leaned me against a tree and kissed me. Then he looked at me and asked, "You want to have kids?"

"God no. I want to have sex. I was kidding about the kids. I'm too selfish for kids. You know this."

"I know you don't want kids *now*, but do you ever?" He pulled away from me then and guided me along another path back towards our campsite.

I'm a person who has a lot of time to think, and one thing I haven't had to think about much is where I stand on children. I know without a doubt in my mind that I will never want children. I simply dislike them, first of all. I find them extremely annoying and ill-mannered, little petri dishes full of germs. I can't stand that they always have dried snot around their noses or crusty food on the corners of their mouths. Kids are pretty much Paige repellent. Let's not even mention what a horrific job my parents did, which is the only parental examples I have to follow, so I decided long ago, no kids for me. Unfortunately, I couldn't say that, so what did I say to B? Well, I said what he wanted to hear.

"Doesn't everyone?"

He smiled at that. We walked back to our campsite hand in hand. Blake cooked steaks on his little portable grill and roasted corn on the cob over the fire. We drank a bottle of red wine, smoked a joint, and sat by the fire talking way into the night. He asked me about my family, but I skirted the question and distracted him with more questions about his.

He has three brothers. His mother had four boys and no girls. He said if you asked her, she would tell you that she spent most of her time as a taxi to him and his brothers, hauling one to basketball practice while another had soccer practice but that it was the time of her life. She loved having the boys in the car where they couldn't escape talking to her. He said he could tell her anything and did. He also told me that she was the strongest person he knew.

I fell in love with his mother that night. He mentioned that he would love for me to meet her, and I shockingly agreed to it, so that's on the horizon for next month. There's the knot in my stomach again.

When we got in the tent that night, Blake unzipped a few flaps and rolled them down revealing a sky sprinkled with thousands of silvery stars. I gasped, lying back on my pillow trying to absorb the sheer beauty of the world above me.

"I told you camping wasn't so bad," he said. He rolled to his side, put his hand on my hip and guided me to my side facing him. "I need you, Paige," he whispered as he started undressing me. His whiskered face brushed up against my cheek until his mouth found mine. His lips tasted like sweet red wine, and I took his mouth, hungry for more. He was gentle and precise, his fingers tracing my jaw.

He shifted me to my back. When I felt his weight on my chest, I welcomed him, wrapping my arms around his back pulling him into me wanting him closer than our bodies would allow. We moved together, two animals in the night, each a source of refuge for the other. In that tent, he was mine and I was his. Nothing else in the universe could challenge that. I forgot about the hard ground, the bugs, the threat of wild animals searching for food. Nothing existed but us, and for the first time in a really long time, I felt like I was home. Home, in the wilderness of all places.

The temperature dropped down into the fifties that night, which to some people would be comfortable, but I'm a Texas girl. When he realized I was cold, he offered me a pair of his flannel pajama pants, but I told him that according to an article I recently read in *National Geographic*, heat transfers better without clothes. We had a two-person sleeping bag, which was purposeful on Blake's part and having him sleep naked next to me warmed more than just my body.

We spent part of the next day hiking. B took me to a small pond and tried very patiently to teach me to fish. Neither of us caught anything, but in those moments, I found myself appreciating the quiet, the gentleness of nature and its subtle way of giving me peace. For a moment, I allowed my mind to rest. Before I knew it, the weekend was over, and as we started packing, I already longed to return.

And now I can't help but wonder. Is this what happiness feels like?

Highs

Dear Stephanie,

Back to life, reality, and therapy. This week, the good doctor was hell-bent on discussing drugs. He seems to think I suffer from addiction and has high hopes of helping me overcome this battle. His words. During a fairly quiet moment in his office, Dr. Love asked me why I do drugs. My answer, "Why not?" He responded with the typical non-drug user's response, "because they're addictive, because they're illegal, because they're bad for your body and your brain."

Stephanie, let's discuss my brain. Short story, my brain is fine. I'm twenty-nine years old which means I've been doing drugs for the last fourteen years of my life. The whole "you'll rot your brain" routine is old news. I don't like to brag, but I'm smart. I graduated at the top of my high school class and scored a 2200 on my SATs. That's only 200 points away from perfect, so I was offered scholarships to several different schools. I originally wanted to go away to college. I was accepted to Dartmouth University, my first choice, but when it came time to pack and get ready to move, I sank deep into a depression, a horrible sinking low.

Getting out of my bed was impossible. Thinking about all of the coming change, the fact that I would have to make friends and learn a new town, and then I couldn't imagine leaving Janie. She planned to stay in Dallas and attend Southern Methodist University. Imagining being 1,800 miles away from her just made me sink further and further. On the day I was scheduled to move, I told my parents that I had changed my mind, that I wanted to stay in Dallas for school. My father flipped out, but in the end, I enrolled at SMU. Janie and I got an apartment, and I declared English my major. I had no idea what I would want to do with my life, still don't really, but studying English meant that I would be required to take a bunch of literature classes, so at least I'd be entertained. I stopped going to school my junior year when I realized how unnecessary having a degree would be in my life, and having to wake up early and attend classes highly interfered with my more favorable activities, i.e. drugs.

From the outside looking in, I probably seem like a slacker because I don't have a job (which I don't need) or because I never really applied my adult self, but it doesn't mean I've rotted my brain. I can go head-to-head with any genius and come out on top, so that theory doesn't work on me, never did. Obviously.

To answer his next concern, yes, they're illegal. So what? So is speeding, which I do, everyone does. I'm not selling drugs to children or stealing money to buy drugs or offering to suck some scumbag's dick for drugs, so the only chance I'll get in trouble is if I get caught with drugs, which I never would because I repeat ... I'm too smart for that.

Also, I have standards. I don't do heroin. I won't try crack or crystal meth, or anything that will rot my teeth or age me. I mean, let's face it. I'm way too vain for this stuff. Plus, I'm not a junkie, and I won't let myself become one. I like the fun stuff. Cocaine, weed, ecstasy, acid, and magic mushrooms because who doesn't like to giggle? And pills, well, pills are my go-to. I love Xanax and Valium, and pain pills are fun mixed with drinks. I've tried Oxy a few times, but I don't love it. It makes me too hazy, too out of control, especially if I mix it with booze.

Which brings us to the addictive part. Are drugs addictive? Of course they are. Am I addicted? Not right now. Can I stop when I want to? Sure I can. I've quit doing drugs numerous times and not only because I've landed in rehab facilities. I have spent a lot of time in those, and I've seen the people who have addictions. I am not one of them.

The thing that people, namely my therapists, both past and current, don't seem to understand is that I don't do drugs every day. I don't wake up needing to get high. I do it for fun, on the weekends, at concerts, at night clubs. I have gone through times when I get cravings, but I am self-aware enough to realize when I'm getting out of hand. I simply take a break. If I want to stop, I can stop. Blake and I have seriously slowed down on the snorting these days, but do I want to? No. Why would anyone quit taking drugs?

I said all of this to my shrink today trying to explain to him that I really don't have a problem. He proceeded to ask me why I do drugs.

Why do I do drugs?

Have you ever felt like you were on the absolute top of the world, completely unmovable, invincible, unafraid, intimidated by nothing, completely uninhibited? It's called *high* for a reason. That is how I feel when I do cocaine.

The first time I tried it, I was fifteen. My parents were of course elsewhere. My brothers were away for college, following Daddy's footsteps and attending NYU, and I was alone and bored. I decided to go for some dinner, so I took my dad's Mercedes and went to this pizza dive that I loved where I ran into someone very familiar.

There was this guy, Toby, who lived a few houses down from me and went to public school. Going to an all-girls school, I tended to find boys anywhere I could, and he was easy since he was conveniently close. He often came over after school to get away from his family. We messed around a little, but I never let him go further than second base. He continually tried to get me to have sex with him, and for whatever reason, I played hard to get. He was cute though, blonde and fair skinned with blue eyes and dimples, so I flirted with him endlessly and basically teased him.

When I walked into the pizza joint, I noticed him immediately. I can't say whether I was relieved or annoyed. When he finally saw me sitting in my booth waiting for my pizza, he left his table and sauntered over. He was horribly arrogant, which annoyed me, so I pretended to be unmoved when he sat down.

He put his arm around me and ran his finger down my arm. Then he whispered in my ear, "I just scored something you might like. Wanna go for a ride?" I was going to take my pizza to go anyway, and being ever so curious, I nodded.

Fifteen minutes later, he was driving my dad's Benz toward my house, which smelled heavenly of my recently purchased pepperoni pie. We went up to my room where he pulled the tiny Ziplock bag out of his pocket and showed it to me. I had never seen cocaine. I was enamored.

Up to this point, my only experience with drugs was some dried up weed. I held the baggie in the palm of my hand, closing and opening my fingers around it, when Toby finally said something and got me out of my daze. "Want some?" he asked, and took it out of my hand.

"That's why you're here, asshole. Of course I want some."

"What are you going to do for me?"

"I'll pay you for it. How much was it?"

"I don't need your money, babe," he said. I hate when people call me babe.

"Then what do you want?"

He walked toward me and grabbed my crotch. "This."

I think I said, "What the hell," or something like that because before I knew it, he was grunting on top of me, sloppily shoving his very tiny dick into me and moaning like I was the best thing on Earth, which was the typical routine with the few high school boys I had entertained naked. Two minutes later, after flushing his too large for him condom, he lined up my first hit of cocaine.

He showed me how to do it first then handed me the rolled up dollar bill. I snorted so hard, I thought my head was going to explode. He rubbed a little over his teeth, so I did the same. My mouth went numb immediately.

A few minutes later, I fell into heaven. We moved into the den, and I turned on some music. I was going through a Ja Rule stage, so he, J Lo and Ashanti entertained us for the evening. We danced for an unknown amount of time, the energy never waning. Everything felt intense. My skin like electricity. My body felt weightless. My joy, endless. My sense of smell was even heightened. I don't know what fabric softener was used to wash Toby's shirt, but it smelled like the air after a summer's rain.

Even the music sounded better. I could hear every instrument individually, the bass mixed with the strings and the horns, which before that day, I never even noticed. Time passed, and eventually the high wore off. Toby left, and I began to wonder. Would I ever feel that good again?

That is why I do drugs, Steph. Because one day, I'm convinced, I will.

Slutoween

Dear Stephanie,

Halloween is my absolute favorite holiday. I love dressing up as someone else and playing a character for a night. I get really into it. I enjoy the entire process of transformation. You're probably thinking that I follow the masses on Halloween and slut it up. Uh ... no. I love scary, gory, bloody costumes.

Janie decided to host a huge party, proceeds benefiting her thirsty children organization, and she told me that I have to come, and I have to come in costume. Her words, "something awesome. There's a costume contest."

What Janie knows is that I'm extremely competitive and that dangling a contest in front of me solidifies my coming to her little soiree. What Janie doesn't know is that B-Large and I are more than just bed buddies now, so I thought it would be a nice surprise to show up with him as a couple. Maybe even a scary couple.

I couldn't wait for Blake to get home so that we could choose our award-winning costumes. I texted him to come straight home after work and to immediately let me know when he arrived. I decided that this Halloween would be the best ... ever.

I kept myself busy that day by cleaning my apartment, making sure everything was perfect because, well, that's just how I am. People often wonder why I don't hire a house-keeper since I can clearly afford one. It's simple really. I grew up with housekeepers. I know what they do when they think you're not looking, and I'm always looking. I don't trust anyone else with my stuff. Call it trust issues. Call it control. Besides, nobody cleans my place to my standards, so I prefer to just do it myself. I mean, if I have anything, it's time, right?

Finally, a ding on my phone.

B-Large: Home. Meet me in my bedroom

So I did. I found him lying naked on top of his unmade bed, smiling with his come-hither grin. I sat on the end of his bed at first, ready to dive into Halloween and a brain-storming session, but B wasn't having it.

"Get over here," he ordered.

"No. Aren't you even going to ask me how my day was?"

"No. I'm going to make your legs shake. Then we'll dis-cuss your day."

Damn, he speaks my language. After some intense leg shaking, he sprawled himself over me and asked, "So, tell me about your day."

I told him about Janie's party and my plan to win the costume contest. He perked up immediately, matching my enthusiasm.

"Sounds like fun. What should we be?"

"I don't know," I said. "I was thinking about maybe Uma Thurman and John Travolta from *Pulp Fiction*."

"Overdone. We could be Bonnie and Clyde."

"Speaking of overdone."

"What do you think?"

I bit my lip. "I don't know. I've thought about a bunch of things, but I want something memorable."

We laid there for a while, both calling out characters from movies and stories. Neither of us yielding to the oth-er's suggestions. Then B sat up. "Dr. Frankenstein and the monster. You'd be a sexy doctor."

"Ooohh!!!" I sat up, too, pulling the covers up with me. "I love that. Plus, we can at least enlighten a few people on the fact that the monster is not Frankenstein. But I want to be the monster."

"No, I want to be the monster." We sounded like two toddlers in a sandbox.

"I'll blow you for it." Well maybe not toddlers.

"Done."

I speak his language, too.

I searched online relentlessly and hired this lady that I found to make our costumes. I told her I would pay her double since she didn't have much notice, and she took the deal. The costumes turned out brilliant.

I also learned that some chick B knows is a makeup art-ist for the Dallas Opera, and B asked her to make me into the monster. I made an appointment, sat down in her chair, and she began the transformation. It might shock you, but I'm not a super friendly gal. I don't chat it up with people I have no intention of seeing again, and something about this girl said, "Don't trust me."

As soon as I sat in her little chair, she pursed her lips at me for a minute then said, "So you're Paige?"

"That's my name. Did you get the pictures that Blake sent?" I asked, not wanting to banter.

She nodded, sort of brushing off the question. "So, you're with Blake, huh?" she asked as she removed my make-up. I couldn't even concentrate because she kept smacking her gum, and sucking it through her teeth, popping loud spearmint bubbles. I guess I didn't answer quickly enough because she went on.

"So, like, are you guys together?" What business was it of hers, right?

"Yes," I said, hoping that she would catch on to the fact that I wasn't interested in a conversation.

"So, like, how long have you guys been together?"

"I don't know. Not very long."

"Wow, because Blake is like, I don't know. He, like, talks about you, like all the time."

I'm not exaggerating the "likes," Steph. She "liked" four times in one sentence. I counted. I still didn't involve myself in her conversation, but part of me wondered how frequently he saw this "like" girl and also the extent of their relationship.

As my eyes assessed her, she blurted, "We used to go out, you know."

"No. I didn't know."

"Yeah, like, a while back. He is so much fun, isn't he?"

"Yeah, a fucking riot." I stared at her boobs for a minute. Total falsies. Hey, I'm not judging. But I know Blake, and he's a total a tit man. This piqued my interest a little in "like" girl. "You dated Blake?" I asked. He didn't mention that when he suggested she do my makeup.

"Um, well. Like, I guess we went out a few times, yeah," which translated to, "I fucked your boyfriend ... more than once."

I'm not a jealous girl, not really, but seeing a former bedmate of my boyfriend in the flesh, well, it sort of made my stomach hurt, and not just a little bit. She kept talking, and told me about the time Blake took her to a Black Keys concert and how much fun they had, and how Blake was "like" the best dancer and that was "like" the best night of her life, and I began to see that this chick was "like" in love with my boyfriend.

And she kept talking and talking and talking as she applied not just makeup but prosthetics to my face. Four hours later, after listening to her tell me everything she knew about my boyfriend other than the size of his dick, she turned my chair around, and just like that ... I was the monster.

"What do you think?" she asked me through the mirror.

"You're amazing."

"Thanks. When Blake sent me the photos, I played around a little bit first so that I could get Frankenstein right."

"The monster," I interrupted.

"Yeah, like isn't that the same thing?"

"Like, no. Frankenstein was the doctor. He created the monster. The monster is like the monster."

"Oh, well, whatever. You look awesome in like a horrible sort of way. Can I take a picture for my portfolio?"

"Sure," and then I got an idea, a really bitchy one, and said, "You should come to the party."

"Really?"

"Sure. It's at that new club on Pearl. You'll love it, but you have to dress in costume."

"Oh, well, I already like bought my costume. Are you sure? Will Blake be there?"

"Of course, he's the doctor." Stupid.

I paid her $500, which was $200 more than she asked for because even if she's stupid, she earned it. Then I rushed home, got into my costume, and waited for Blake to knock on my door.

I wish I could describe his face when he saw me. To say he was awestruck doesn't even begin to describe it. "Holy shit, Paige."

"I know."

"Come on, monster," he said with a smile, offering me his arm, "let's go win a costume contest."

As we were driving to the club, I slipped in my little surprise. "I enjoyed meeting your girlfriend."

"You're my girlfriend," he said without looking at me, but I could see the smile turning up the corner of his mouth.

"Your like girlfriend like had a lot of like interesting like things to like say about you."

"Oh? Like what?"

"Like how like awesome you are and like how much like fun you guys like always had, and how like big your dick is."

"Shut up. She did not."

"No, she didn't go there, but dude, she loves you."

"Did she say that?" he asked.

"No, she didn't have to."

"Well, yeah, she wants my ass."

"Shut up! I was kidding."

"It's no secret, Paige. I'm a catch. I'm beating bitches off with a stick," he said as his grin stretched across his face. He was in a great mood. It was contagious.

"You arrogant ass."

"Don't worry, this is all yours," he said and grabbed my thigh, laughing.

"I invited her to the party."

All of a sudden, his expression hardened.

"What? Why?"

"Because, I wanted to see you squirm with both of us in the room. Are you mad?"

"A little. Paige, that's not cool. I don't want to see her."

"But I thought you were friends?"

"We are, Paige, but you should have asked me first before inviting her. Really. It's not cool."

"I didn't realize I needed your permission."

"Come on, Paige. Be reasonable. Would you want your ex-boyfriend at a party you were looking forward to?"

"I don't have an ex-boyfriend."

"God, why are you so weird?"

"Lighten up, B. It will be fine. She probably won't even come."

"Oh, no. She'll come. She's already there. Trust me."

And she was. We walked through the entrance and were immediately greeted by a bumblebee. And by bumblebee, I mean Blake's ex-girlfriend who took slutty Halloween costume to an all new level. She wore a yellow and black striped triangle top bikini that barely covered her nipples and left her (apparently recent) implant scars right out in the open, and her skirt, short doesn't even begin to describe it.

Blake whispered in my ear, "She needs two haircuts to wear that skirt." And then to her, he said, "Happy Slutoween ." Those words earned him a hearty laugh from me, and probably another blow job.

We left the slutty bee at the bar and headed to find Janie who also celebrated Slutoween only with a little more class, and by class I mean that I couldn't see her ass in her witch costume. She immediately recognized Blake. "Hey, Blake.

I didn't know you were coming." Then she turned to me. "I'm Janie. Blake sucks at introductions."

I smiled and extended my hand. "Paige Preston. Nice to meet you."

"Holy shit balls, Paige. You look amazing."

"I know."

And even though Blake's girlfriend shot daggers at us all night, we ended up having a great time. Janie was all too pleased to find out that Blake and I were actually a couple, so much so that she hugged B a thousand times. I even caught them whispering about me in a corner at one point, but it was too loud, and I was too drunk to make out what they were saying.

Unfortunately, we just drank, no drugs, since B had to work the next day, but surprise, surprise. We won the costume contest, and when Janie announced our names, I watched the bumblebee make her way through the crowd toward the exit.

When we got home, I tried to talk Blake into sex with the monster, but he said he couldn't do it. I looked way too scary. He helped me remove my make-up/prosthetics, and gave me a simple kiss good night. Then as I began to feel sleep tugging at my eyes, he said, "Please don't ever invite one of my ex-girlfriends anywhere again."

"I won't. Do you forgive me?"

"There was never anything to forgive."

"Okay, night, B." I said as he pulled me into his chests and kissed his spot on the back of my neck.

Like I said, I'm a little competitive, and it looks like I won more than just the Halloween contest.

Oikogeneia (Family)

Dear Stephanie,

It's official. I've met the Oikogeneia of my boyfriend, and they are all big fat Greeks. When B decided he wanted me to meet his mom, one thing lead to another, and I spent Thanksgiving with his entire family, brothers and wives, nephews and nieces, aunts and uncles, mom, dad, and yia yia.

It all just sort of happened. Blake mentioned meeting his mom on our camping trip. I agreed, expecting an afternoon coffee with the two of them, but Blake had other plans. When he learned that I planned to spend Thanksgiving with a book and a bottle of vodka, he insisted, through lots of arguing that I join him and his family instead of spending the holiday alone. And I said yes. Because I can't say no to this guy.

The next minute, I'm walking into their huge ornate living room filled with laughter and voices and children's squeals. I can't lie. I was overwhelmed. Even on a good holiday, my family never grew larger than maybe ten, and that included my dad's parents and a business associate or two, but this was off the scale. I mean, people were lined up wall to wall, talking with one another, hugging, yelling at kids.

B's family lives in a pretty big house, but there seriously was standing room only. It went a little like this.

We pulled up to the house, which sits on the end of a cul-de-sac, as I realized how many vehicles were parked on the street. Blake decided then to tell me that it was going to be a little more than just his "folks" (his word). He proceeded to tell me that Thanksgiving is a huge deal to his mom, Claire, and since she doesn't have any family nearby (hers live in Michigan or something), she invites all of his dad's huge Greek family who travel from all over the place to come for Thanksgiving. So, basically, he said, "you're going to be meeting about thirty people today, give or take."

"Give or take? Keep driving, B," I said through hyperventilated breaths.

"Don't be scared, Paige. My family is harmless."

"Then why did you wait until we were here to tell me there would be so many?"

"Because I knew you wouldn't have come," he said as he placed his Tahoe in park and hopped out of the truck like it was no big deal.

I watched him jog around the front then open my door. "Come on, beautiful. You're going to love them."

"I can't, Blake. C'mon let's just go back to your place, order Chinese, do this another time." My anxiety level was mounting, palms sweating, heart racing.

Just as the last word came out of my mouth, a tiny woman appeared in the door way.

"Is this her, Blake-darling?" she asked, wiping her hands on her apron. Then she jogged to the car.

"Yeah, mom. This is Paige," he answered as she reached my side of the Tahoe. Blake reached up to help me out of the truck. "Paige, this is my mom, Claire."

"Welcome, Paige. Blake's been talking about you for over a year now. We're so glad to finally meet you. Please come in."

Over a year? I wondered what exactly he's been saying to this woman.

And with that, there was no turning back, I held the petite hand of my boyfriend's miniature mother as she guided me through her front door. She led me into the great room and said, "Everyone, this is Paige. Please make her feel at home." Then she looked at me and said, "There's about a billion people waiting for some food, so if you'll excuse me, I have to get back to the kitchen. I'm really so glad you came." She squeezed my hand and then disappeared down the hall.

I looked over at Blake who wore an exaggerated smile as he started going through the line of people. "This is my yia yia." (He leaned down and kissed her head) "Yia yia, this is my girlfriend, Paige."

I reached down to shake her hand, but she wrapped her arms around my waist and whispered, "Welcome to our family, love."

I looked at Blake who continued to beam with excitement. My heart threatened to pound out of my chest.

"This is Ryan, my brother, and his wife, Sara, and their new baby girl, Lily." Blake shockingly took the baby out of her mother's hands and held her like a boss. He carried her with us as we went through the rest of them, no longer offering me his hand for support. "This is my brother, Mark, and his fiancée Brooke." Smile, shake hands. "This is James, my younger brother and his wife, Sidney." More smiling, more hand shaking, stomach twisting in knots as he introduced me to Aunt Sandy and Uncle Myles, Uncle John and Aunt Jan, Cousin Brandon and his wife, whatever, Aunt whatever, Uncle whatever. "And Paige, this is my dad, Robert. Everybody calls him Big Bob."

Big Bob stood up and towered over me. I thought Blake was tall for a Greek, but now I could see where he got his height. Easily, he stood six foot six, big burly belly, dark curly hair like Blake's with little hints of silver around the temples and forehead, and Blake's beautiful green eyes.

"It's nice to meet you, Bob," I said as I shook his enormous hand.

"Paige, sit. Have a drink. What's your pleasure, wine? Vodka? Or are you a scotch girl?"

"I'll just have a glass of water for now ... Please."

Blake looked at me confused. "Water?" he mouthed, shaking his head.

I nodded a confirmation. There's no way in hell that drunk Paige was going to screw this up. The baby started crying, and just like that her dad came in and rescued Blake from the screaming. "She probably just needs a fresh diaper," he said to me. Blake kissed her head and handed her off to her dad who placed her on his chest, patting her little bottom as he walked out of the room.

Blake shuffled me into another den where there were only half as many people to meet and then asked if I wanted a tour of his house. "Absolutely," I whispered as he took my clammy hand and walked me around his childhood home. He showed me the kitchen where his mother was working like crazy, fretting from one side of the kitchen to the other. "Are you showing her around, honey?" she asked Blake.

"Yeah, Mom, just giving her a little tour."

"Make sure you don't go into Ryan's room. Bobby's taking a nap in there." Then she addressed me, "Bobby's our three-year-old grandson, and you don't want him around if he hasn't had his nap."

"Okay, got it, Mom. Do you need any help?" He walked over to the stove and looked over her shoulder at the contents of a pot, putting his arm around her waist. She laid her head against him and patted his hand.

"In a bit, maybe. I'll need you to come in and make your famous gravy, but show Paige around first."

I smiled at her as our eyes met. Then she winked at me and shooed us out of the room.

We walked into a few different rooms. Then he showed me the room where he spent his boyhood. I sat down on the navy and green plaid comforter and took a deep breath. Then I leaned over and put my head between my legs and tried to talk myself out of throwing up. "You okay, Paige?"

"Not even slightly okay. I'm freaking out. I haven't had Thanksgiving dinner like this in years, and I think there were maybe eight people there, and that included the caterers." The one good thing about Thanksgiving is that the bars usually stay open, knowing that most people need to unwind after forced conversation with relatives. I just usually unwind without adding the relatives to the equation.

"Paige, this is my family. They're harmless."

"Yeah, you mentioned that. I'm just not good with parents, Blake, or family really. I'm so nervous." I admitted for the first time, a weakness.

He came over and sat down next to me. Then he pulled me down so that we were lying side by side on his queen-size bed, our feet still on the floor. "Shhh," he whispered. "My mother is already as in love with you as I am."

I think he said love, didn't he?

"That's because she doesn't know me, B."

"But I know you, Paige. Give them a chance."

"Okay, but can we leave when I'm ready?"

"As long as you're not ready until after the Cowboys game."

"Football, really?" I sighed. He pulled me on top of him and kissed me.

"We better get out of here," he said with a smile, "before I get caught having sex in my room again."

"Again?"

"Yeah, just wait. My dad loves to tell this story after he's had a few scotches."

"I think I'm going to like your dad," I said as he guided me out of his room.

We ended up having a great time, and he was right. His family was harmless. His brothers were like him, charming and witty with quirky senses of humor. And his dad ... well, he may very well be the reason why Blake is so cool. His dad was hilarious, full of funny stories that embarrassed B along with his brothers.

His mom and his dad took turns telling me all about Blake as a child, talking about first ski trips and the time the boys caught the kitchen on fire trying to cook breakfast for their mom for Mother's Day. When Big Bob got too boisterous, Blake's mom would simply place her tiny little hand over the top of his giant hand and squeeze. Then they would make eye contact, and his dad would change the subject.

After lunch, everybody went into the den to watch the very long and drawn-out football game, and I noticed something that I found so endearing. We had been in there for a bit, while Blake's mom and Sara cleaned the kitchen. She refused to let me help. When she came into the den, Big Bob looked at her and motioned for her to join him, and she did.

She walked over to his leather recliner and sat down right on his lap and watched the remainder of the game from there. I was mesmerized at the open display of affection. He snuggled into her and kissed the back of her head half a dozen times, and I realized that this was where B-Large grew up. This was the home where he learned to love, so if he did mean it when he said the dreaded "L" word, maybe it might not be the worst thing in the world.

I don't want to jump ahead, but part of me already has.

Perfection

Dear Stephanie,

Dr. Love seems to think I'm obsessed with perfection. I don't even know how to respond to this. I mean, yeah, I'm a perfectionist. What's so wrong with that? Today in therapy, he brought it up to me like this ...

"As you know, Paige, I've read your medical file."

"Yes."

"Want to tell me about the plastic surgery?"

"I didn't think that it was relevant to my mental health, doc."

"Everything is relevant to your mental health, Paige." He said using air quotes around mental health and matching my sarcastic tone.

I sat there twirling my hair, staring down at my recently manicured toe that rested against my favorite fuschia Jimmy Choo sling-backs.

"Paige? Are you going to talk to me today?"

"Um, you're asking me to talk to you about my boobs. Why don't I just take my shirt off and show them to you and save us both a bunch of time because, trust me, they are fabulous?"

"I'm not talking about your boobs, Paige. I want to talk to you about your decision to have plastic surgery. Tell me about that."

"Which time?"

"Well, the first time is a good start." He took a deep breath and crossed his leg so that his foot rested on his knee. I could see the hair on his legs through the gap in the bottom of his pants. I noticed he could use some lotion. He doesn't wear a ring, so I knew he probably wasn't married, but it is clear now that there is no woman in his life. Ashy skin is a clear sign of the absence of a feminine touch. My attraction for the doctor to this point was waning with the whole new world of my relationship with Blake, but I still have eyes and a vagina. I couldn't help but wonder how he was single. Single and wanting to know about my boobs. Jesus.

"Seriously, Dr. Morea, I really don't want to talk about this. I already know what you're going to say, and frankly, it won't make a difference."

"When you become the psychiatrist and I become the patient, you can decide what we talk about." He's trying the tough love approach apparently.

"What was the question again?"

"Why did you decide to have your first plastic surgery?"

"Because I had small boobs, and I wanted big boobs."

"Okay, good enough. Why did you decide to have your second plastic surgery?"

"Because I liked having big boobs, so I wanted bigger boobs?"

"What about the surgery between the two breast augmentation surgeries?"

I almost forgot about that surgery. I was still in college at the time. After getting my first boob job, I got into a very short relationship with one of my dealers who ended up breaking my nose one night during a heated and very drunken argument. He didn't hit me. He was actually trying to leave my apartment.

We had a very volatile relationship, and we fought all the time. I can't even remember what it was about, but I was having a complete hysteria fit and wouldn't let him go. I wanted to keep fighting. As he tried to walk away, I grabbed his arm with all of my drunken strength. He yanked it away, and when he did I stumbled and fell face first onto my marble tile in my kitchen leaving me with a ridiculous imitation of Rocky Balboa's nose. The next day with a pounding head and throbbing nose, I called my plastic surgeon and scheduled surgery for the next week.

"My nose needed to be fixed."

"Why did your nose need to be fixed?"

I told him the story, leaving out the drug dealer part.

"Okay, so you had breast augmentation, rhinoplasty, breast augmentation again, and then what?"

"Jesus Christ, Doc." I blew my hair out of my face. I could feel myself growing more agitated, my fingernails leaving marks on my palms. "I had another boob job."

"And?"

"And I had my chin chiseled down a little."

"How frequently do you get Botox?"

"Frequently." I've been getting Botox for four years now, every six months. It's more preventative than maintenance. I don't have wrinkles, but I also don't want them. Thank you, botulism.

"What about laser hair removal?"

"What? That's not in my medical file."

"I know. I took a guess. Botox isn't in your file either."

"Asshole."

"Why am I an asshole, Paige? I just want to know what makes you feel like you need to change yourself."

"Do you like what you see?"

"That's not the point, Paige, though I think you are quite pretty, and the more you tell me about yourself, the more I see your inner beauty, too, and inner beauty lasts forever."

"I guess."

He leaned in the way he does when he wants me to take him seriously and told me that he thought maybe I was striving for a perfection that might never exist in my mind and that it might be a battle I won't win. He did tell me that he thought I was pretty, a compliment I didn't, couldn't ignore. He also said that he worries that I have an addiction problem, not just to drugs, but to anything that makes me feel good and that plastic surgery can be a major addiction for some people.

He gave me another task to add to my journaling. He said that he wanted me to say a daily affirmation aloud to my reflection every night before I go to bed, something genuine and true that I think is good about myself. Does this guy think I suffer from low self-esteem? Has he seen me? Good grief.

My mother had low self-esteem. She let herself become a person who lived through another. Her opinion of herself rested in the mind of an egotistical pervert who couldn't have appreciated her if she had stayed twenty years old forever, and she tried. She used expensive creams on her skin. She started getting gray hair at the ripe old age of thirty, which is exactly when she started seeing Gilberto, her hair stylist who kept her shiny straight black hair, straight and shiny, and most importantly ... black.

She had a facelift at one point, but she did it overseas, so I never really even noticed. I just heard her tell her friend about it over the phone one day. My mother was an American Indian in all of the good and bad ways. Unfortunately for her, her skin weathered young, and her hair grayed far too early, and to a woman desperately trying to hold on to a man who wants only younger women, this became a constant struggle that would haunt her until her near fatal fall. Once she began to age, she never felt confident again. I heard her on too many occasions voice how much she missed being beautiful. Funny though, I thought she was even more beautiful with the lines, but she couldn't see that.

Confession ... I had my first surgery because I wanted bigger boobs. No other reason. Genetics gave me tiny A cups, but I had unlimited access to money, so since I could easily buy what I wanted, I bought some C cups. I thought that would be enough. I scheduled the typical three consultations and did my research to find the right doctor.

I was sitting in the exam room at consultation number two when Dr. Godfrey walked in. He asked me if I would be okay if one of the residents from the medical school came in to observe. I had no problem with that, and fifteen minutes later, Prince Plastic Surgery walked into the exam room to stare at my tiny breasts. He was gentle and sweet, almost demure. He and Dr. Godfrey began discussing my breasts. He started to touch one but quickly pulled back his hand and asked permission first. Of course, I said yes, so he gently lifted my left breast.

At this point, I expected him to ask Dr. Godfrey to politely excuse us, but instead he said something like, "this one is smaller than that one." Um, not exactly what I wanted Dr. Amor to say to me or about me, I'm not sure which. They then got a tape measure out and started measuring me, moving me here and there, until they finally came up with a plan. All of the time I could think of nothing more than Dr. Mendoza doing much less scientific things with my breasts, but I held it together until the end of the appointment. Dr. Mendoza excused himself, shaking my hand and telling me how lovely it was to meet me. I wanted him immediately.

Dr. Godfrey was very thorough and mostly conservative. He suggested that I get at most 300cc, which would get me to about a C cup. I told him that I wanted to look natural, like I was born with them, so he felt this would be my best option given my slim build and my height. He offered the choice between silicon and saline. I chose saline because I heard horror stories of women with silicone implants having them explode in their bodies leaving them deformed for life.

Two weeks later, I walked into the outpatient surgery center and had my first surgery. Janie drove me and promised not to tell my parents what I had done. We had an apartment, so she basically nursed me back to health, bringing me the beautiful pain pills right on schedule. She even made a spreadsheet. She brought me take-out and together we sat on our couch watching old movies, trying not to laugh because laughing hurt like hell. The next day, she drove me to my follow-up appointment where I got a second chance to talk with Dr. Mendoza. And fall deeper into his trance.

He took the bandages off and stood behind me as I got the first look at the new me. I was swollen and a little bruised, but I can honestly say, I never felt more beautiful. He reached under my arms and pointed out the fullness at the top, explaining that when they dropped, the fullness would be more even and not look so strange.

"Strange?" I asked. "I think they're beautiful."

"They are beautiful, Ms. Parnevik. You were an excellent candidate. I can't wait to see what you think when you are fully healed."

And that's where it started. This beautiful, gentle man, who spoke quietly with a slight Latin accent began my addiction to plastic surgery. What I purposely left out of our conversation during therapy with Dr. Love was that it was more of an addiction to the Latin doctor than the plastic surgery, but it became my obsession to have him.

For the next six months, I was required to go back in for check-ups. Each visit, I saw both Dr. Godfrey and Dr. Mendoza, and I would stand topless in front of a mirror, while the two of them stood on either side of me just a step behind discussing their masterpieces, and they were fabulous. Perfect. Dr. Godfrey even got my permission to show my before and after photos on his website.

Dr. Mendoza took more of a front seat as I progressed in my healing. On my last follow-up appointment, Dr. Godfrey had the flu, so Dr. Mendoza examined me. He walked into the exam room not in his typical green surgical scrubs, but a beautiful black pinstriped suit accented with a light green tie and a huge grin spread across his face.

"Good morning, Ms. Parnevik."

"Good morning, Dr. Mendoza," I replied with a smile I could not avoid.

"So, what do you think? Let's take a look."

He led me to the mirror and gently pulled off the robe to reveal my healed C cups. "They're perfect," he said as he walked around me to stand in front of me.

"I think so."

"Well, you're done. You don't have to keep coming back here." He rocked back on his heels a bit.

"I know," I said with obvious disappointment.

"You should be excited. It's summer time, bikini weather. You need to spend your time shopping for your new suit, not hanging out here."

"I know. I think I'm going to miss you," I said as I bit my lip.

He looked at me confused, and then he opened his mouth to talk but stopped. He sort of shook his head then cleared his throat. "Well, you're perfect now, Paige. You won't need to come back here again," clearing his throat again, "I mean, unless you notice any pain or swelling, loss of feeling, etc."

"Okay," I said as I took a deep breath, "Thank you, Dr. Mendoza."

"My pleasure, Paige."

And with that, he left. I heard his shoes tap on the floor as he walked away from me forever.

I did what he suggested and went straight to Neiman Marcus to buy new swimsuits with a disappointed and deflated feeling in my gut. I questioned whether or not I flirted enough. Did I wear the right clothes? Remember, men are my specialty. I usually get what I want when it comes to the other sex, so standing in the dressing room, donning a tiny teal bikini, I let the demons in my head take over for a brief moment. Then I looked at my reflection and decided there was plenty of opportunity out there, and my new gifts needed some attention.

I moved on and forgot about him. I spent the summer at the pool with Janie, soaking in the warm Dallas sun as she applied ridiculous amounts of sunscreen to her only slightly pink skin. School started back in the fall, and I toured around the frat houses a bit, and before I knew it, over a year had passed since my surgery. I started screwing my dealer, who was really only another pretty boy from school, but I liked calling him my dealer since he scored me what I needed. I broke my nose and ended up in Dr. Godfrey/Dr. Mendoza's office. By this time, Mendoza was licensed and legit, so he performed my rhinoplasty, giving me the exact nose I never knew I always wanted.

Again, I continued to go back to the office for follow-up appointments where Dr. Mendoza and I would flirt and giggle, but still, he made no move. I knew our meetings were coming to an end, so I decided to "consult" with him on a second boob job. He argued with me at first saying that he didn't think it was a good idea, that he thought we achieved our goal the first time, but as history suggests, I got my way, and we scheduled surgery for the next month where he replaced my 300cc saline implants with 400cc silicone implants. He swore they would look better and feel more natural. He clearly leaned to the side of silicone, explaining that they were no longer unsafe and were the premier implant, and since his hands were the ones I wanted on my breasts, he won.

Another round of follow-up appointments followed, and flirting progressed. When we got to the six-month mark, and he hadn't made his move, I walked away disappointed and more than a little irritated. I met up with Janie at our favorite dive bar to get smashed and wallow in my pity.

She was all stressed about this upcoming benefit that she was organizing for starving children or something and couldn't stop talking about how she hadn't sold enough tickets, and how it was going to totally suck if she didn't get some more pledges to come. A very bright idea light bulb flashed on over my head, so I told her the plan. She agreed. We toasted our Patrón shots, got smashed, and went our separate ways to pass out.

The next morning, I woke up bright and early, drank a gallon of water to rinse out my elephant shit mouth, dressed in my favorite dark denim jeans, with a white peasant-style low-cut billowing blouse and knee-high brown suede high heel boots. I spritzed some perfume between my breasts on my wrists and on my neck and headed out to find some charity for my BFF.

I walked into the office, greeted the staff who knew me by my first name at this point and asked to speak to Dr. Mendoza privately. He looked puzzled when he saw me sitting in the lobby but escorted me to his office anyway. I told him why I was there to save starving thirsty children. He looked confused at first but humored me and listened to my sales pitch. I suggested that he buy at least two tickets for the dinner so that he could take a date, and then it happened, "Paige, would you be able to join me?"

"Well, I already pledged for one ticket, but I wouldn't mind having some company."

"Then it's settled. Do you want to meet me there?" he asked.

"No, actually, I've reserved a car, so I'll just have my driver swing by your place to get you."

And there it began ... our relationship outside of the surgical center. I called Janie and told her that we had to book a trip to New York, and visit Barney's immediately to purchase our benefit attire because if you can't buy it at Barney's, it's not worth buying, right? Or so says my favorite stylist. We sipped champagne and tried on at least fifty dresses until I found the exact one. I walked out of the dressing room to see Janie's giant blue eyes grow. I twirled around to give her the full view of the most beautiful red silk gown I have ever worn.

Picture this. Deep V halter with two thick red silk ribbons that come together and tie at the back of my neck leaving a trail of red down my bare back, catching the dress where it hugs at the base of my spine, low enough to reveal my entire back without showing any of my nether areas. The skirt was shorter in the front and long in the back, leaving a trail of red silk on the floor as I walked. My breasts were made for this dress, or rather, maybe the dress was made for my breasts, but either way, I looked gorgeous. Sold. We

completed the dress with a pair of silver and rhinestone be-
dazzled Valentino three-inch sandals.

I went home and plotted for a week, which felt more
like a month, on how I was going to make Dr. Mendoza
mine. I wondered if I would end up at his place, if he would
make the first move, if I would have to corner him and show
him I'm a sure thing. I imagined our future. I wanted nothing more than to bed him, not love him, so in my head, I
played several scenarios of us naked. The date couldn't get
here quickly enough.

When the day of the event finally arrived, I spent it at
my salon getting beautified. My hairdresser decided on a
simple bun at the crown of my head. I argued telling him to
leave it down, but in the end, he won, and I must admit, it
was perfect. The dress needed nothing else. I wore diamond
stud earrings, and no other jewelry. I took my time getting
ready when I got home. I wondered how I would greet Dr.
Mendoza, who at this point, had yet to give me his first
name, Guillermo.

When the driver buzzed me from downstairs, I peaked
at my reflection in the full-length mirror. "Perfect," I whispered to myself. I stepped out of the door and walked past
B-Large's place. He was coming in as I was leaving, and he
whistled at me as I passed. At that point, we were just bed
buddies.

When we got to Dr. Mendoza's house, a cute little cot-
tage-style home on the M streets, I let my driver go to the
door and waited in the limo. As he got into the car, he
smiled and said, "Stunning."

We sipped champagne in awkward silence all the way
to the benefit which was at a newly renovated historic hotel
downtown. When we reached our destination, he got out of
the car first and then leaned down to help me. He tucked
my left hand under his right arm and ushered me into the
banquet room where a grand piano played by an older woman in a long sleeved black sequined gown tenderly sang the
sad melody of Beethoven's Moonlight Sonata. The host
showed us to the table, where we sat quietly listening to the

soft melancholy of the piano. He squeezed my hand under the table. I looked at him, and he smiled as he said, "The sound of a piano is kind of soothing, isn't it?"

"It really is beautiful. Beethoven must have been so sad to come up with such soul wrenching music."

His left eyebrow raised, and he looked at me again with confusion, "You surprise me, Paige."

"Big boobied blondes can appreciate art, too, Dr. Mendoza."

"I know. I'm sorry. I didn't mean to offend you. I just ... er ... you just ... nevermind. Would you mind calling me Guillermo?"

"Sure. No problem." It was awkward.

We ate the first course mostly in silence, making small talk with the other couples at our table. When the main course arrived, we'd each had a glass of wine, making things a little less stuffy. I couldn't get over how nervous we both were. At his office, our rapport was playful and easy. I started to wonder if I needed to take him somewhere and show him my boobs so that I could get the cute, flirty doctor that I was used to, not this timid guy.

He squeezed my knee under the table to get my attention. Then he motioned to the exit and whispered, "We paid our dues. Do you want to get out of here?"

No need for a reply from me because with that, we were off. We walked out of the banquet hall and into the lobby of the hotel.

"Want to get a room?" he asked.

"Here?" I replied, puzzled.

"This is a hotel, Paige." I stood shocked for a minute. Who was this forward hot Latino, and what did he do with the jittery guy from the benefit? He continued, "I hate tuxedos and pretension, and this whole night, all I can think about is getting you out of that red dress, so if I've read you wrong, or if I'm coming on too strong, just let me know. I'm not good with hints or games, and I don't mean to be disrespectful in any way."

"No. I think you read me just fine."

I waited in the lobby while he secured our room at the front desk. As soon as we were in the elevator, he pulled me into him and kissed my neck. "Mmmm. You smell amazing." I am genius with perfume.

We barely made it into the room before he reached up my dress and pulled my panties off. "Get out of this dress." I did, and we made good use of the bed ... all night. What is it about hotel rooms that make a girl insatiable?

We began a short sexual affair. Neither of us wanted anything more, so I would frequent his place where we would take what we needed from each other periodically. He was super busy with the practice, so he didn't have time for a girlfriend, a title that terrified me anyway, so we agreed to keep it casual.

One night he was looking through some before and after pictures and showed me some pictures of women who had their bones shaved on their chins. He called it chin chiseling. I was immediately enamored with the process and how subtle but remarkable the change was. "I want that done," I said to him.

"Paige, you don't need that. Your face is flawless."

"I want it. Will you do it for me?"

"I really don't think you should."

"Why?"

"I just think you've done enough. You don't want to become a woman who is unrecognizable."

"I'll go to someone," I said as I rolled away from him in the bed.

"I think you're being ridiculous. You're acting like a petulant child."

"No, I'm acting like a customer who wants something, Dr. Mendoza."

"Let's talk about it later. I need to get some sleep." He took the photos and put them in a file, turned off the light, and five minutes later, he was asleep.

I crept out of his house and went home. The next morning, I made an appointment with Dr. Mendoza for a consultation the next week.

When I arrived for the appointment, he walked into the room and rolled his eyes at me. "Why are you so stubborn?"

"Because when I want something, I get it. I'm not good with the word no," I said with a grin.

"Fine. We'll get you scheduled, but for the record, I think it's pointless and stupid, and I'm only doing it because of your persistence." He kissed the tip of my nose. "Don't sneak out of my house again, by the way."

"Fine," I replied, and two weeks later, I walked out of the surgery center with a new chin, a perfect one, for the record.

I don't really know what happened to the relationship, nothing really. It just kind of fizzled, and we lost touch with each other. A couple years ago, I decided to pay him a visit and get my last, or rather, my most recent boob job. I met this girl at the spa who had the most amazing breasts I have ever seen. We started talking about our surgeries, and she told me that she had 500cc's. I had total titty envy, so I scheduled an appointment to get my boobs redone. When Dr. Mendoza came in, he laughed. "Preston, huh? Did you get married?"

"No, just needed something new."

"Like new boobs?"

"Yeah. I want 500cc's."

Again he argued, telling me that I was being ridiculous, but he finally let me win, and we scheduled the most recent surgery. Everything went well, and here I am. Several surgeries later, I'm mostly happy with my appearance. I love the chin, and I love the boobs. They're big, but I don't look ridiculous, pornish, or clownish. I'm a DDD. They fit my height and my frame. I won't go any bigger than this. I can't really think of anything else to do for now, but I'm quickly approaching thirty, and who knows what gravity will do to my body? I will never say that I won't have another surgery because the truth is, I've enjoyed the transformations I've undergone. Even the recovery isn't so bad because plastic surgeons are not afraid to prescribe some powerfully awesome pain meds.

I guess Dr. Love and I were at a stalemate with this topic. I am seeking perfection. For now I have it, but beauty is fleeting.

The best I can do for him is the affirmation he suggested, so I stood in front of the mirror and said to myself, "I am beautiful with a perfect body, and my chin is awesome."

There's some affirmation for you, doc.

Christmas

Dear Stephanie,

Nothing says kill yourself like yuletide cheer. Christmas ... a huge overly commercialized holiday that drives lonely people like me to lose themselves in the dark places of their minds. I just spent a week in Manhattan. With B-Large, no. I went alone. I needed to get out of town, so I went to New York under the guise that I had to do my Christmas shopping, which I had done, but mostly online.

I needed to be with strangers, to enjoy the snow, walk through the bustling streets of New York in a big wool coat with a scarf and gloves. Feel the cold air on my cheeks. Winter never really starts in Texas until after the first of the year, and even then, it never gets cold like it does in the northeast. Sometimes I just need to feel winter. The cold, unforgiving wind, the chill all the way to my core. I hate the cold, but I needed a change of scenery, one that would possibly distract me from the voices in my head.

It's Christmas, and everyone is all, "what are you plans for the holiday?" And my answer is to shrug my shoulders. My brother invited me to his place for Christmas dinner, which was more of an unvitation than anything else. A text message:

Paul: What are your plans for Christmas?

Me: I don't have any.
Paul: Well, come over if you want. Kat is making a prime rib.
Me: I'll let you know ...

So, he can go on feeling like he's reached out to poor single Paige who doesn't have a husband, or kids, or friends, or parents, or really anyone, and he won't have to feel guilty as his snotty nose twin toddlers are ripping paper from their boxes on Christmas morning while his wife sits on the floor blowing her hair out of her face giving him the evil eye because like any normal day, he can't please her, especially on Christmas where he might have gotten her a tennis bracelet instead of diamond earrings like she hinted for but didn't actually ask him for, just assumed that my idiot brother would be able to read her pretentious fucking mind ... or something like that. Not to mention that I'm sure my father will be there.

No thanks, Paul. I'll pass.

Janie gave up years ago trying to get me to join her family for the holidays. I can't stomach being in the same room as her sister. She and I have never spoken since the night I caught her with my father, and seeing her happy with her husband and children it just too much for me. I'd rather be alone.

Nobody knows this, but normally on Christmas, I go visit my mother. She doesn't speak, so the secret is safe with her. I bring her an afghan every year from Nordstrom's. It's the same one she used to carry into our theater with her to keep her warm while she watched movies. I know. I'm thoughtful. What do you get for a woman trapped in a body who lost her ability to communicate when her husband pushed her down the stairs? An afghan to replace the one from the previous year, every single year. Last year they served cold ham, mashed potatoes that clearly came out of a box, canned green beans, and some sort of Jell-O mold. It was a beautiful spread, and I fed it to her myself.

She sat staring, which is what she does, with her dry, cracked lips pursed and looking through me. When I touched the spoon to her lips, she parted them and chewed.

Wash, rinse, repeat, until she finished the meal. I didn't talk to her. I never do. I didn't know what to say or even if she can hear or understand me. She couldn't talk back anyway, so what would have been the point?

I untied the silver ribbon from the box and pulled the afghan out, draping it over her legs. I always take the one from the year before and give them to the nurses to put in their common room. Then I gave her shoulder a squeeze and left.

This Christmas, I'm having a hard time thinking about my plans. It's so hard to see her like that, helpless and mute. I get a lump in my throat with the thought. I know, Paige has feelings. Who knew?

I keep half expecting B-Large to invite me to have Christmas with the Greeks, but so far, I'm hearing crickets. It's not like I've brought up the subject or anything. Maybe he assumes I'm doing something with my family. That's possible considering that I still haven't introduced him to my fucked up past. I want to approach that very delicately. After seeing him with his family, I'm afraid he might run away from me when he hears about mine. Could I lie and just say they're all dead, that I'm an only child whose parents were tragically killed? That's an idea. I certainly don't want to tell him the truth.

It might not even come up considering that I haven't even seen B in almost two weeks. I know, I went to New York, but before I left, I saw him a total of one time that week, and since I've been home, he's been too busy with work and then traveling for work. I think I'm going through withdrawal, and I'm sort of freaking out about it.

Don't get me wrong. I'm totally fine with being by myself. I've been alone for almost thirty years, and I've managed quite well, but since B came into the picture, I've gotten used to having dinner with someone, sleeping next to someone, caring about what someone else did that day.

It's driving me fucking mad. I'm swooning over a guy. Janie's done it a thousand times, for which I gave her a lot of grief, and now here I am wondering why the man who said he was falling in love with me is so painfully absent all of a sudden, and then I wonder why I care, and what the fuck happened to me. Seriously, I don't understand why people couple. I have never been so confused.

Typically, when I feel down like this, I call B, and we do blow and screw like maniacs. The less time I spend with him, the more I start thinking about my other go-to when I'm down, and for the first time, I don't want to do it. I have pills of every variety in my medicine cabinet. I keep going into my bathroom to make sure they're still there, taking them out to count them.

My first suicide attempt happened completely spontaneously, as a reaction to what happened with Mr. Preston. Every other time, it's been calculated, planned. I get this feeling in the pit of my stomach, a dull ache, and then slowly, darkness begins to surround me, and the voices in my head start, whispering at first, and then gradually their volume increases to screams until I feel like I am at the bottom of a hole with no light, and I'm suffocating, unable to take a deep breath, unable to focus, and unable to make it stop.

Then a calmness comes over me, the voices hush, and it feels like warm honey being poured over my head until my body can feel again, and I know what to do. Sometimes it comes slowly, and sometimes more rapidly, but every time, the answer is the same. Depression is a monster. He seeks me and haunts me and tries to pull me into the darkness.

I keep getting the dull ache. I know it's there. I feel it, and I can't shake it. The voices, they whisper, "You know what to do. Do it. Do it. Do it." The voices convince me that the world is better off without me, that I'm doing myself and everybody who knows me a favor by making my exit, and most of the time, I believe their words.

This time though, I don't want to believe it. As much as Blake makes me happy, I can tell I do the same for him, or at least, I did until he disappeared.

To distract myself, I've tried reading but can't concentrate. I went out for martinis by myself last night, but it didn't help. The crowd couldn't drown out the voices, no longer whispering, "Do it. Do it. Do it."

I shush the voices with thoughts of Blake. I beg him in my mind to call me. I walk past his empty apartment and want so badly to go inside, to feel him warm against me, his weight on my body. I want to wrap myself in his contagious and infectious happiness, but he's not home. I rest my hand against his door and close my eyes. Where is he?

All I want to do is call him and ask him to hang out with me, but I can't dial the number. I won't let myself. It was so much easier before he was my boyfriend. Now there's a game involved, and I'm losing. Janie has too much on her plate right now to deal with me, so I don't dare call her. I don't know what to do. I am so sick and so afraid. I keep writing the same text message and deleting it.

B, I need you. Please come home.

Introductions

Dear Stephanie,

As it turns out, I was over-reacting, typical reaction from a girlfriend, apparently. According to B, he's been super busy with work, end of year stuff, yada, yada, yada. He finally talked to me about Christmas. He asked what my plans were. I told him that I would be having lunch with my mom but didn't go any further. He asked if I would like to come to his parents' for Christmas Eve, spend the night there so that we could wake up Christmas morning to "Santa," and then we could go to my mom's. That's right, "we."

I decided that I would let him go along with the idea that he too would be having lunch with my mother and then last minute, drop an excuse bomb on him about why it would be best for him to just sit this one out. Then he sent me a text:

B-Large: Hey–shopping ... what does your mom like?

Me: Why?

B-Large: Um ... shopping. Thought I made that clear.

Me: For my mom?

B-Large: Yes. Gifts are customary on Christmas, right?

Me: Music

Music. That was all I could say. I sat at my bar in my apartment, sipping a vodka martini, wondering how in the world I would get around this. Remember, B doesn't really know anything about my family or my past. He just accepts me, present alone Paige. How in the world would I explain all of this without making him run, not walk, away from the Parneviks?

Two hours later, another ding on my phone.

B-Large: *What kind of music?*

Me: *Don't worry about it. Just come home. I'm bored.*

B-Large: *If you will quit being so difficult, I can get this done and wrapped. Then I promise, no more boredom ;-)*

Shit, I thought. And just decided to keep up this charade.

Me: *Paul Simon, Crosby, Stills & Nash, Led Zeppelin, stuff like that ... come home!!!!!*

B-Large: *Soon, baby.*

I slid my phone across my bar and threw my head back. I got myself into this. Now what?

By Christmas Eve, I still had not come up with an excuse. I didn't want to lie to B. For whatever reason, I couldn't. To this point, I have never lied, and I didn't want to start now. Plus, on any given day, Blake is giddy, but he was in an all-time state of excitement. It's as if he still thought Santa came down the chimney and left treats under the tree. I didn't want to be the one to deflate his enthusiasm.

We packed our bags and headed to his family home where we were greeted by his tiny mother and his giant father and of course, the rest of his big Greek family. Christmas Eve was spent in the den around the fire drinking egg nog and listening to stories of Christmases past where B and his brothers would wake at 4:00 a.m. and creep into their parents' room begging them to wake up and see what Santa had brought. I imagined the little green-eyed boy with a big mop of black curls in footed pajamas sneaking down the stairs to see if he could get a glimpse of the mythical elf, and my heart swelled (three sizes) in my chest at the thought.

I went to bed that night (alone in the guest room) with the nastiness of dread beginning to form, tossing and turning, uneasy, unable to sleep, knowing that in the morning

I would wake to more warmth and love and then ruin it all when I left to go see my mute mother.

B crept into my room after I had finally drifted to sleep and knelt down next to my bed.

"Wake up, sleeping beauty," he whispered.

"No," I replied and rolled away from him.

A very cold hand crept under my covers and grabbed my inner thigh, then squeezed.

"What is it?" I asked rolling back toward him, pushing his hand off of my leg. His skin looked blue in the dark room, and as my eyes adjusted, I could see his eyebrows furrow and then relax.

"I'm nervous about meeting your mom tomorrow."

"What?" I sat up in the queen-size bed and tried to focus on him. He wore only pajama pants, the curly hair on his chest shining in the moon light coming through the window above the bed.

"You don't have to go."

"What is she like? I know absolutely nothing about your mom. I'm just afraid she won't like me," he said as he slid into bed next to me, sitting up against the headboard.

"Has anyone in the history of the world ever not liked you, B?"

"Paige, I'm serious. This is a big deal. You're so tight-lipped about your family that it makes me wonder. I don't know. I'm just sort of stressed about it."

I sighed. In all the time I've known Blake, I had never seen him stressed. He mindlessly rubbed the back of his head.

"I told you, Blake, you don't have to go. Seriously, especially if it's causing you stress. I don't want that." I reached my hand out and traced a circle around his belly button, willing him to say that he didn't want to go and be done with it.

"Of course I'm going with you, Paige." He put his hand on mine and said, "I just want to know what to expect. I don't even know where she lives." I thought about the night we had spent with his family, the way they made me feel so welcomed, like I was part of it, part of his world, part of him, and here he was trying to be part of me.

I sat up in bed next to him, and I told him what I could about my mom, that she was gentle and elegant, that she was beautiful and complex. I explained her Native American heritage and shared some of the things she told me about my grandparents, who I only ever met once because she refused to take us to the reservation where they lived, and they refused to leave it except for the one time when they came to visit. Then I told him about her accident and that she was no longer the mother I knew but just a body with the same sad eyes.

"And your dad?"

"He's gone, B."

"Like dead gone or left gone?"

"He's dead," I lied, "And can we please not talk about it? Let's just tackle one of my parents tonight, okay?"

"Okay. Sorry." He ran a finger down my cheek and then touched my lips. I kissed his finger and pulled his hand to my chest.

Sometime later, after we sat in silence while Blake absorbed the monstrous pile of information I just laid in his lap, he leaned down and kissed the top of my head and whispered, "I love you, Paige."

"I know," I whispered and actually felt relief, the earlier tension disappeared, and I folded into him and sought shelter from the unexpected.

He stayed with me in the guest room and held me while we slept. The next morning, we were awakened by one of his nephews squealing in the hall, "It's Christmas! It's Christmas! Wake up everyone!!"

B looked at me from his pillow and raised one of his eyebrows at me. "Merry Christmas," he said with a smile.

"Merry Christmas, B," I replied with the same warmth I felt in my heart while sitting by the fire with his family the previous night.

We got up and headed downstairs where we were quickly engulfed in boxes and paper with B's family still in pajamas sporting bed head and scruffy stubble. The children were all excited and couldn't unwrap their gifts fast enough. It all went by too quickly.

Blake opened the Cartier watch I bought him and put it on his wrist immediately. Then he handed me a box wrapped in gold paper with a beautiful red ribbon perfectly tied around it. I pulled the ribbon away and then slowly opened the box, unfolding the tissue paper from its contents. Inside was a fairly tattered hardback of *To Kill a Mockingbird.*

I lifted the book out of the box with the ease of someone handling a bomb that's about to explode. "Open it," Blake said. I opened the cover and turned to the dedication page where I immediately saw the signature of Harper Lee.

I gasped, quickly covering my mouth with my hand. "Thank you," I whispered breathlessly knowing he must have spent a fortune on it. I felt the sting of tears fill my eyes and took a breath trying to keep them from falling.

"You like it," he said with a satisfied smile. Not a question, a statement.

"I love it," I replied, suddenly realizing that the entire room had hushed and all eyes were on me. I silently begged the tears not to fall in front of the family. B realized my discomfort and quickly took the attention off of me by asking one of his nephews to demonstrate how his remote control car worked.

I helped his mom pick up all of the paper and trash while Blake and his brothers took the kids outside to ride their new bikes and play with all of the other new treasures they had received. Blake's mom, with a handful of tissue paper in one hand, grabbed my hand with her free one and squeezed it. I looked up from my own pile of trash into her kind eyes.

"You make him so happy," she said and squeezed my hand three quick times. I stood there absorbing her words. I wanted to say that it went both ways, that he made me happy, too, that for the first time in my entire life, I actually could define the word happy, but before I knew it she took a deep breath and glided out of the room.

We had a quick breakfast, cleaned up, and then headed for "the home," which was the term I'd given to my mother's residence years prior.

As far as nursing homes go, the one where my mother lives is upscale, very expensive, and only for the elite. This, however, doesn't change the fact that no matter how much money a person has, at a certain time in his life, he may end up in a place where he pisses and shits himself on a consistent basis. Thus was the case on this particular Christmas day.

Blake parked his Tahoe in a space noticeably far from the door. We walked together silently, holding hands, a package in his free hand, a package in my free hand. Tiny snow flurries began to fall. I looked over at Blake whose hair was catching some of the small white flakes and smiled.

I lead him through the double doors where we were assaulted with the putrid odor of lemon trying to mask urine. We walked past the nurse's station where Blanche, a nurse who was only moments away from living there herself greeted me, "Hello, Ms. Parnevik."

"Merry Christmas, Blanche. You look well," I lied, pulling Blake along behind me.

"Parnevik?" Blake asked.

"Long story," I replied, shaking my head.

I opened the door to my mother's room. She sat in her chair with her back to us, staring at the unexpected snow falling outside her window. Staring, always staring. Nerves mixed with last night's egg nog and this morning's eggs threatened to wretch my already nauseous stomach. I paused in the door, taking a deep breath, stilling my heart, swallowing the bitter taste in my throat. Blake reached for my hand again, from which I gathered a little strength and moved closer to her.

"Hi, Mrs. Preston, I'm Blake," he said nervously.

"Parnevik," I replied.

"What?" he asked confused.

"Her name is Parnevik, not Preston," I said with a little too much irritation. "She can't talk."

"Well, I can," he said making his way to meet my mother face to face. "Merry Christmas, Mrs. Parnevik. I'm Blake Demopoulos, Paige's boyfriend, and you must be why she is so beautiful," he said taking her hand.

I walked around her bed and stood just behind Blake, like a kid experiencing stranger danger hiding behind a parent.

He began to tell her what he did for a living, where he was from, what school he went to, all about his brothers and mom and dad. He told her how we met, leaving out all of the racy details of our life. He talked to her like they were having a conversation, with ease, charm, and respect. Then he grabbed the package he bought for her and opened it. Inside was an iPod and a Bose SoundDock System.

"I loaded the iPod with the music Paige said you liked." He then looked at me, "I took a risk hoping that she was like my mom and didn't have one already." He started to take everything out of boxes and get it situated and set up on her bedside table. I looked at the wrapped box still holding the afghan I bought and wondered if I should just shove it under her bed.

"I'm not sure they'll allow music in here," I said.

"It doesn't have to be loud," he said dismissing my concern as he plugged the system into the wall. I sat on the edge of the windowsill watching him get everything in order. He placed the iPod on the dock and then hit play.

I listened to Paul Simon's voice dance through the tiny speakers, watching my mother. She turned her eyes to the music, and I swear to God, she smiled. I felt tears in my eyes. Blake leaned in and whispered, "I figured this was a good start since you listen to 'Kodachrome' all the time. Loudly." He winked. Apparently expensive apartments don't put much into the insulation.

I didn't visit often, but since the day she "fell" down the stairs, she had not shown a bit of emotion, and now, joy? We stayed for several hours going through the playlist that

Blake made for a woman he didn't know but apparently understood better than I ever had. He gently and patiently showed her how to use the remote to switch the songs, change the volume, and how to turn it on and off, and surprisingly, she could do it.

She's not a vegetable. They told us that from the beginning. I mean, her hands work. She can feed herself and walk and can move, but she never seems to *want* to do any of that. She hasn't said a word since the accident, but according to all of her many MRI's, her brain looks normal, with just a tiny spot that indicates a minor stroke. They think it probably occurred during her accident.

She's had numerous therapists and specialists work with her, and most seem to think that she can talk, but that she refuses to speak. It's one more thing to blame on my father. I'm certain that if she spoke, she would probably incriminate him.

I've watched her for years just lie in her bed or sit in her chair, but the music ... it seemed to sort of revive her, and for the first time since her fall, she looked alive. Blake and I kissed her good-bye, leaving her in the company of John, Paul, George, and Ringo.

On the way out, I met with Blanche and told her about the music and her reaction. She smiled and brushed her hand down the back of my upper arm. "That's great news, dear. I'll make sure she gets to hear some music every day."

"Thank you, Blanche," I replied feeling almost happy about my visit with my mother.

We drove home in comfortable silence, Blake's long fingers wrapped around his steering wheel stiffly at ten and two.

"Thank you, B," I said and leaned over to kiss his scruffy cheek.

He looked at me and smiled then reached over and squeezed my hand three quick times, just like his mom had done that very morning.

"What's that?"

"What?"

"The three squeeze thing. Your mom did the same thing this morning."

"Oh, did she?" he asked with his crooked grin.

"Yes, she did."

"Three squeezes. Three words ... I"—squeeze—"love"—squeeze—"you"—squeeze.

Sigh.

On Christmas night, I stayed at Blake's. We ate leftovers on the floor in his living room next to his small sparsely decorated Christmas tree, talking about the day and about our New Year's plans. After a very comfortable tumble between his sheets, we laid in his bed quietly, my head resting on his chest, feeling the rise and fall with each of his breaths. I reached down and grabbed his hand. Then I squeezed it three times. I could feel his smile as he pulled me even closer to him.

"I know," he whispered.

Bulletproof

Dear Stephanie,

Blake says I love you often. He tells me that sometimes just when we're sitting in his kitchen eating dinner. Those three words just naturally flow from his mouth, like thank you and okay. I'm not like him. It's just not something I can throw out there. "I love you."

I didn't grow up in a home where the phrase was tossed around like in B's house where every time he talks to his mom on the phone he ends it with, "love you, too." But I think I feel it. I think this tug at my heart, this need to be near him, this comfort, I think it's love, but I have nothing to which I can compare it.

There's also a fear with saying it. Everyone I have ever loved has left me, and I can't risk giving Blake a reason to run. I feel this need for him, this physical pull, and it's not just the sexual chemistry. It's a full body need, a longing to be with him when he's away, a comfort in having his presence. He makes me better, almost forcing me to believe that I deserve to feel ... happy.

For New Year's Eve, B made plans to take me to our favorite night club that was hosting a private party. Acting almost as giddy as he had on Christmas, Blake made reservations at one of our favorite restaurants for us to have dinner before the party and procured a nice bag of white powdered fun for the evening. Before we left for dinner, we each took a small bump. B always gets everything ready for us, and when I complained at its miniscule size, he reminded me that we had a long night ahead of us and that we needed to pace ourselves. He was right.

I wore a short, fitted black leather strapless dress with red pointed toe Manolo Blaniks. B gasped when he came to my door. "How is it even possible that I'm spending New Year's Eve with the most beautiful woman in Texas?" he said as we got onto the elevator in the parking garage.

"Just wait until you see what's underneath," I whispered in his ear as I tucked a stray black curl behind it. We kept up this banter all through dinner until finally we had to rush to his Tahoe and have a quickie before we got to the night club. The short dress came in handy, wink, wink.

The night was off to such a great start. We were having a good time, a little high, a little tipsy, and you know, in love. We got to the night club a few minutes after ten. B loaded another line in the car, and with that, we were off.

We ran up the steps to the club hand in hand, giggling like two teenage girlfriends. I could feel the music, the throbbing of the bass before we even walked in the door. The place was packed already, but we had a table and bottle service reserved in the VIP room. B had thought of everything. We sat down at the round booth and each ordered a vodka martini, his dirty, mine with a twist.

He leaned in and tried to say something in my ear, but the music pounded in the background making it impossible to hear him, so I scooted over closer until our thighs touched. "What?" I yelled.

"Who is that guy staring at you over there?" He gestured with a nod of his head. I turned my eyes in the direction of his gaze but didn't see anyone.

"How the fuck would I know?" I yelled with a laugh. We ordered a couple of Patrón shots next. Then B realized the DJ was playing my favorite song and guided me to the dance floor. I swayed my hips and threw my arms in the air mouthing my anthem: MGMT's "Time to Pretend" until the song blended into Steve Aoki's "Pursuit of Happiness." And there we were jumping, twirling, bass thumping, lights strobing, spinning, dancing, laughing as if we were the only two people on Earth.

Then the song slowed, B pulled my back into his front, wrapped his arm around my waist and yelled the words into my ear. I felt the vodka warm in my belly, cocaine soaring through my nerves. The piano hit the chords, speeding up the beat again, and we jumped and sang along letting the alcohol and the cocaine fill our bodies with a synthetic electric euphoria. And we felt it ... happiness. Happiness and love.

We danced and danced and danced until the DJ's voice said, "Everyone get your champagne ready, one minute to midnight." We walked to our table where our champagne was waiting for us. Then the countdown began, "Ten, nine, eight ..." B grabbed me by the crook of my arm and pulled me into him, standing behind me with his free hand wrapped around my waist, his other hand swaying his champagne back and forth as we yelled at the tops of our lungs, "Five, four, three, two, ONE!!!" B spun me around, set his glass on our table, and grabbed each side of my face. Then he pulled me into a soft, sweet kiss. "I love you, Paige Preston," he whispered. "Happy New Year, baby."

"Auld Lang Syne" played in the background, silver and gold foil confetti falling all around us, and for a moment, I'm pretty sure the world stopped spinning. I squeezed his hand three times.

We stood in an embrace for a minute, until I started to get the feeling someone was staring at me. B tensed a little and said, "Your admirer is back." I turned around, and my knees turned to putty. B caught me and held me up.

"What's the matter, Paige?"

I couldn't speak. My heart banged wildly in my chest. I lost the ability to breathe, and all the while, he just stood there with a sick grin on his face, staring at me. Then for whatever reason, he started to walk toward us. I turned to Blake and mouthed. "We have to leave."

"What's wrong, Paige? Who is that guy?"

I nervously reached up and felt the scar on the back of my head from where he rammed me up against the brick wall in the alley. "Nobody. Can we please just go? I think I'm going to be sick."

"Well, hello. Paige, right?" He said as he leaned against the booth and cocked his head to the side.

"Hey, man. I don't think Paige is very interested in talking with you right now," B said and actually made it sound polite.

"I think you should ask her ... man."

"Let's go, B. Please. Let's go," I begged.

"What's wrong, Paige. Does your little boyfriend here not know what a whore you are?"

"Listen, asshole. Get the fuck away from us." B, no longer being polite, took a step toward him, shielding me with his body, towering over the taunter, the scum who raped me.

Then it all happened so quickly. I'm not sure if it was Blake or the scumbag who hit first, but punches were thrown around, and the rapist ended up on the ground. Bouncers were on us in no time, ushering us towards the door. Even the owner, Chris, came to pay witness to the unexpected New Year's violence. Blake looked at him and apologized for getting physical. "That prick was talking shit on Paige, man."

"Hey, that guy's a dick," Chris said, "but you know the policy. We have to ask you guys to leave." Then he looked at me. "I'm sorry, Paige."

I still couldn't talk.

As we walked to the car, the prick still taunted us. "You're a slut and a cock tease, Paige Preston, and you know it."

Blake opened my door for me and helped me to get into the car. Then he got into his seat and slammed his door shut.

"You gotta talk to me, Paige. What was that all about?" He gripped the steering wheel with both hands then stretched his fingers, curling around the wheel, then stretching again, repeatedly.

I didn't say anything. I just sat there trembling and looking out my window at the cold Dallas night.

"Paige, seriously. I'm about to lose my shit. Who is that guy?"

"He's nobody, B. Please take me home."

"If he's nobody, then why are you shaking so bad, and what the hell was he talking about?"

"It's not like it's a secret that I'm a whore, Blake."

"You are not a fucking whore, Paige!" He pounded his palm on the steering wheel.

"Yes I am, B. I know you think that I'm some prize or something or that I am even slightly worthy of being with you, but Blake, I ... am ... a ... whore. I've had sex with so many men, I can't even keep count, and even with you. I had sex with you the first day we met. I didn't even know your name. That's the definition of a whore, Blake. Please quit making me into something that I'm not. It's who I am whether you can admit it or not."

"Did you fuck that guy or something?"

I didn't answer right away. Then quietly, I said, "He raped me in an alley by our building, Blake, so if you count that as fucking, the answer is yes."

He took a deep breath and started the car. Silence filled the air as he drove home, making my stomach hurt even more, and before I knew it, I felt tears in my eyes as I continually swallowed the bile that kept creeping up my throat. I looked out the window willing the tears to stop, but they kept coming, breaking my emotionless mask. I knew I had ruined it with B. He knew that I slept around and that I was in no way a virgin, but now he knew the ugliest of my uglies.

We pulled into his parking spot, and as I started to open the door, he stopped me, grabbing me by my bicep, pulling me back into my seat.

"He should be in jail, Paige."

"I know."

"Why didn't you tell me?"

"Because it's disgusting, Blake. And I'm ashamed."

"You're ashamed? You're ashamed? That motherfucker raped you, then tried to humiliate you in public, and you're ashamed? God, Paige, you are so fucked up," he said with a nervous laugh.

"I know." Raped, suicidal, depressed. Fucked up for sure.

He got out of the car and came around to open my door. When we got in the elevator, the space between us terrified me. He always has his hands on me in some way, either holding my hand, or with his arm around my waist, or even just with our arms laced, but now between us, space. It felt like miles. We walked down our hallway toward our apartments. He stopped at his. I kept walking to mine.

"Where are you going?"

I turned around, confused. "Home," I said.

He took another deep breath and sighed. "Come home with me, Paige," he pleaded. Then he held his arms out to me like a mom coaxing a toddler. I ran to him, almost tripping in my four-inch heels and fell into his arms, sobbing into his neck.

He stroked my hair and shushed me, saying, "It's okay, baby," over and over again. Then he guided me into his apartment, through his living room, and into his bedroom, where he took off my shoes and started to undress me. When he peeled my dress away, he saw the tiny panties I had teased him about before our night was ruined. He looked at me and smiled. "Rain check?"

"What do you mean?" I said and gave him my "let's do it" look.

He shook his head. "Not tonight." He grabbed a tank top and a pair of my pajama pants that I had left at his place from his dresser and tossed them to me. I went in the bathroom and threw up my dinner that had been threatening a reappearance for the last hour, then washed my face, brushed my teeth and got dressed. He followed me, grabbing his tooth brush. When we got into bed, he pulled me to him, the way he always does and started tracing his fingertip up and down my arm.

"Good night, Paige," he whispered.

"Good night, B."

I rested my head on the pillow, taking deep breaths, trying to make my heart stop racing with no luck. I'm not sure how long we lay there, but at some point, B broke the silence and said, "If I ever see that motherfucker again," he paused, clearing his throat, muscles tightening around me. I held my breath waiting for him to continue. "I will kill him."

"Thank you, B, for sticking up for me."

"Don't thank me. I'm sick I didn't do more. If I had known ..." he trailed off. I felt him tense up again.

"Can we not talk about it anymore?" I asked.

"Gladly," he said and kissed his spot on the back of my neck. "I love you, Paige."

"I know," I said and eventually fell asleep.

Today, after a couple of weeks of debating what I should do and watching B struggle with anger, yes, actual anger over his lack of action that night, I went to the police station and filed charges against the man who raped me. I was terrified to talk about it and kept my sunglasses on to shield my face. Thankfully, the wonderful officer who helped me was a beautiful olive-skinned woman with kind eyes and a soft voice. She went over everything with me in painstaking detail.

I actually have a chance of putting the douchebag in jail. Since I attempted suicide the night of the rape, I was rushed to the hospital where they did a rape kit, and his DNA would most definitely be uncovered since he didn't wear a condom. Also, pictures were taken of the gash in my head before and after stitches, which she explained would show a struggle. She said they would issue an arrest warrant immediately.

I left actually feeling relieved. I never wanted to go to the police about the incident. I tried to forget about it. When

I was alone, and the memory crept back into my mind, I would pour myself a drink, take a few pills, distract myself however I could. I've even used Blake for that.

The truth is, however, that when someone violates you, rapes you, takes away your freedom, your safety, and your dignity, he doesn't just disappear. He's always there, lurking in the back of your mind, ready to jump out and startle you when you least expect it. I want him punished. I want some giant prison inmate to make him his bitch. Eye for an eye, right?

Bugs

Dear Stephanie,

I started to my therapy session with Dr. Love with hopes of letting him in on a few things that I'd been keeping from him, but I never made it. I couldn't stop vomiting. In all of my life, I have never been so ill. I called the doctor (psychiatrist, that is) and shared my symptoms, telling him I'd reschedule when I felt better. He wished me well, but before he got his sentence out, I was puking again. Then again. Then again.

I stayed in bed for a week, didn't let B near me for fear that he might catch my stomach flu. When I still didn't feel any better after a week, I decided to make another appointment with Dr. Love and just suck it up.

I drove rigidly to his office with a trash bag wrapped around my steering wheel ... just in case. Thank God I didn't have to use it. I walked into the good doctor's office feeling green but hopeful. For the first time in a week, I had gone an entire morning without regurgitating my empty stomach.

"Wow, Paige, you look ..."

I sat on his couch, exhausted from the climb up the stairs, held up my hand, and shook my head. "I know. I'm still sick, but I have to talk to you," I huffed at him.

"Let me get you some water," was all he could say. I must have looked more than a little putrid.

He walked over to a mini fridge in the corner (somehow I never even noticed it) and came back with an ice cold bottle of water with a napkin wrapped around it. I immediately took the damp napkin and blotted my forehead. Feeling a tad bit more in control, I started to talk, but Dr. Love interrupted me. "Paige, when was the last time you ate? You're so thin."

"I can't keep anything down. B keeps trying to feed me, but everything makes me sick. Everything. I can't even stand the smell of food right now."

"B?"

"Blake, my boyfriend."

His eyebrows shot up in surprise. I've been keeping Blake a secret from Dr. Love. I just haven't felt like getting this relationship psychoanalyzed

"I know. That's why I'm here. I have to tell you about him," I started, but before I could get any more out, I felt the vomit rising in my throat. I ran to his trashcan and wretched into the clear plastic bag the water I had just swallowed moments before.

"Paige, I think you might need to see a doctor." I hate going to the doctor. Going to a therapist is bad enough. I make one appointment with one doctor a year, my gynecologist to keep my birth control in order. Of course there's the Botox, but that's done at a plastic surgeon's office, where there are no sick people. Sick people give me the creeps.

"Well, you're a doctor, aren't you?"

"I don't treat the body, Paige."

"I know," I sighed, feeling deflated and sunk into the couch, resting my dewy forehead in my hand.

"How long have you felt like this?"

"A little over a week, maybe two," I said, blowing my hair out of my face, regretting my decision to come to the appointment.

"I think you should eat something," he said and walked over to his little refrigerator and came back with a package of peanut butter crackers. My mouth started to water a little when he handed them to me.

"Thank you."

"You're welcome. Eat your crackers, and tell me about this boyfriend."

He sat down in his chair grabbing his pen and pad. I started to tell him about Blake, leaving out our extracurricular activities involving chasing lines.

"When did this all start, Paige?"

"Um, well, about the same time I started coming here. We've been friends for a while but only then did we become," I paused considering the word for us, "romantic," I finished with a smile then popped another cracker into my mouth.

"Romantic," he repeated, summoning his pen to his yellow pad. "Are you intimate?"

I looked at him, chewing my cracker. "Yes, although I think that is highly irrelevant."

"Everything is relevant, Paige. For how long have you been intimate with Blake?"

I didn't like how he said his name.

"A few years," I answered.

"I thought you said you just started seeing him recently."

"No, doc, I said that we only recently became romantic. Before, we just slept together, no strings attached."

"And now there are strings?"

"Yes," I replied irritated that he was giving me the third degree about the one thing in my life that made me happy. I looked down at the now empty wrapper in my lap, wishing there were a few more.

"Tell me something, Paige. Have you told him about yourself? About your treatment? About your medication?"

"No, well some of it. He knows about my mother. I let him meet her, but I have no intention of telling him about everything else." I made a circle motion around me and laughed, that much was obvious.

"Everything else?"

"Um, depression, suicide, little blue pills."

"Depression is nothing to be ashamed of, Paige."

"I didn't say I was ashamed, but I just don't think it's necessary to tell Blake that I want to kill myself."

"Do you want to kill yourself? Have you thought about suicide lately, Paige?"

"No," I lied. Everyone has suicidal thoughts at Christmas, right? I mean the holidays are brutal.

"Well, that's good. That's progress, Paige." He started writing stuff on his pad. God I sometimes wish I could read his notes. "How's your stomach?" he asked as he wrote.

"Actually, I feel okay right now. I need to tell you about something else." I wanted to steer this talk away from Blake. I didn't want Dr. Love to ruin him for me.

"What is it?"

"I had a run in with the guy who raped me."

"What do you mean by a 'run in'?"

"Blake and I were out for New Year's Eve, and the asshole was there, too."

I told him everything and how Blake interceded. He said he was glad Blake was with me and that I really need to quit drinking so much, especially at night clubs. I'm sure he's right.

"I went to the police."

He looked up at me, shocked.

"I'm glad. When I got your file, I read that you were adamant that you didn't want the police to be involved. That's common for a lot of victims, so I didn't press you on it. What made you decide to finally turn him in?"

"Blake."

"Oh?"

"Doc, Blake was so upset. I had to do something. I don't want to lose him." I didn't add that B said he would kill the guy if he saw him again, and I believed him. It's also one of the only things Blake has wanted to talk about since it happened. He asked me repeatedly to turn him in, that not doing so was basically like letting a rabid dog out on the loose in a park. What he was trying to say is that I could prevent this guy from raping anyone in the future. What I heard was, "if he rapes again, it's your fault." Blake can be very convincing.

"Paige, it sounds like Blake might be good for you, but you might want to slow down a bit. I don't want him to become another addiction. I don't want you to get hurt."

I sighed. I knew that was coming. Every therapist I've ever had has basically told me to slow my roll when it comes to men. I wanted to tell him that Blake was different, but part of me was scared to believe it.

He told me to keep him up to date on the progress of the rapist, if he got arrested, etc. He said he wanted to help me through the process, that it might bring up some pain. Then he walked over to his desk and came back with his prescription pad.

Little flutters filled my heart. What could this be? I love prescription pads but only when they're full of fun little pills. Could he be giving me an anti-anxiety because of a potential trial? I started running through my inventory in my mind. Xanax—about half a bottle left. Valium—two, maybe three. That would be money if he gave me a prescription for Valium. With refills, my heart would be content.

"I think you should stop by the store on your way home," he said, folding the piece of paper in half before handing it to me.

I nodded and headed to my car. I waited until I was in the driver seat before opening my little prescribed gift. I unfolded the paper and gasped.

In Dr. Love's almost illegible scribble were the words:
Pregnancy Test
Take one and call me with the results tomorrow.
What?
Fuck.
Fuck.
Fuck.

Positive

Dear Stephanie,

I woke up this morning and after throwing up again, took the test. I said a silent prayer to a God I didn't know was there before looking at the result. A plus sign. It's positive. Fuck, I'm pregnant. What the fuck, Mirena? I immediately googled "can you get pregnant on Mirena?" I read countless, no kidding, pages of real life entries of women who got pregnant on Mirena and were now holding their DD. Had to look that one up, too. DD—Dear Daughter. Good grief.

You don't get a period on Mirena, so there's no way to know if you're pregnant unless you have symptoms, which I never have had ever ... until now ... because I am motherfucking pregnant. There's a bun in my oven, and I can't even register that. I've worn permanent marks into my rug in my living room from pacing back and forth, back and forth, back and forth. I don't want to deal with this.

Why did this happen? Did my happiness upset the cosmos? Are they reminding me that I don't deserve it, that happiness is out of my reach? It's like a bomb. Boom! Time for my world to shatter. Again.

I don't even know how to tell B, or if I even should tell him. I've never been pregnant. I've been really lucky. Mostly,

I've used protection, and I started taking the pill at sixteen to regulate my period, according to my mom, but probably because she knew even then that I was a sex addict like my dad. A couple of years ago, my doctor suggested that I try Mirena. She thought that I would appreciate not having my period. Sold. I started it then and have used it ever since.

Things are going so well with me and B. And even with me, things are good. The monster, my monster, has left me alone lately. I'm happy, and I'm even beginning to think one day I'll be brave enough to tell B how I feel about him and then maybe even tell him about me and my demons, and now I'm pregnant? What am I going to do? In the back of my head, the answer screams at me, but fear and dread loom with that prospect. I know I can't have a kid. No way. I can't. I am not fit to be anyone's mother. Ohmigod, ohmigod, ohmigod.

Jesus, Steph, you're no help. I'm calling Dr. Love.

Decisions

Dear Stephanie,

I called him, and Dr. Love has all the answers, doesn't he?

Apparently, he's a dad. I know. Who would have thought? He said his wife, that's right, wife, who apparently doesn't care if her husband wears a motherfucking wedding ring, had terrible morning sickness with his kids. Yep, kids, plural, so when I walked into his office sick to death and spurting news of a boyfriend, he added two plus two and developed a theory. That's why he brought me the crackers. He told me to keep something in my stomach to keep the nausea at bay. I've feasted on saltines for another week.

Since he's married, I refuse to use my pet name for him. I don't give myself very many rules, but married men are off limits. Period. I won't even flirt with them, so from now on, he's Morea. Adios Dr. Love. I promised Dr. Morea that I would make an appointment with a doctor to see how far along I am before making any final decisions.

I told him about the option that I still don't want to write and that if I chose to do that, I wouldn't even have to tell B about it. He doesn't think it's a good idea. He says I need to start being honest with him if we are going to have a real relationship.

I don't know why I'm so scared to tell him. I go through it in my head, how to break it to him, but I can't get up the nerve, and every day that I don't tell him, I lay another brick on an imaginary wall of dishonesty that I'm building between us. He wonders why I'm not drinking, but I just tell him that I'm detoxing, trying to lose a few pounds, while my boobs have already grown a cup size.

I have to do something before this thing wreaks more havoc on my body. As it stands, I still have a flat stomach, which I attribute to the constant puking, but if I don't make up my mind, the belly is going to pop, and I'll have to spill the beans to B for sure.

Honestly, I'm not afraid that he will be mad or disappointed. That's the weird part. I'm terrified he will be happy and want it and try to talk me into wanting it, too, and I have such a hard time telling him, no, so instead I hold it inside.

A baby? No. I can't. I will never do what my parents did and bring a child into this world that was never wanted to begin with, a child who will be a burden and an ornament more than something that is actually cherished and loved. I won't put another human through what I went through, and the one way I can prevent that is to not have one at all. What have I gotten myself into?

I've thought about it all. The good, the bad, the impossible.

Sometimes my mind wonders to an unknown land where I imagine a little boy with Blake's dark hair and green eyes walking hand in hand with me. I see myself bend over and pick him up tossing him in the air over my head as he squeals and giggles, dark wavy hair falling in his face.

Then another thought brings the image of a little girl with curly blonde hair, brown eyes, and dimples on her elbows sitting in B's lap, laying her head on his broad shoulder. She wears a ruffled dress and black Mary Janes, and smiles at me through my imagination. I have to squelch those thoughts almost as rapidly as they fire in my mind. I can't get attached, or I'll never be able to do it. Something else haunts me in the pictures of the children I see in my mind.

But then again, haven't I always feared love?

B-Small

Dear Stephanie,

The cat is out of the bag, or at least, the baby is. I'm eleven weeks pregnant. That's the way it works. They do it in weeks. I always thought it was months, but I'm learning all kinds of new things. I finally made an appointment with my doctor, and after waiting two weeks to piss in her cup, she confirmed the truth.

She smeared warm jelly over my stomach trying to see something through a sonogram. When that didn't work, she rubbed some lube over a dildo looking wand and had me shove it into my vagina. A few seconds later, she said, "Meet your baby, Paige."

She gestured to a black and white swirl on a screen with a little fluttering dot in the middle. She pointed to the dot. "That's the heartbeat. Would you like to hear it?" I nodded, unable to voice any words. A couple of clicks later, and the sounds of a rapidly beating drum filled the tiny dark room. "The heart rate is 167. That's good." She waited for a reply, maybe a reaction. I gave her nothing. My heart was pounding almost as loudly as the baby's. I looked at the swirl on the screen, and I couldn't even breathe. Inside my belly, this thing had a heartbeat and apparently a spine. I made myself look away.

She went over the measurements with me using doctor lingo that I paid no attention to until she said, "looks like you're about eleven weeks, maybe twelve."

"Do I still have time to ...?" I choked on my words. I still couldn't say it.

Her expression hardened a bit. She took a breath and said, "You can still terminate the pregnancy if you choose to, but I don't recommend you wait much longer."

"Do you ...?"

"I do not perform abortions, but I can refer you to someone who does." She said matter-of-factly, handing me a print out of my sonogram.

"Would you like to take this home? You don't have to."

"I think I would," I said through a shaky voice.

I came home and sat at my bar staring at the baby blob in the picture. It didn't look like a baby. It was still considered a fetus, I rationalized with myself. I pulled out my laptop, got online and googled all of the drugs that I had taken in the last three months and their side effects on babies. My stomach dropped to the floor. This kid had potential to be utterly fucked up, and that didn't even include all of the alcohol I consumed in the last eleven weeks. Once I googled that, my decision was made. I pulled out my phone and texted B.

Me: *Gotta talk, STAT. Call me when you're home. I'll come over.*

My phone dinged immediately.

B-Large: *Everything ok?*

I didn't respond. I got in the shower and cleaned the doctor's office off of me scrubbing away as many germs as I could as scalding hot water warmed my skin to a flushed shade of pink. I decided I needed to look my best for B, to try to keep him in my good graces, so I dressed in one of his favorite outfits, indigo J Brand skinny jeans and a gray cable knit sweater from J Crew. The jeans were difficult to button. Another sign I was making the right decision.

I applied my make-up carefully, blow dried my hair shiny and straight, and spritzed B's favorite perfume, Shalimar, on my neck, my wrists, and my breasts. Then I waited.

At 5:24 (I looked at the clock), I heard B's door open and close and then a ding on my phone.

B-Large: *Home, come over.*

I slipped on my favorite Lanvin black ballet flats and headed to B's place where I was greeted by a boyishly happy Blake who immediately engulfed me in a huge hug lifting my feet off the floor.

"God I missed you. Are you hungry? I can make you dinner," he rattled off as I got lost in his attention, "Whoa, Paige, you smell delicious," he said with his crooked fuck me grin and nibbled my neck.

He kissed me, deep, and started pulling my sweater over my head. I let him, thinking that he might take the news better in a post-coital glow. He lifted me up and wrapped my legs around his waist as he carried me into his room and dropped me onto his unmade bed. He tugged at my bra clasp, finally giving up when I reached back to unclasp it myself. Then he took my tender breasts in his hands and pushed me back down onto the bed. He quickly wriggled me out of my too tight jeans and undressed himself. Then he took me. Passion, love, hot, glorious sex erupted, and I cried out as the orgasm shook my body. He followed right behind me then collapsed on top of me.

"I was about to burst," he chuckled.

"Clearly," I said rolling away from him so that we were facing each other lying sideways on the bed.

"You've been so sick that I didn't want to come near you, so I've been forced to handle things on my own lately. I've missed this," he said, and patted my vagina.

"Well, my vagina has missed you, too."

"Please tell me you'll never get sick again."

I started to say that I wish I could, but he interrupted me. "What did you need to talk about?"

I sat up and reached for my clothes. He pulled me back down to the bed.

"No clothes tonight. There's more to come, baby."

I smiled, then realized what I had to do and said, "Well, B," I paused waiting for his eyes to meet mine, "you put a baby in me."

He sat up, open mouthed, brows furrowed, "What?"

"I said that you," I pointed to his crotch, "put a baby in me." I patted my stomach. It was now or never time. The decision was made. Time to fill him in. Honesty, right? Then he got all soft and sweet with me. He reached down and traced his fingertips across my belly.

"Are you serious?" he asked with a smile. A smile. I know. I began to prepare myself for the most challenging conversation of my entire life.

"Yes," I answered, clearing my throat.

"Wow."

"I know."

"I thought you were on some kind of birth control?"

"I am. Apparently, it's sucky birth control."

"Paige, what's wrong? Are you okay?"

"B," I took a deep breath, shook my head and closed my eyes so that I wouldn't have to look into his, "I can't."

"What do you mean, you can't?" he said, not realizing the news dynamite I was about to ignite. He hopped up and sat on his knees, looking down at me as I lied on my back.

"Paige, this is great. I'm thirty-five. It's about time I start acting like a grown-up. This is good news."

"Don't get attached, Blake, please."

"What do you mean, don't get attached?" he asked confused.

"I mean, I'm making an appointment tomorrow ... to get rid of it."

"You're what? No, Paige." He ran his hands through his hair ruffling out his curls into a halo of frizz. "Paige, are you even going to consider me in this?" I jumped off the bed, grabbed my clothes and frantically started getting dressed. Blake pulled on his boxers but stopped there.

"Listen, man, it's my fucking uterus, which means, it's my fucking business," I spat the words at him. "You don't have to carry it, or birth it, or change your entire fucking life for it. I've told you, Blake, I can't do kids. I can't."

"No, Paige, you told me you could. You told me you wanted them eventually. Why else do you think I've stuck around in this?" His voice was calm with an edge. I thought back to our camping trip, the night when I said that, the weekend where new feelings and emotions took over my normal guarded heart.

"What do you mean this?" I asked.

"I mean your secret fucked up world where you hold all of your shit in and don't tell anyone anything. I hardly even fucking know you, and I still love you. You can't make a decision like this without me, Paige." No longer calm, straight up shouting. "You are so fucked up. I don't deserve this."

"You're right. I am, Blake. I am fucked up, and you don't deserve this. I'm sorry this happened. Really, really fucking sorry. I am poison. This thing," I pointed to my stomach, "is half me, which means that I should spare the world something that has me flowing through its veins." I stormed out of his room trying to make a break for it before the tears came.

"Paige, wait." He came up behind me before I made it to the door. "Please, Paige, for the love of Christ. Please talk to me. I'm not letting you run off this time. This is real, what we are. It's the realest thing I've ever known, and this decision that you've made ... without me," emphasis on without, "... it's not cool, and it's not fair, and if I mean anything to you, you owe me a conversation, not a fight, an honest, no lies, no secrets, straight truth conversation. Then you can go. You can run. You can hide, but you're not going anywhere until you give me that. Now sit the fuck down and talk to me." His nostrils flared, his skin turned red, and his naked chest heaved up and down as he yelled.

I took a deep breath and sat on the arm of the couch, not quite yielding yet, still able to sprint if necessary.

"So, you're pregnant, and you're sure? Have you seen a doctor?"

"Yes, today. Eleven weeks."

"What does that mean?"

"Pregnancy is forty weeks, so I'm a little over a quarter of the way there. I can still have an abortion, but my doctor recommends that if I choose to do it, I should do it soon."

He rubbed his eyebrows, pushing them back and forth. "Okay," he came over and sat on his ottoman in front of me and grabbed my hands, "listen, I'm sorry I freaked out. Thanks for not going."

"You're welcome."

He looked up at me with sad green eyes. "I can't figure out what to say, Paige. What can I say?"

"I don't know. Say you'll support me."

"I can't support you doing that, baby. I can't. It's your body, and I understand that it's ultimately up to you. You say it's half you. Well, it's half me, too, right? I mean, you're sure it's mine?"

"Yes, asshole."

"Sorry," he shrugged his shoulders. "Okay, look, help me understand. What would be so bad about having a baby?"

"Well, for starters, I don't want one." I twirled my hair around my finger trying not to look at him. I fought my nerves, my temper, my heart. I just wanted this conversation to end, and he was having none of that.

"Well, you didn't want a boyfriend either, but you're getting pretty used to me."

"True." Tension filled the air between us. He held my hands, nervously rubbing his thumbs over mine. He took one of his hands and brushed a loose curl out of his eye.

"I want kids, lots of them, actually." He paused. "I'm not scared, Paige. I'll be here. You won't be alone. I promise. I'll wake up in the night. I'll change shit diapers and all of it, and listen, I can't think of anything better than having something that is half you. You're smart and sexy and wildly uninhibited." He flashed a quick sideways smile before he continued, "I love you, Paige. All of you. And I don't even care that you don't say it to me. I almost love you even more for that. Don't you see, Paige? I love that you're all fucked up and secretive, a map I can't read."

I stared into an intense green glare.

"I'm in." He got up and started pacing back and forth, rubbing his hand on the back of his head. "I'm in even in if you're not. You can run. I'll stay. Have the baby. I'll take it. No strings attached."

Silence ensued. I listened to my own rapid breaths fighting the argument taking place between my heart and my mind. Then a moment of answer, a light bulb.

"What about the drugs?"

"What did the doctor say?"

"I didn't tell her." He sat back down in front of me, confusion written all over his face. "Look," I said to him, "you want to admit you do drugs, be my guest. That's not in my bag."

"Well, I guess it doesn't matter if you're planning to kill it anyway."

"Why are you being so hard on me, B?"

"That's my fucking kid in you, Paige. I'm not sure I could live with," He trailed off. I swear to God I thought he was going to rub a bald spot right into the back of his head. "Just think about it, Paige. For me, can you *please* just think about it?"

"I have thought about it, Blake. That's all I've done for the last couple of weeks, thought about it, since I took the test. Waiting for that goddamned appointment was torture for me. Plus, B, there's so much you don't know that might change your mind about me." Like the fact that at that very moment, all I could think about was the smorgasbord of pills awaiting me in my bathroom.

"Well, Paige, why don't you enlighten me? You might be surprised," he said, biting the inside of his bottom lip.

Now it was my turn to pace. Trying to still my rapidly beating heart, I took a few deep breaths. No help. Then I decided, fuck it, he's going to be history soon anyway, so I let it fly.

"I'm crazy, B, batshit crazy. Suicidal, actually," I looked up for a reaction, nothing, "Therapy, pills, treatment, hospitals, *mental* hospitals, B, all of it. That's me. That's the big fucking secret that you don't know." I threw my arms up in the air in surrender.

"What makes you think I don't know that?"

I looked at him, trying to read him.

"I know, Paige," he said calmly, "I was here last summer when they dragged you out on a stretcher. I followed the ambulance to the hospital, and I stayed there with Janie waiting to find out what was happening to you. I know you had to spend some time away. I figured you were in some sort of treatment center, inpatient, or something. I'm not an idiot. I know you take pills. You've practically moved in here. You can't hide everything from me. I just don't say anything because for whatever reason, you don't seem to want me to know. Paige, I don't care about any of that. So what? You're depressed. You and more than a billion other people. It's not the first time I've witnessed it. I can handle this, all of it. I just want you, and the baby, our baby, if you'll have me." He motioned to my stomach again. "You're it for me, Paige. I need you to trust me."

I tried to swallow the big pill he just fed me. Thoughts ricocheted in my head: Blake said he knows about me. He knows I'm fucked up. He has never said a word about it and still wants to be with me. I had no idea he was there when I attempted suicide. I can't believe Janie never said anything. I made a mental note that she needed an earful of Paige. In my mind, I battled with the thought that he was at the hospital that night, and still wanted to be there, here, standing in front of me.

I looked at him once more. "Fine," I resigned, and then I opened my optical floodgates and let them poor down my cheeks.

He came over and pulled me into him. I showered his naked shoulder with my tears. I held on to him, and sobbed.

I sobbed with grief for the past I couldn't admit was mine. I sobbed with relief that someone loved me in spite of it, and I sobbed with hope for the rest of my life to not be heartbreaking. I cried into my rock, my new foundation, my something to live for, my future.

When his shoulder was drenched with my tears, I pulled away and retreated to his bathroom where I grabbed some tissue and tried to put myself back together. I stared at my reflection in the mirror, debating with myself, looking into my own sad dark eyes. I took three deep breaths and shoved myself away from the counter. I walked out of the bathroom and met him back in his living room. He had pulled on a T-shirt and some basketball shorts, which for some reason made me smile.

I looked at him and met his eyes again. He appeared hopeful, the last hour's anger dissipated. I walked over to where he sat, and reached for his hand, tracing my thumb over the crooked knuckle of his middle finger. "I'm in, too," I said swallowing the monstrous lump in my throat.

He bared his tease of a crooked grin at me and said, "Well, you should probably call your doctor then, and let her know what a druggie you are." He pulled me down onto his lap and wrapped a long arm around my waist.

"Oh, God. Please don't start nagging me. What are you my wife?"

"No, I'm your baby daddy," he said with a chuckle. Suddenly, an aha look took over his face, "B-Small," he said with another grin. "We will call him B-Small."

I had no words I leaned in and kissed his cheek, grateful for his presence, grateful for him.

Because in one hour he took me from abortion to B-Small.

Change

Dear Stephanie,

I don't do well with change. I am a creature of habit. I like things my way, perfect and in order ... my way, but I no longer get a vote apparently. Let me start from the beginning. B said we need to tell my doctor about the drugs. That's not something with which I'm even slightly comfortable.

I'm a pretty face with a good body who looks nothing like a girl who *dabbles* in illicit recreation, so just having to admit this out loud to someone who isn't snorting it with me is about as terrifying as meeting the masked guy from the *Texas Chainsaw Massacre* at summer camp ... I'm not even slightly kidding. But I made the appointment anyway, and I made Blake promise to come with me. I saw a few "dads" in the waiting room last time, so I figured we might as well get this out of the way.

I almost ripped the receptionist's head off when I called to make the appointment. "Ms. Preston," she said in a condescending tone, "you don't need to see the doctor until next month. Weren't you *just* here?"

"Yes, I was just there yesterday, but I need to talk to the doctor about some things, and I'd like to schedule an appointment to see her."

"You can leave her a voicemail."

"What is your name?" I asked about ready to strangle her through the phone.

"Miranda."

"Listen, Miranda, I called to make an appointment, so I'm going to need you to do that ASAP. I need to see the doctor, and it's not something I can accomplish through voicemail. It's urgent."

"Why is it urgent?"

"None of your business, Miranda. Just do your job and make the goddamned appointment." Seriously, this bitch.

I heard a long sigh and typing. "I can schedule you in two weeks."

"Not good enough. Urgent: adjective: requiring immediate attention or action."

"I'm sorry, Ms. Preston. That's the best I can do. If it's an emergency, you should go to the emergency room."

"Do better, Miranda."

More typing. Another sigh. "I'll squeeze you in tomorrow at 8:00. She doesn't usually take appointments this early, but I'll make sure and let her know you said it was ... urgent. Is that better?"

"Yes," you fucking cunt. I scheduled the appointment, quickly texted B the time and started pacing around my apartment, and then I had a panic attack.

All of me was coming to surface. First with Blake. Now I had to tell my doctor. Even Dr. Morea didn't know everything. My secret world began a quick descent that I felt sure would eventually crash down on me.

I ran to my bathroom and pulled out an orange prescription bottle. With hands shaking, I tipped over the bottle and let a Xanax fall into my palm. I threw it in my mouth, turned on my faucet, filled up a glass, and then I spit out the pill. "You can't take fucking Xanax when you're pregnant, idiot," I said to my reflection.

I replaced the lid and stared down at the bottle. I have a ton of self-control about a lot of things, but when I'm tense,

I need a pill. I don't know how I will make it nine months, or I guess seven more, really, without a pill. Jesus.

I decided to call Dr. Morea. An hour later, I was sitting on his purple couch. Thank god I'm a priority patient, and he had a free hour. I told him about my freak-out and then about not taking a pill and that I didn't know how I could do this.

"Back up, Paige. So you told Blake about the pregnancy?"

"Yes. I told him about everything."

"Everything?"

"Yes, doc, meds, suicide, hospitals, that his girlfriend is batshit crazy, all of it."

"You're not batshit crazy, Paige."

"That's what he said."

"So then, you decided to keep the baby."

I sat twisting my thumbs together.

"Yes, I'm keeping it."

"We need to talk about your medication, then, Paige."

Holy shit, another change was coming. I sat up and leaned forward, letting my head fall between my knees.

"I can't take my meds, Dr. Morea?"

"I don't usually recommend it, Paige. There are some risks and complications that could occur for the baby. We probably need to slowly take you off of them. I'm going to give you a prescription for a lower dose. We will treat your depression with therapy during your pregnancy. We'll work on relaxation and calming techniques for your anxiety. You can have a standing appointment every day. I'm a little more conservative with medication when you're pregnant Paige. I think it's best."

Meditation? Great. I could only imagine sessions of Gandhi inspired calming techniques. Ugh. This wasn't news to me. I knew he was going to take me off of them, after my own internet research, but I had really hoped that I could be an exception.

As it stands, I can't drink alcohol. I can't smoke (which I really never do anyway, except for when I drink or when

I'm nervous), I can only have limited amounts of coffee. I can't eat sushi. I can't eat goat cheese or Brie. Clearly cocaine is out of the question, and now I can't take my meds. If they tell me I can't have sex, I swear to God I'm going to cunt punt someone.

We talked about my depression, suicide, all kinds of stuff, and I left feeling anxious and tired. I went home and fell down on my bed and slept until I heard the ding on my phone.

B-Large: *Home. Come.*

Me: *Too tired. See you tomorrow.*

B-Large: *You need to eat. Come over.*

Me: *Too tired.*

Then I heard him knock on my door. "Paige, open the door," he yelled from the hall.

I staggered off of my bed and sulked to the door. I opened it to B standing in his basketball shorts and a T-shirt with a little white gift bag in his hand and his ridiculous boyish grin spreading over his face.

"I got you something," he handed me the little white bag. I pulled out the pale pink and blue tissue paper and then the contents. Tiny yellow baby socks.

"Oh my God," I said looking at the sweetest little socks I had ever seen.

"I know," Blake gleamed. "I passed this store at lunch and went in to get you something. As soon as I saw these socks, I had to have them. Can you believe anything can be this small?"

"No," I whispered, running my thumbs across the soft tiny socks. For the first time, I pictured the baby and his little feet. I felt tears in my eyes. I cleared my throat and swallowed my emotion. "Thank you, B."

He smiled. "Come on. Let's go eat. I don't feel like cooking tonight."

Over dinner, Blake decided to spring yet another monumental new thing in my lap.

"I've been thinking. We need to look at houses."

"What?" I asked, choking on my pasta.

"Seriously, Paige? Where are you going to put a baby? In your closet? In mine? One bedroom apartments aren't really made for kids. Plus, we can't raise a kid in the city." He said all of this like it was no big deal, like he was telling me to order marinara instead of alfredo.

"What?" I could feel the tension build in my body. Frankly, I hadn't thought about it. I've lived in my apartment for seven years. It's all I've known since I left the apartment Janie and I shared in college. It was my home. And the city? The city was everything to me. "What are you saying, B?"

"Just that I think we should look at getting a house, maybe in the suburbs." He said the last part fast, knowing I was about to have a monumental explosion of freak out.

"You know I fucking hate suburbs, Blake. I'm not moving out of Dallas. What do you want to get a house in the neighborhood with the rest of the douchebags you work with?"

"It crossed my mind, yeah. But I know you wouldn't go that far. What about Highland Park or Lakewood? They're both in the heart of Dallas and close to downtown. You can still be to your hair salon in minutes."

I rolled my eyes at the hair salon comment.

"You're manipulating me, and I know it." I looked up at him. "Way to throw out suburbs to get me to consider your other options. Well played, B."

"Thanks," he said, slurping a noodle through his lips.

"I'll look, but I can't promise anything."

"Good enough." And with that, he talked me into looking at a house. I can hardly even believe it.

The next morning, after a fairly sleepless night for both of us, B kissed my shoulder to wake me. "Good morning, momma," he said. He's started calling me all sorts of new things. "Baby momma" is his favorite at the moment. Good grief.

"Good morning." He sat on the edge of the bed shirtless and handed me a glass of ice water.

I gulped it down. Since finding out about the pregnancy, I have been horribly parched. "Better get up and get ready. We need to leave in about an hour. Traffic will be a nightmare today."

I laid my head back on the pillow and sighed. I had almost let myself forget about the dreaded appointment. "Come on, sleepy head. Get up. I'll make you breakfast while you get ready."

"I hate doctors, B," I whined.

"It will be over before you know it. Come on, get up." He pulled the duvet off his bed as he walked out of the room, leaving me naked and cold. I had no choice but to get up and shower.

A couple hours later, we pulled into the parking lot of the medical complex that housed my doctor's office. Blake held my clammy hand as we walked into the building. I let him touch the buttons to the elevator this time, quietly grossing out at the amount of sick people's germs now living on his index finger and making a mental note to hold his left hand and not his right.

We sat nervously in the waiting room, watching pregnant woman after pregnant woman walk in and hobble to her seat. Then they called my name, and we were ushered into an exam room. B was back to rubbing the back of his head bald. I twirled my hair around my finger sitting on the edge of the exam table, knees shaking, stomach clenched, waiting. B got up and started pacing. I sat and watched him, wondering how freaked out he was that his kid was going to come out with two heads or two noses, or one toe. I certainly had the images, but neither of us had voiced that fear out loud. I studied the sonogram picture trying to see if my child looked normal, but still all I saw was a blob.

My doctor quickly knocked on the door three times before opening. B resumed sitting in his chair, knees spread, elbows resting on them.

"Hi, Ms. Preston. What's going on? Miranda said it was urgent." She looked from me to Blake. Neither of us spoke. I tried to swallow the cotton that had formed in my mouth wishing I had brought a bottle of water from Blake's fridge. B looked at me and raised his eyebrows at me silently willing me to speak.

"I need to talk to you about um," I paused.

"Go ahead," she said and sat down on her little stool in front of me.

"I've done drugs." I rushed the sentence. "Lots of them."

"Since you were pregnant?" She set my file on the counter behind her.

"Yes, well, no, well, yes. I did them before I knew. I haven't done any since I found out, other than my prescription medication for depression." I took a deep breath, relieved that the sentence hadn't made my head explode.

"Okay, what have you taken?"

And I told her. I told her about the cocaine on New Year's Eve, about the several different times I had taken sleeping pills, especially when I was vomiting at the beginning, and about the prescriptions, and I told her how much alcohol I consumed before finding out about the baby. She did not panic, was mostly unmoved. She said that babies tend to be resilient and that she is not really worried, but to be safe, she suggested that I have sonograms at every appointment. She said she didn't want me to panic but that she was going to categorize my pregnancy as high risk, which did make me internally panic. Big time.

I read about high risk pregnancies, horror stories. I pretended to be as calm as she while we mapped out my pregnancy. She wants to see me weekly rather than monthly, and she agreed with Dr. Morea about the depression meds. She said she prefers no drugs during pregnancy, unless they're absolutely necessary, and she handed me for the second time a list of medications that I would be allowed to take. None of them are any fun.

B and I walked back to his Tahoe in silence, purposely not holding hands since I was certain he used his left finger on the elevator. He opened my door for me, gently kissed my cheek, then jogged over to his side and got in the driver's seat. "You, okay, babe?"

"I hate being called babe," I responded. Everything was changing, so quickly, and I felt myself spinning. Without having a single go-to or crutch, I don't know what I'm going to do. I can't even take ibuprofen.

Messages

Dear Stephanie,

After that appointment, I sort of checked out for a bit. I turned off my phone and just stayed in my apartment for a few days. B couldn't reach me, and knowing the state I was in, panicked and came to my door. I let him in and lied to him telling him that I was tired and just needed to rest. I don't think he was convinced, but he let me have my space and left me alone for two more days.

Finally, he came over and demanded that I at least turn on my phone. By this point, I had wallowed and sulked and done all that I could, except off myself, so I decided to just give in to him. I told him to go home and cook, that I was going to shower and that I'd be at his place in a bit. I plugged my phone in while I got ready.

When I picked it up, I couldn't believe the amount of voicemails and text notifications. I threw the phone on my couch and headed to Blake's. I couldn't deal with anything else, and I needed me some B-Large.

He left the door unlocked, so I let myself in. Spices filled the air of his apartment making my stomach growl. I walked into his kitchen where he was busy making tacos, singing along to New Order's "Temptation." He obviously didn't hear me come in.

I quietly sat at his bar watching him dance around, chopping lettuce and tomatoes, sprinkling cumin and chili powder over the meat. Beautiful perfection right there in front of me. I just sat there drinking him in like the vodka martinis I missed so much.

"Boo," I said, just above a whisper. He dropped the knife on the cutting board.

"Jesus, Paige," he laughed. "How long have you been sitting there?"

"Long enough," I smiled at him. He smiled back.

"Can you take a break from cooking?" I asked and pulled my shirt over my head.

"I'll meet you in my room in two minutes," he said and leaned over the bar, biting my bottom lip.

I didn't move. I waited for him to turn burners down and cover the vegetables. When he started out of the kitch-en, I looped my arm around his waist and pulled him to my bar stool, wrapping my legs around his torso. I missed him.

In all of my selfish tantrum throwing, I forgot that he was my most favorite addiction, and he was allowed, so I took a hit. I pulled his basketball shorts down, got down on my knees and took him in my mouth, every inch of him, until he grabbed my hair, twisting it in his hands, pushing me down further, begging me to not stop. It felt delicious, and raw, and I loved the control I had over him. I let him finish in my mouth, and I drank in all of him. He sagged to the floor and grabbed me around my waist. "Your turn," he said with that sexy smile of his.

"Nah, B, I'm good. Let's eat."

He looked at me confused. I'm pretty selfish in bed. I live by the rule that I come no matter what, so normally if he were to "finish" first, he would take care of me. I under-stood his confusion, but I didn't know what to say. It felt nice to just give him something and not expect anything in return. I made a mental note to do that more often.

While we were eating our tacos, B asked me if I got his messages. I told him about all of the voicemails and texts, and he convinced me that I shouldn't avoid them forever, so I went to my apartment and stopped avoiding while he stayed back to clean up the kitchen.

In two days, Blake had left me about a dozen, effing stalker. Janie left three, mostly of the tune "Call me. Blake is flipping out." Dr. Morea left a couple, but there was one on my phone that I listened to repeatedly.

"Ms. Preston. This is Lieutenant Sanders. We arrested him today. He's in jail."

I dropped my phone. I know I should have been relieved, but I wasn't. The pit of my stomach fell to the floor. I wanted him arrested, clearly, but I knew once they did, he would get a trial, and I would be forced to see him again. Dr. Morea warned me of this. I wanted desperately for a Xanax and a vodka martini. I silently cursed at my unborn child.

I could feel the panic rising in my chest, making it difficult to breathe. I tried to force myself to take deep breaths like Dr. Morea and I practiced in therapy, but with every breath, the more I felt like I was suffocating. Before I knew it, I ran to my kitchen sink where I threw up my tacos. Blake came in while I was cleaning out my sink with bleach.

"Hey, should you be using bleach?"

"Jesus, Blake, are you going to audit everything I do for the rest of this pregnancy because if you are, then I might lose my already precarious mind," I screamed at him. He threw his hands up and slowly backed away from me.

"Geez, Paige. Sorry." He started to walk toward my door that I had apparently left unlocked. He doesn't have a key.

"No, Blake, I'm sorry. I just threw up. I clean with bleach. I'm not sure if I can use it or not, but I haven't read anything that says I can't, so I used it. I'll add that to the list of questions you have for the doctor."

"What's the matter with you?" he sort of barked at me.

"Where should I begin? Let's see. I just got some," I took a deep breath, "News. Normally, I'd call you and we'd drink ourselves into oblivion, snort some shit up our nose, and pretend we live in a make believe world where everything is perfect. Or I would take some sleeping pills and sleep until I didn't hurt anymore. Or I would let this news take me into the dark depths of my twisted head and try to fall asleep forever, but I can't do any of that because you put a fucking kid in me, so I threw up, and I'm cleaning up the mess, but apparently, I can't do that either."

"Wait, Paige. Please just calm down. Take it easy."

"Take it easy? Are you kidding me? Take it easy?" I screamed.

"Paige, please. Please just try to relax." He started walking toward me, slowly, treating me like a rattlesnake about to attack. He grabbed my shoulders and pulled me into him, wrapping his arms around me protectively. "Come here. It will be okay. I promise," he whispered, and we stayed there until I pulled away. I went back to my counter, placed the lid on the bleach, and put it in the cabinet under the sink.

"You gonna tell me the news?" he asked.

"No."

"So we're back to secrets again?"

"No," I said weakly, and walked past him to the living room where I plopped down on my couch. I grabbed one of the throw pillows and held it over my chest. He followed me to the couch and lied down, resting his head in my lap, and looked up at me with his emerald eyes.

"You have to talk to me, Paige. We're in this together, baby."

"They arrested the guy who raped me."

He sat up, positioned himself next to me and put his arm around my shoulder. "Wow. Well, that's not the worst news I've ever heard."

"He'll get a trial. I'll have to be there," I said with a sigh while sinking deeper into the crook of his shoulder.

"You won't be alone, Paige. I'll be there for every single minute. Don't worry." He kissed the top of my head. He always knew what to say. The more we talked about it, the more I realized how relieved this made Blake. I had no idea that this ordeal had weighed so heavily on him. With the pregnancy and all, I'd mostly pushed it away, but Blake said he thought about that guy every day and how he should have done more. We sat on my couch for a while. After many attempts by Blake to change the subject, we ended up sitting together in silence, comfortable with the simple presence of the other. Sometimes words are unnecessary.

When he was sure that I was sane again, he got up and stretched then asked me to go back to his place with him, but I declined, and I didn't offer for him to stay. It's just not an option for me, so I went to bed alone and found myself wide awake and anxious. At 3:13, I looked at the clock, still completely unable to sleep, I reached for my phone and sent B a text.

Me: *Can I take you up on that offer?*

It took about fourteen seconds for the reply

B-Large: *I left the door unlocked. I knew you'd come around.*

I crept over to his place in my T-shirt and panties and slid into his bed. He rolled over to face me. "I couldn't sleep either," he whispered and pulled me closer to him. I buried my face into his chest and breathed him in, wrapped my arm around his waist and fell asleep instantly.

Home

Dear Stephanie,

I'm fourteen weeks pregnant now and am having a love hate relationship with the pregnancy. Some days I love it. I mean, my skin is unbelievable, and my hair is so soft and shiny, and Blake is eating me up. He's ridiculously happy. So all of that is good, right?

I still don't see myself as a mother though. I imagine this little baby, and I can see Blake with him, holding him, fathering him, but I can't see myself with a baby. Still. I keep hoping it will change, that I'll have some sort of epiphany and all of my natural maternal instinct will kick in, but mostly, I just look at my reflection, at the visible changes on my body and wonder what's going to happen when this thing is born.

Maybe it's the pregnancy, but lately I miss my mother terribly. I long to hear her voice and have made it my mission to get her to talk to me, so I visited the home a couple of days ago. I passed Blanche at the nurse's station. She stopped me.

"Oh, Ms. Parnevik, that boyfriend of yours is a pistol, isn't he?" she chuckled and used the back of her hand to gently slap the other nurse standing next to her.

"Sure he is," I replied trying to avoid any more conversation.

"What was it that he said the other day when he was here, Joclyn?" The other day?

"Oh, Blake, Guurl, he's funny! That boy always has somethin' up his sleeve, don't he? Bet he keeps you on your toes," Jocyln said to me.

I stood watching these two old nurses giggle about my boyfriend wondering what in the world they were talking about.

"What do you mean?" I asked.

"Guurl, he comes here on his lunch break, bringing that guitar of his, playing music for your momma and all of those old women in there. He's got a few fans, too. They see his pretty green eyes, and those old ladies start droppin' their Depends left and right," Joclyn giggled and made her voluptuous breasts jump up and down.

"Joclyn," Blanche scolded. She looked at me shaking her head, "nobody has dropped any Depends, but he does have some fans."

I had to laugh along with them. "He comes here to visit?" What the hell?

"You don't know?" Blanche blinked at me through her glasses smiling with her mouth and her eyes. "He's been coming here on Tuesdays, usually around lunch since you brought him at Christmas." Since Christmas? That's three months my boyfriend has been visiting a nursing home without my knowledge. "Sometimes he comes on other days, but we all count on his being here every Tuesday. He's been really good for a lot of our patients, especially your mother. He sits in her room, and they listen to music together. He's such a sweet boy." Boy? He's thirty-five years old, for Christ's sake.

"They practically have traffic jams in their wheelchairs every Tuesday, and it smells to high heavens of cheap perfume. Old Hilda even puts her lipstick on. He's a good one, that boy. He's the only thing some of these old girls have to look forward to, his visits on Tuesdays. Then he pulls out that guitar, and we all get the treat of hearing him sing. He's gotta a good voice, too. Nobody knows the songs he sings, though, 'cept maybe your momma. Mr. Duncan even sometimes dances. You should come with him some time."

I sort of got the impression that even Joclyn had the hots for my boyfriend. And what was this about a guitar and a voice? B-Large had his own secrets.

"Interesting," I said to Blanche. And that was that. Joclyn and Blanche resumed their discussion of my boyfriend's ass as I walked into my mother's room. She wasn't sitting in her chair like usual staring through the window. Instead, she was lying in her bed, staring at the ceiling.

I rolled a chair next to the bed and sat down next to her, grabbing her hand. I normally don't talk to my mother when I visit, but I figured if I wanted her to talk to me, I would have to take the lead.

"Mom ... I have news." I said. She didn't budge, just stared.

"Okay, so ..." I choked on my words as tears filled my eyes. I never imagined telling her what I was about to say, and the rawness of my emotion was unexpected, I guess. "Mom, I'm pregnant. I'm going to have a baby." I cleared my throat. "With Blake." I looked at her eyes. She turned her head and looked at me as tears filled her beautiful brown eyes and spilled out onto her pillow.

She was in there, in her silent body, and she was happy. For me. We sat there in silence for a while, my hand still holding hers. I got up and got the remote to her sound system to kill the silence with some music.

I stayed for about two hours, listening to music with my mother. While Peter Gabriel sang "Solsbury Hill," I lost myself in the lyrics, reliving his spiritual journey, and a realization came over me as he sang about taking things and going home.

I kissed my mother's forehead, whispered my good-bye and got in my car. I sent B a text.

Me: *Find a realtor. We need to start looking for houses.*
B-Large: *One step ahead, baby ... always*

Me: *What's this I hear about a guitar?*
B-Large: *Guitar? I plead the fifth. Who told you?*
Me: *Could have been any one of your groupies. I'm no rat ...*
I smiled at my phone thinking *I'm in love.*

If I ever want my mother to come back to me, to talk again, how can I leave her in the home, the depressing place where people go to die? Thus begins my new plan. I'm going to take her home, to my home.

News

Dear Stephanie,

It's official. We've told people about the pregnancy. First my mom, then Blake's parents.

We met them for dinner at a little Thai restaurant near their house on Friday night. They were already there when we arrived. I could hear Big Bob's loud voice echoing through the tiny restaurant the minute Blake opened the door for me. We walked to the table where his parents were already seated.

While Blake pulled out my chair, the waitress came over with a bottle of red wine. She began her wine presentation, but Robert looked at her with his big green eyes and told her not to waste any time on productions and just get to opening the wine. She proceeded to pour a glass for his mom. She then started to pour a glass for me. My mouth watered, but before the first drop hit my glass, B promptly moved it letting her know that I'd take a Pellegrino instead. Good grief.

We sat making small talk until everyone had ordered their dinner and appetizers were served. Big Bob looked at me and said, "So what's the big news? Blake said you guys have something to tell us. Did he propose without telling his old dad?"

I spit out my water.

"No," I cleared my throat and squeezed Blake's leg under the table willing him to break the baby news himself.

He wiped his mouth with his napkin and set it gently on his lap, smoothing it over his leg. I could almost see his nerves. Blake's being nervous was a new thing for me. "Actually, Mom, Dad," he paused, "Paige is pregnant. We're having a baby." There was that smile again, which made my own mouth twitch in response. Pure elated joy and nothing more from my B.

"Okay," his mom started as she looked up from her plate. "This is kind of sudden. I mean, you're not even married."

I took a deep breath summoning the courage to tell his mom that was not going to happen, but before I could get it out, B took the stage.

"Mom, we don't have to be married to have a baby. We're really happy about this, and we want you guys to be happy about it, too. I need you to say you'll support us and not hound us to do anything else. This is a big enough step for us." He looked at me. Blake, my hero. Then he continued, "We'll get married after the baby is here, and we've had time to settle in a bit." I spit out my water. Again. Blake and his plans. Does he not realize that marriage is completely out of the question for me?

"Blake, honey, I expect you to me more responsible than this," Claire said, taking a small sip of her wine.

I couldn't believe my ears. I did not foresee this happening when I pictured how things would go down with his family. I figured they would just jump up and down and hug us, congratulate us, pull out their phones and start running through the Greeks on their contact list. His mom looked so disappointed. I felt kind of ashamed.

"Mom?" Blake looked deflated. "Can't you just be happy for us?"

"Blake, baby, I love you. You know that, and I support you no matter what. I just want what's best for you. Paige, I know he loves you. Do you feel the same?" She waited for me to answer. Blake looked at me waiting, too. I nodded. Sure I love him, but do we all have to scream the word at each other all of the time? Geez these people.

She continued, "I support you, baby," she said to Blake taking his hand from across the table. "A baby is a lifelong commitment. You need to do what's right for this baby and for Paige, and take responsibility, whether it's now or later. You know what I mean."

"I will, mom." Blake squeezed my leg under the table three times. I knew he was trying to tame the beast inside of me, but nothing would work at this point. I needed to bolt in the worst way. Then Big Bob came to my rescue.

"Sugar," he said to Blake's mom, "I couldn't be happier. Congratulations, guys." He got up and walked around the table. Then he scooped me up from my chair and enveloped me in a massive hug, the kind that is impossible not to love. "When are you due, sweetheart?"

"Early September."

"Oh, Paige," Bob laughed, "Pregnancy and Texas heat ... better you than me, sweetheart."

I laughed. "I know." We all laughed, our fake laughs, finished our dinner making casual conversation about plans for the baby, and then headed our separate ways. In the Tahoe on the way home, Blake asked me what I thought about what his mom said.

"I'm not asking you to put a ring on me or anything, B. You know that's not what I want."

"I know, Paige, but maybe she's right."

"Blake, please, I need to take baby steps here, and all I can handle is the actual baby right now. Please don't add anything else."

He drove the rest of the way home in silence. I could see the wheels turning in his mind. I closed my eyes and silently begged him not to do anything crazy. Blake has a lot of respect for his parents, and frankly, so do I, so I couldn't help but wonder what he was going to do with what his mother said. Is there any better candidate for a husband than Blake?

No. He's loyal, faithful, honest, kind, beautiful, all things good. Too good, actually. Too good for me.

* * *

Telling Janie was so much more fun than telling anyone else. I did it our traditional way, in a note with a list that I left taped to her car outside of her office.

Top 5 Reasons Why You Really Need to Call Your BFF

#5. I need an update on your douchebag boyfriend who likes dry humping you in night clubs.

#4. You need an update on my awesome boyfriend and his magical penis. (Did Paige just say "boyfriend?" Yes, yes she did.)

#3. Dude, hold onto your horses ... Blake plays the guitar. I know!!! And he sings. Are you thinking what I'm thinking? Hootenanny ... STAT!

#2. You still have my pimp-black minidress, which you swore you would return the next day ... it's been like 6 months, and it better not have jizz stains from said douche-bag mentioned in #5.

And the number 1 reason you need to call your best friend is ...

I HAVE NEWS!!!!!!!!!!!!!!

I texted her...

Me: *Check your car. Left you a note.*

Janie Juggs: *Stalker*

Five minutes later my phone rang.

"Hello."

She began reading the list out loud, per the rules. When she finished, she simply blurted out, "Send me a pic of the ring."

"There's no ring."

"Then what's your news."

"B put a baby in me."

"I'm coming over." And I heard the three dial tones telling me she ended the call.

She used her key and walked into my apartment twenty minutes later. (She is the only one in the world I trust with a key). After about a ten-minute hug (Only Janie is allowed to hug me, well and Blake), she asked, "You okay, Paige?"

"Sure I am, Juggs."

"Don't lie to me."

"Well, I've had my fair share of freak-outs, but I've got it under control." She pulled a rubber band from her wrist and pulled her long silky red hair into a high pony tail.

"Wow, Paige. I need a drink." I waited for her to realize what she was asking. "Oh, sorry, Paige. Shit. You can't even drink. How are you dealing with that?"

"It's miserable. I can't do anything. I can't even eat goat cheese."

"I know. Melody has kids, remember." Melody. Janie's older sister. I hate that woman. Still.

"Yeah. Want a Pellegrino? That's the best I can do because there's no way you're allowed to drink in front of me. I have some flavored ones."

I pulled two out of my refrigerator and slid one across my bar to Janie. She twisted the cap off and took a big drink, then turned to me and berated me with questions. "When are you due? How much weight have you gained? Are you sure it's Blake's? How big are your boobs now?"

My boobs are growing so fast I'm pretty sure they will need their own zip code by the end of my pregnancy. Clearly it's noticeable.

We sat at my bar, drinking our sparkling waters catching up, and I realized how much I missed my best friend. I had sort of checked out on her since Blake and I started seeing so much of each other.

"Well, can you get a pedicure?"

"I think so. Nobody's said no yet. We better get going, though, before B finds out and tells me not do it."

"So what's this about a guitar?" She asked as we were walking out the door. We passed Blake in the hallway. Janie gave him a big hug and congratulated him. He beamed at her, smiling at me.

"Where are you guys off to?" he asked still holding Janie in a tight hug.

"Happy hour. Where else?" Janie said pulling herself away from Blake.

"She can't drink." All serious ... what is happening to my fun B-Large?

"I'm kidding fucko. We'll be back in a bit. You can get your panties out of a wad while we're gone."

He play-kicked her in the ass and then grabbed me and pulled me into him. "Be good," he whispered into my ear. Then he kissed the back of my head and shooed me to my best friend.

"I'm keeping the black dress until you're skinny enough to get back into it. I don't think your boobs are ever going to fit into it again, though," Janie said as we exited my building into the cool afternoon.

The thing about Janie and me is that we're always able to pick up right where we left off the last time. We don't have to talk every day, or even every week, but when we do, it's as if no time has passed. Janie is of course in love with the d-bag from the club. Unlike Blake and me, she and her beau are taking it slow, and I reinforced her devotion to condoms, too. We can't have two illegitimate kids on our hands.

Once our toes were beautified, we stopped at a little café near my house for dinner. I had been dying to ask her all night and couldn't formulate the question, so I finally just came out with it.

"What am I going to do with Blake?"

"You're going to marry him, Paige," she said shaking massive amounts of salt over her salad.

"No way."

"Paige, you're happy. I can see it." She arched a dark eyebrow at me.

I sighed. "I am happy, but I'm also really scared. I mean, I'm going to have a baby. I've never even held one."

"So what? They teach you that shit in the hospital. Stop being afraid of everything, Paige. You're one of the smartest people I know, but sometimes, you're just clueless.

"I am not clueless."

"You can't see what's right in front of you, can you? Blake has loved you since the moment you two met, and he's been your little lap dog for years." She wiggled in her chair and stuck out her tongue while making a dog panting sound. "You need to realize what you have here, Paige, and quit being a selfish asshole. Look, it's okay to be happy. It's okay to be in love. In fact, it looks pretty amazing on you."

"I am not in love."

"You, my dear, are a terrible liar," Janie laughed.

"I don't even know how to love, Janie." I rested my head on my hand on the table.

"Yes you do. You're doing it right now. You love him. Admit it."

I nodded. I do love him, but saying it out loud and feeling it are two different things. I mean, the pattern speaks for itself. I love somebody, and they leave me. It's pretty simple.

"Paige, Blake and you are right. You work. He puts up with your narcissism and even loves you for it, and you. I don't even recognize you."

"That's because I'm getting fat."

"No, it's because you're being real. I think this kid might be just the right medicine for your ..." She trailed off, but I know what she was thinking. I always know with Janie. Maybe she was right. I felt a little tingle in my chest for a minute. With Janie's support and even blessing, I began to wonder if I could truly make this whole thing work.

It was the best night I have had in a long time. I really do love my Janie Juggs, but after our talk, I couldn't wait to get home to B.

Popcorn

Dear Stephanie,

Looking for a house might be my least favorite thing to do. Blake has this realtor, Mark, who has been his friend since high school. I think Mark's high school girlfriend must have blown Blake behind his back or something because he clearly has some sort of vendetta against B since he has shown us about two hundred shitty houses. Blake says that nothing is good enough for me, and he's right. Nothing is good enough for me. I hate them all.

When I bought my apartment, it was brand new, pristine and beautiful with a view of the Dallas skyline, I looked at it and signed the paperwork the same day. I expected to fall in love with a house the same way, but I do not love any that we've seen, and frankly, I'm sick of looking, so I told B to give me a break, and it's been kind of nice not having to deal with anything.

I'm eighteen weeks pregnant. B-Small is about five inches long, and apparently, my uterus is approximately the size of a cantaloupe, or at least that's what B-Large tells me. He's bought a bunch of books and always has his nose in one learning everything there is to know about his boy ... or so he thinks. We decided not to find out the sex of the baby. B thought it would be a fun surprise. I don't usually like surprises, but this one isn't so bad. I mean it really doesn't make a difference to me what it is. I just want it to have ten toes and one head.

So far, my appointments are going well. "Baby looks great!" is all my doctor ever says. She really thinks he's going to be fine, but we're still being cautious. I've gained a little weight, but I'm still not showing too much. Just a little food baby, as I used to call them. Crazy now it's an actual one.

I go back and forth with how I feel about this whole thing. I realize now that I'm no longer taking the little blue pill every morning, that maybe it never really worked. Maybe I just thought it did. I certainly got depressed on the medicine, even tried to off myself a few times while taking it, and now without it, I can still feel the apathy reaching for the dark hole of my mind. B does what he can to try and pull me out, to try and make me feel better, and he somehow can sense when it's happening. I don't know how he knows me so well, but he does, and when I'm with him, I can often quiet the voices.

I think loneliness plays a big role in depression. Having Blake around certainly fights the lonesome blues, so maybe that's why. Most of the time, I want to live, and that's more than I can say for me two years ago. Between having a purpose, and Dr. Morea, I'm beginning to understand myself a little more. I still find it challenging to think about the future, actually having a baby, living in a house, but the new and improved Paige doesn't need a Xanax at the thought. That's a big step in some direction, hopefully the right one.

Sometimes I actually enjoy being pregnant. The other night, I sat next to B on his couch pretending to care about some documentary he couldn't wait for me to see. We sat side by side eating popcorn, drinking water, because that's what we drink now, watching some lame true story when all of a sudden I felt something. I sat up. "Popcorn," I said to B. He mindlessly handed me the bowl, not taking his eyes from the television. "No, stupid, popcorn," I said again, standing up and pointing to my stomach. I rolled my pants down showing him my tiny baby bump.

"What?"

"It feels like popcorn popping in my belly. I think it's B-Small." The name stuck. I can't help it.

He reached over and put his palm on my belly waiting. "I don't feel anything."

"That's because he's tiny. I can feel it though." I sat back down, and snuggled into Blake relishing the first tiny flutters from the baby as I rested my hand over my womb.

Blake smiled with his whole face. "That's so cool. Hey, small, don't be too rough on mommy," he said to my stomach. I know it's kind of cute, but it really annoys me when he talks to my abdomen. I pushed his head away and put my hand back on my stomach waiting for more.

He didn't move anymore that night, or at least I didn't feel it, but it's crazy how often he startles me now and wiggles inside of me. It's almost like he's kicking some sense into me reminding me why I'm giving up everything. That's when I feel at peace. I silently reassure myself that I can handle this and hope that I'm right.

Even if I can't, I know Blake can. He said it, remember. "I'm in, Paige. Even if you're not. I'm in."

He's on cloud nine most of the time. He buys something for B-Small every time he leaves the house. Every day he comes home from work with a new gift bag for me. He's gotten onesies, pacifiers, a little stuffed dog that barks, a bib that says, "I love daddy" and a bunch of sweet little blankets. He's going to be a great dad. This I know for sure, the kind of dad every child should have, the kind I thought I had. B-Small is going to have a dad who's head over heels in love with him and with his crazy mom. How did we get so lucky?

Bingo

Dear Stephanie,

I found our house. That's right. I found it, not that dick, Mark, who keeps insisting that we look in the suburbs, a minimum drive of thirty minutes from Dallas for Christ's sake. Me, Paige, the chick with no job and endless amounts of time to surf through house after house after house on the internet found our fantablous house! I love a good project.

When I was a little girl, there was this house on the way to my school that I always loved. It was older and dark and a little bit foreboding, but it also looked welcoming and lived in. I didn't realize that was what I was looking for until I came across our place.

It's an older Tudor style home in Lakewood, four bedrooms, three baths with a two bedroom guesthouse out back that has its own kitchen, bathroom, bedroom and living area. The patio is covered and has a brick fireplace (not that I think that's necessary in Texas, but it's a nice touch). It has handscraped hardwood floors throughout, a study with floor-to-ceiling book shelves equipped with one of those rolling ladders like you see in libraries so that we can reach the top shelves, makes me tremble with excitement just thinking about stocking the shelves with my favorites.

Of course, B's favorite is the kitchen, which is fully load-ed with a stainless steel Wolf cooktop, Sub-Zero refrigerator, and a Thermador double oven, beautiful granite counter-tops with a stone backsplash and rubbed bronze accents. A wine cove nestles just to the left of the kitchen, which at the moment competes with the study as my favorite part of the house. It's amazing. We fell in love as soon as we got out of the car.

Last time I visited my mother in the home, I decided that maybe that's not the place for her. Looking around at the empty tan walls, the hospital bed, the tiny table next to it where her stereo sits, I decided she deserves better. She left the dump where she grew up to live an extravagant life with my dad, and one fall down the stairs landed her in a place where even a healthy soul would die, so I toyed with the idea that she could live with us, and when I talked to Blake about it, he completely supported me.

Perhaps getting her out of her drab surroundings would entice her to use her voice again, to communicate with me, with the baby. Maybe she feels like we've left her there to die. Maybe she feels abandoned. She may have left me alone, to figure out life for myself, but that's no reason to do the same to her, so with the new house, she can move into the guest-house. I can hire a nurse who can take care of her and live onsite. It's the dream home I never knew I always wanted.

Mark suggested that since we loved the house so much, we make an offer quickly. We offered more than they were asking to ensure that we would get it. They accepted imme-diately, and we close in two weeks. The couple selling the house was getting a divorce, so they both wanted out quickly and seamlessly. When I suggested that we just pay cash for the house, B was shocked. "How rich are you, Paige?"

"Rich," I responded spreading out imaginary cash in my empty hand to try and make light of it.

"I know you have money, but are you telling me you have enough money to pay cash for this house?"

"Yes, B. I have a lot of money and more than enough to pay cash for this house."

"Wow. Thanks, moneybags, but I want to do this together. I'd like it to at least be half mine."

"Ok, Blake. Whatever." I really don't see the point in making house payments, but if that's what he wants. B's the one who manages money for a living.

"How much money do you make, Blake?" Since we're talking about cash flow here.

"A lot, but maybe not as much as you." And then he pulled out his empty pockets and shrugged his shoulders. Blake and I have never discussed our finances, but between the two of us, we can afford this house and maybe even another should we change our minds.

Speaking of changing our minds, I haven't told Blake that I have no intention of selling my apartment. I'm keeping it. With all of the other changes I'm dealing with, he can't take this away from me, too. I think he'll understand ... if I ever tell him.

I guess it's time to pick out some furniture and hire an interior designer. Big things are happening, Steph, and I am more than a little excited about it all. I think maybe Janie is right, maybe I can handle all of this. Maybe I even want to.

Interrobang

Dear Stephanie,

Where do I even start? Well, I guess I'll just go with the beginning. We closed on our house, and after we signed the paperwork, B suggested we head straight there to figure out what we were going to do with the place. I happily complied and drove in my newly purchased pearl white Range Rover singing along with The Killers, windows rolled down, open sunroof, enjoying a nice warm spring evening. Blake and I met at the title office to sign the papers, so we arrived at the house separately. I noticed his Tahoe already parked in front of the house when I turned the corner of our new street. I smiled to myself at the sight.

I used my key to unlock the front door, a little surprised to find it locked, pushed the big wooden door open, stepped into the large empty foyer, and took a deep breath, soaking it all in. B interrupted my moment and beckoned me into the large and also empty great room. When I walked in, he was standing in the middle of the room waiting for me looking dapper in navy flat front dress pants and a baby blue long sleeve dress shirt. He had removed his tie, opened his collar, and turned the cuffs up on his sleeves. He was positively breathtaking looking at me with his beautiful boyish grin.

"Welcome home," he smiled, motioning to the empty room.

"I guess I can say the same to you," I said as I walked over to him. He wrapped his arms around my waist and held me to his chest for a minute. He smelled like, well, he smelled like Blake, a perfect mixture of sweet and spice that is his truly unique scent. A few seconds into the hug, I heard music begin to play. Otis Redding's soulful voice filled the room with "These arms of Mine."

"Dance with me," B whispered into my hair, taking my right hand into his left, swaying his hips into my protruding belly. I laid my head on his shoulder and closed my eyes. "I have loved you since the day we met. Do you remember that day?" he asked, also in a whisper.

"How could I forget?" I giggled into his chest.

My mind drifted back a few years when I was wild and free and completely self-absorbed, even more than I am now. I met Blake Demopolous around this time. I knew that the apartment down the hall from me had recently been purchased by a guy. Curious as to who this mystery man was, I watched closely waiting to catch a glimpse of the new owner.

Then one day, I heard some voices in the hall, so I peered through the peephole to see this beautiful man with wavy dark brown almost black hair down to his collar and a perfectly grabbable ass standing just outside of my door. My mouth watered. I wanted to lick him.

He left shortly after that, so I called down to the door guy, Carl, and asked him to tell me everything he knew. He knew very little, but he was able to give me a fairly valuable piece of information that I could use to my advantage ... the move in date, which would be the next day.

It was a sunny Tuesday in July. The temperature had to be in the triple digits. I, per the usual, had a plan. I decided that I needed to get his attention, so I got up early and made myself perfect. Then I put on my very tiny red bikini, a pair of gold strappy sandals, and a long sleeve white button down shirt, unbuttoned of course. I mixed up a pitcher of margaritas and threw it in my refrigerator. Then I waited, and waited, and waited.

Finally I heard some activity, but upon closer inspection, it was just movers, so I waited some more, continually peeking through my peephole to see if he was there. Finally, I saw him. He clumsily carried a box, wearing a T-shirt and basketball shorts, flip flops, and a baseball cap, backwards. I forgave him for the douche outfit, and decided to make my move.

As soon as I saw him set the box down, I opened my door as wide as I could to give him a full view of the inside of my apartment. I had placed the margarita pitcher in a cooler and my towel by the door, so I purposely displayed myself as I bent over to grab my necessities and headed out into the hall. I watched him drink me in for a bit, making eye contact. Then I pulled my Oliver Peoples shades down over my eyes and breezed by him. He let out a sigh as I walked past.

It was probably about thirty minutes later when I heard the door open to the rooftop pool and I watched him walk through. He had changed into a pair of very bright green board shorts and was no longer wearing the dumb backwards cap. His hair was a little longer then, and all I could think about was grabbing on to it and wrapping my legs around his tight, trim waist. Christ he looked like a god. A tall, toned, tan, Greek god.

He glanced over at me offering his crooked grin from the other side of the pool, peeled his shirt off and threw it on the ground, revealing a torso of nicely cut abs, and then dove into the pool. He swam underwater to the side where I had set up camp for the afternoon. He rose out of the pool and rested his arms on the edge. His curly hair dripped onto his broad shoulders as his green eyes undressed me with a raw sensuality. I needed to dive in to cool off at this point, but I couldn't break my game.

"Hi, neighbor," he said with that fuck me smile of his.

"Hi, neighbor," I replied, trying to remain coy when all I could think of was his stubble grazing my inner thigh.

He pulled himself out, without using the ladder, offering me a closer look at his beautifully tight chest and stomach. His chest hair clung to his skin. I imagined myself biting it, licking it, scraping my nails across it. A hot pool of desire surged through me. I needed to have this man, and I needed him immediately. I could hardly catch my breath.

He pulled a lounge chair next to mine and laid down on his side, propping himself up with his elbow, facing me. Then he reached down and retrieved my margarita out of my hand. He took a big drink, never breaking his gaze into my shaded eyes. Then he reached over me and set the drink on the table next to my chair.

As he pulled back to his chair, his chest touched mine. I let out a small sigh. Being the predator that I am, I couldn't wait any longer. I grabbed him through his shorts. He paused for a minute, pulled my sunglasses off of my face, and raised one asking eyebrow at me. I nodded, so he then planted himself on top of me, taking me into a hot and hungry kiss, his wet body covering mine completely.

"You are incredible," he said between kisses as I untied my bikini top and slid it away from my body, dropping it next to the margarita. I pushed my hips up against his silently begging him to take my bottoms. He followed my lead, and forty-five seconds later, we were both butt naked and banging on a lounge chair at our rooftop pool, and it was UH-MAY-ZING. Luckily we were the only ones enjoying the pool that afternoon. When we finished, redressed, and caught our breath, he jumped up from his lounge chair and pulled me with him. "Let's go get a drink," he ordered, and started pulling me toward the door.

"I know just the place, and we don't even have to change." I said as he continued to tug me forward, grabbing his shirt when we passed it. The sight of him pulling it over his head made me a little light-headed.

We grabbed an elevator to the first floor, walked through the front door, and to my favorite dive bar. B held my hand the entire way. He pulled my stool out for me, waited for me to sit, pulled his stool out, sat down, and held out his hand.

"I'm Blake," he smiled, shaking my hand.

"Nice to meet you," I shook his hand back. "I'm Paige."

"Nice to meet you," he smiled, and brushed my knuckles with his kissable plump lips, "Paige."

I smiled at the memory and made myself step back into the present.

I listened to Otis sing the last line of the song, thinking back to that day when B-Large walked into my life. When the song ended, I felt B place something in my left hand. I wrapped my fingers around it and brought it to my waist, looking down to see what it was.

B leaned in, placed two fingers under my chin to guide my eyes to his, and placed his forehead against mine. Then he kissed my nose and said in a voice just over a whisper, "Marry me." A statement, not a question.

I looked down at my hand and squeezed the little blue box, taking a deep breath, but before I could answer, I felt a gush of warm liquid soak my jeans.

"I think I just wet my pants," I said to B with a giggle.

He pushed me away from him holding me at arms-length and looked at me. His eyes widened as he said, "Oh my God, Paige. You're bleeding."

He scooped me up in his arms and carried me to the Tahoe. He placed me gently into his passenger seat then ran to the driver's side. I watched his hair bounce as he ran in front of the car and couldn't help but think about how perfect things were just moments before. Then I passed out.

I don't know how long I was out, but when I awoke, I found myself lying in a hospital bed with B holding my hand. I noticed immediately that the foot of my bed had been raised up slightly higher than my head. I felt like I was on some strange amusement park ride. I looked at his worried eyes and suddenly realized what was happening. I reached down to feel my belly, which was still there, but I had to ask anyway.

"How's B-Small?"

B looked at me with sad green eyes and swallowed. I watched his Adam's apple bounce in his neck, and held my breath, bracing myself for what he was going to say.

"He's okay for now, but they have you on medication to keep you from having contractions. You're blood pressure is out of control, and your amniotic fluid is dangerously low. They're only holding off to give him some more time, but it could happen any minute now."

"What could happen?" I asked trying figure out how to make my bed sit up.

"You have to stay that way, with your feet elevated. I can't remember why, but it helps."

"You didn't answer my question, B."

"You could go into labor any time now, Paige." He squeezed my hand. I could hear the terror in his voice.

"But it's too early." Nineteen weeks too early.

"I know." He laid his head in my hand and let out a little throaty cry but quickly pulled himself together. "I need to let the nurses know you're awake," he said as he got up and walked out of the room. To see Blake so concerned and so unplayful, terrified me.

After he returned to the room, a nurse came in and took my vitals, making a huge fuss about everything. I was on magnesium sulfate, which made my skin burn as if I was strapped to a stake, but even that didn't distract me from my biggest fear. The nurse offered me something to eat and some water, but all I could think about was that my baby wouldn't make it. If he was born now, he would not survive. I started to panic. I asked Blake for my phone. He pulled it out of my purse and handed it to me. I texted Janie.

Me: I'm in the hospital. I'm okay, and so is the baby, but I need you.

Janie Juggs: What happened?

Me: Long story. Can you go by my apartment and bring me some things? And please hurry.

I texted Janie the things that I needed including my laptop and my hospital bag, which I packed just a week earlier and placed it in my closet, just in case. Sometimes being a control freak comes in handy.

I sent her the name of the hospital, and she was here in my room an hour later.

She held my hand and tried to control the fear that was written all over her face. She kept saying, "You'll be fine. The baby will be fine." But Janie is a terrible liar, and she and I both know that the situation is dire at best.

I was told that I will be on bed rest for the remainder of my pregnancy and that there is no chance of being released from the hospital any time soon. It looks as though I am stuck in this bed, feet over head for a very long time. There are about a thousand things that I can imagine being mind numbingly miserable. Bed rest is one of them.

What's even worse is that I still haven't given B my answer. I know what I would have said had my body not broken there in our new living room, but maybe the cosmos had other plans. Until then, my focus is B-Small and keeping him in my uterus until he's fully cooked. And when I look at Blake and see his furrowed brow, his worry, his fear, I know I only have myself to blame.

Sometimes I wonder what kind of sick joke it is that I've never been able to kill myself. I just keep causing pain everywhere I go. Even things that are unbreakable, break when I touch them.

Ennui

Stephanie,

Word of the day: Ennui. Definition ... basically it means boredom. Want to know how I know this? Because ... oh my god. Boredom might be more miserable than depression. Have I mentioned how much I hate TV? Well, I absolutely despise it now, thanks to this family who seems to think that every name has to start with a K. I will never wear Louboutins again. They've bastardized them.

The only saving grace is that Blake keeps me company most nights, and Janie is up here a lot, and then of course, there's Dr. Morea. He has been coming to the hospital for my sessions since I can't go to him. God bless him. He's terribly worried about what this is doing to me, but the good news is, I can't kill myself because I'm not allowed to get out of my motherfucking bed.

I'm stuck here, day in and day out, with my feet propped up over my head, wearing a thin cotton gown unable to even get up and go to the bathroom. This is bed rest, and it is not for me. I stare at the same four walls all day. I can feel the irritation creeping up my spine. The sheer pressure in between my shoulder blades makes me want to scream, and everybody tip toes around me. I can't stand it. I want to punch someone, or shake someone, or just be left alone.

Until I'm alone, then the thoughts start bouncing around in my head. I put my hand on my womb and try to wake B-Small, to get any sign of life even though the machine that I'm attached to twenty-four hours a day tells me he's fine. I'm scared. I'm terrified. And I'm sick of this bed, and this room, and the nurses, and Blake, and Janie, and every single person who looks at me with those pity eyes silently affirming, "Hey, sorry you fucked up your baby." Is this what losing my mind feels like?

Blake bought me a Kindle and loaded up all of my favorite books along with a bunch I haven't read. It's only been a week, and I'm halfway through them all. I have no idea what I'm going to do for the next eighteen weeks. I'm determined though that this baby is not going to come early.

They keep two monitors attached to my belly that display any contractions and the heart rate. I can hear the thumping of his little heart fill my room. I can't even believe how much I love this kid, and I haven't even looked at him.

I've spent hours on the internet reading stories of women like me. Thank god or Wi-Fi. Some share happy endings. Some are sad. I want mine to be happy ... so badly ... I want mine to be happy. Don't I deserve this? Or maybe I don't deserve a happy ending. Maybe I've fucked with fate too many times, and Karma's a boomerang, right? Maybe I'm getting back what I gave. I don't know.

As much as the nurses drive me crazy, they're all really great. They show both concern and care when they're in my room, and they all seem to have compassion for my fragile mental state. I'm sort of a basket case these days, especially for someone who has always had an amazing way of keeping her emotions hidden.

I cry all of the time. All of the time. I cry even on good days. I cry because I'm sad. I cry because I'm so unbelievably tired, and every time I drift off to sleep, another nurse comes in and tickles my toes or takes my blood pressure, which has stabilized by the way. I cry because I'm so ridiculously uncomfortable, and lying with my head down, I feel sure, is quickly sending me over the edge of crazy. And I cry because I miss the feeling of B next to me. I can't believe I'm saying it out loud, but I hate not sleeping with him. So much for my mask.

I so badly need to feel him on top of me, and not just because my libido hasn't slowed in the least, but because he's my addiction. Dr. Morea was right. I'm addicted to B-Large. I'm addicted to the way he smells, the way he tastes, the way he feels when his coarse leg hair brushes mine between the sheets, the way he feels when his chest is up against my naked back, the feel of his lips on the back of my neck in the morning when his alarm goes off. I'm addicted to the noise he makes when he loses control during sex and reaches his climax.

I'm addicted to the way he loves me, the way he looks at me so full of hope and adoration, and the way he holds me. So I guess this is B-Large withdrawal. Because, he's distant, and although he's here every night, I feel his heart slipping away from me.

What is going to happen to us? I'm terrified, and yet, I still can't say the three little words to him that I know he so desperately wants to hear, much less acknowledge his proposal. What is wrong with me?

Scout

Dear Stephanie,

I awoke suddenly the other night to nurses hoarding into my room like rats in a sewer in the dark of night. One raised my head, another pulled out the chart. I heard the beep beep beep of a monitor going off. Which one was it? Was it mine or the baby's? Nobody would answer me. Where was B? I couldn't see him. Then I realized it was the middle of the night. He had gone home to get some sleep. "What's happening?" My voice finally worked, still in a fog from sleep.

"You're in labor again, honey. We need to check you."

I had felt the sharp pains all day and tried to ignore them. It wasn't the first time. They usually came in and administered some meds into my IV to stop it, which they had already done earlier in the evening. But normally there was one nurse. This time seemed suspect. The nurses were not their usual calm scurrying around my dark room with a sense of urgency, flicking on lights and moving things around.

"I need to call Blake."

Nobody stopped to get me my phone.

"I need to call Blake."

Still nobody stopped fussing with all of the monitors and my bed.

"I really need to call Blake." I cried out. Finally a nurse came over and placed her hand over my hand which gripped the bed rail trying to help me ignore the surge of pain in my spine.

"He's on his way, honey," she said, "I need you to calm down."

"Then somebody better tell me what is happening," I screamed at her.

I felt like vomiting. The pain in my lower back rolled through again. I squeezed the rail and let out a moan.

I heard two nurses arguing. "Didn't you check her earlier?" one said.

"Yes, her monitor must have come loose or something. She was fine two hours ago." I heard the panic in her voice.

Another nurse who had her hand between my legs looked up at me from between my knees. "You're nine centimeters dilated. Your baby is coming."

"No. No!" I screamed. "It's too soon. He's not ready. Please. Stop it. Make it stop again. Give me more magnesium sulfate or whatever. I don't care. Please make it stop."

"We can't stop it, honey. Your baby is coming now."

I cried out in anguish, hopeless and alone. And terrified. I was finally sitting at a normal level, no longer was my head below my feet, but it didn't matter because they were telling me the haunting news that my baby was going to be born, and there was nothing they could do about it. I was twenty-three weeks and six days pregnant. I read everything there is to read about this. One more day, and he had more hope. Viable ... that's what they call it. Twenty-four weeks would make my baby viable. Why couldn't I just make it to twenty-four weeks?

Blake came running into my room and grabbed my hand and kissed it as they were wheeling me through the door. "It's going to be okay," he tried to convince me all the way to the operating room. I knew better.

They ushered Blake into a room where he put on paper scrubs and a paper cap. I felt his absence immediately. I was so relieved when I saw him enter the room and come to my bedside.

When the doctor arrived, she pulled on her gloves and tried to calm me. "Listen, Paige. We have the neonatal team ready. We're going to do everything we can to help your baby. I need you to stay calm. On your next contraction, I need you to push. I'll tell you when."

"No," I yelled at the doctor. "We have to keep him in. I will not push him out for him to die. I know his odds. Please. Make this stop. Surely you can sew my cervix shut," I pleaded. "I've read about that on the internet. Or elevate my feet even more. Let gravity help. Please. Do something. Please. Please." I sobbed, body trembling. I imagined all of the babies I had read about who were born blue and black with lungs too premature to breath and hearts full of clots, and fluid in their brains. "NO!" I screamed, but it didn't help. My body had other plans, and as the pain I had been ignoring finally wretched in my abdomen like a gunshot firing off, I felt the sudden and undeniable urge to push.

Blake held my hand. I pushed two times. That's all it took. Two times for my tiny baby to make its entrance into this cold dark world. There was no sound. They quickly took the tiny limp body to a team of strangers who would now be faced with the task of saving his fragile life.

Blake leaned in very close to my ear and whispered through a stifled sob, "B-Small's a girl." A girl.

She was born at 11:47 p.m. She weighed one pound one ounce. She still had yet to make a sound. I couldn't really see what they were doing to her. I held my breath. So did Blake. We waited for anything. Good news. Bad news. Just news. It seemed like hours that we watched, like spectators, at the action taking place before us, waiting for someone to say something.

They started to leave with her, still not saying anything to us. The looks in their eyes said enough. Finally, Blake looked at me, still holding my hand. I knew what he was asking with his pleading green eyes.

"Yes. Go to her. Please go be with her."

He left me in the room where I wept. My doctor tended to me and finally when she finished, she said she would send someone to get an update. I continued to weep. I reached down and placed my hand over my once full belly, now deflated, and I cried out to the empty room and cursed my broken body.

I wanted more than anything to inflate it again with my precious little baby who might be dead on the other side of the hospital. I stopped myself from those thoughts. No. My daughter would fight. She would live. I lay in my blood soaked bed looking up at the tiled ceiling and said another silent prayer to a God I knew had to intervene.

"Please let her live. Please." Huge hot tears stained my face.

They came in and moved me to a clean bed then wheeled me back to my old room. Blake returned some time later, rubbing the back of his head. He walked in the room and took his place in the chair next to mine. He grabbed my hand and kissed it.

"She's so beautiful," he said, eyes full of fear and tears. He swallowed hard. "She's alive, but barely. There are so many tubes and wires, Paige. She's so tiny. Her feet," he choked on the word, "Her little foot isn't even as big as my thumb." He held out his hand to show me his thumb. His long elegant hands didn't seem so large anymore.

"She's in a little box. I can't even touch her," He couldn't hold back anymore. He sobbed as he tried to tell me about her. "Nobody will really say anything, but Paige," He cleared his throat and ran a hand through is hair, "She's perfect. She's so perfect, baby." He lost it then and big giant tears poured out of his eyes. We silently cried together. I felt his tears on my hand. I looked away. I couldn't stand to look at the once playful eyes that were now blanketed in grief because of me. "They said if you felt like it, to bring you down to meet her."

I didn't respond.

"Paige, I don't think she has much time. You should meet our daughter."

I shook my head, and turned away, facing the wall, thinking to myself that everything I love disappears, and I couldn't let my curse fall on her. She has Blake. That's enough.

He dropped my hand and left the room.

I tried to sleep. Sleep would mean escape. Escape would make it feel less real, but sleep didn't come, just wakeful nightmares. A nightmare with a doctor shaking his head, mumbling in a low voice. A nightmare where Blake's smile disappears forever, his smile, that smile. A nightmare with a blue tiny baby alone in a room. I lay in my bed, sick to my stomach, begging the nightmares to fade when I heard footsteps at my door. I turned my head expecting to see Blake, but instead, I looked into the kind dark eyes of Dr. Morea.

"Paige," he said, somberly. Just hearing my name forced me into another hiccupping cry. He came over and sat in Blake's chair. He rubbed my back as I sobbed. When I finished my crying tantrum, I turned and looked at him. Even he had sadness in his eyes.

"For Christ's sake, can anyone please look at me like we have some sort of hope?"

"Paige, she's still alive. Of course there's hope."

"Have you seen her?" I wiped more tears from my swollen eyes.

"No, Paige, I'm here to see you."

After another short tantrum, I let him take my hand.

"You need to prepare yourself for the worst, Paige ..."

"I'm already planning her funeral, doc. I guess I'm one step ahead of you," I interrupted. I wondered what songs we would play, who would attend, how we would manage, at what point Blake would decide to walk away from me, to abandon the woman whose body killed his baby.

"You didn't let me finish," Dr. Morea interrupted my thoughts, "You need to prepare for the worst, but it's okay to hope for the best."

"Nobody has even told me anything."

"Have you asked?"

No, I hadn't asked. I wasn't sure I could handle the answer. The way Blake looked was all the answer I needed. Even my sweet, optimistic B-Large, looked defeated. Hope? Hope is a double edged sword. Hope shatters and cuts in its wake. No, I can't hope.

"I haven't even seen her," I confessed.

"I know. Blake used your phone and called me. He thinks I can help you to understand that you need to go to her."

"Well you can't, so if that's why you're here, you can go."

I turned my head again and continued my stubborn stare, wondering how B figured out that Dr. Morea was D-Love in my phone.

"You don't have a lot of regrets, Paige," he said to my back. "You talk about the things that have happened in your life like you're telling someone else's story. This is real, Paige. If you don't see her, you will regret it, and it will haunt you for the rest of your life."

I had already decided that the rest of my life would not be much longer. As soon as I was released, I planned to end it and eliminate myself from hurting another person, from wreaking my havoc on anyone else. I continued to stare at the wall, and eventually I heard Dr. Morea quietly leave my room. When he left, I cried some more.

Blake came back in the next morning in the same clothes he wore the day before, with more than a five o'clock shadow and a mane full of unruly black curls. He didn't say anything for a long time. Then he finally broke the silence. "She's considered a micro-preemie," he said in monotone to my back. "The statistics for survival are extremely low, but they've gotten better over the last couple of years. She has a long and painful road ahead of her, but the Neonatologist said that it's possible. It's possible that she can survive."

He waited for a response from me.

"Did you hear me, Paige? She can live." Finally some feeling in his voice.

I didn't move.

He shook my shoulders. "Snap out of it, Paige. She's your fucking daughter, and she needs you to live. They said you need to start pumping milk. Something about the lining in her stomach. Your milk will give her antibodies to help her fight. I can't keep it all straight. All I know is that you can't be selfish right now, Paige. She needs you. I need you to just try and do this for her ... for me. Christ." If he could read my mind, he would see that the most unselfish thing I could ever do was to rid myself from the both of them, but if there was something that I could do to help her first, I would.

I rolled over to face him. He looked exhausted. Dark circles surrounded his bloodshot eyes and a huge line seemed permanently etched between his eyebrows. This time, he couldn't look at me. I took a deep breath.

"What do you mean pump milk?"

"You know ... out of your breasts. She needs your breast milk."

I hadn't planned to breastfeed. Actually, I hadn't thought much about it, just assumed that since my boobs had been through so much surgically it wouldn't be an option. I pressed the button to call the nurse.

When she came in, she just looked at me and said, "What is it you need?" What did I need? How about a baby who wasn't fighting for her tiny little life.

"Somebody said something about breast milk. I need to know what to do."

"I'll call a lactation consultant."

Fifteen minutes later, a tall brunette glided into my room and introduced herself as "Lauri with an i, the lactation consultant you called for." She had a bag over her shoulder. I was shocked when she came in and sat on the end of my bed, pulling the strap from her shoulder, and laying the bag between us.

She explained to me that I had to stimulate my breasts to make milk and that since my daughter was so premature, it would take some work. I informed her of my multiple surgeries. She looked closely at my boobs through my paper thin hospital gown. "Well, we won't know 'til we try. Let's get you attached." Attached? I know.

She told me to unsnap my gown and pulled this plastic funnel looking thing from her bag and placed it on my naked breast over my nipple. "That looks like a good fit. Wow, they really are huge. Just wait 'til your milk comes in." Well, at least she was honest.

She pulled a little plastic bottle from some plastic wrap. Then she twisted the funnel looking thing onto the top of the bottle, and attached one end of a clear rubber hose to the funnel and the other end of the hose to a yellow box. Without a word, she put one hand under my breast and placed the funnel over my nipple again. Then she turned the knob of the yellow box.

Immediately, my nipple was extended and sucked into this weird funnel. The room was silent except for the whoot whoop of the box. With every whoot, it pulled my nipple in, and with every whoop, it let it out. Lauri with an i, Blake, and I watched in fascination at the process. I felt very much like a dairy cow, only nothing came out of my udder.

"It's normal for it to take a while, especially the first time," she said unconvincingly.

Blake began to rub the back of his head again. Lauri with an i sat there holding the funnel and my breast, and I concentrated, willing my body to make milk. It was wildly absurd, but in all honesty, it was a nice distraction from my reality. When nothing continued to happen, Lauri with an i placed my hand on the funnel and with her free hand turned up the whoot whoop. I felt more pressure on my nipple. I waited. Still nothing.

"Himm," she said, pursing her lips, "let's try the other side." She moved to the other side of the bed strapped my right breast to the mini torture chamber. Whoot whoop began her song, and we waited some more. Lauri with an i started to twitch her right foot, shaking it back and forth. "How are you feeling, Paige? Are you stressed?"

Are you freakin' kidding me? "Yes, I'm stressed," I said to Lauri with an i all the while thinking that my very tiny baby was not even a day old, born seventeen weeks early, and I was supposed to supply something for her that I couldn't seem to produce. Stressed didn't even begin to describe it.

"Keep holding this," she said as she placed my hand on the funnel. She stood up and walked toward the head of my bed. She lowered it, telling me to stay sitting up. She got behind me and sort of straddled me in my bed. Then she began to massage my lower back, which I hadn't even realized was aching.

Whoot whoop sang in the background. B rubbed his head. I watched with undying fascination as a drop of yellow liquid dripped into the little plastic bottle. "Look. It's working." Lauri with an i continued to rub my back. Liquid gold continued to drip from my nipple, and B gave the back of his head a much needed rest.

I pumped only half an ounce, and that was after we strapped the funnel to my left breast again, but Lauri with an i assured me that it was perfect and a great start. She convinced me that my production would only increase if I kept pumping. As Lauri with an i began packing up her stuff, she took my hand and held it for a minute. Then she said, "I'm leaving my number. If you need me for anything, even if it's just to rub your back, you call me. Day or night." Another tear assault followed leaving me unable to even tell her thank you. Blake walked her to the door and thanked her enough for both of us.

Finally, I allowed myself to feel a glimmer of hope. I had a mission. My baby needed my milk, and I was going to supply that for her, even if I couldn't offer her anything more.

Blake kept me company in my room, going back and forth between me and the baby. He started to gain more of himself, but his eyes were still circled with fear. That night, as I lay in my bed trying to will myself to sleep, B climbed in behind me and held me to his chest. He whispered, "Thank you."

"For what?"

He waited a second, pulled me even closer to him and said, "For her, Paige."

I took a deep breath in, and we cried together, making the bed shake beneath us with the force of our sorrow and our fear. It was becoming our way of life, crying together. But at least I could feel his warmth, and finally we both drifted into sleep, and we were left alone to rest. For a moment, it felt like we might make it through all of this.

* * *

Two days and several ounces of milk later, I made the decision that I needed to meet my daughter. We still had yet to name her, and I couldn't give her a name without seeing her face. Blake kept pressuring me that she needed one. He still called her B-Small when he talked about her, but he said she deserved something written on her birth certificate, something on the card above her box. Something instead of "Baby Girl Demopolous." But I knew what he really meant. If it happened, he didn't want to name her after. I could give him that. I had a few ideas, but it was something that we hadn't really discussed together.

When I told B that I was ready, he jumped up and ran out of the room. He returned with a wheel chair. He placed me in it and wheeled me down the hall to the elevator. They had moved me to the floor where mothers were taken after their babies were born. Most of the babies didn't live in NICU, where my daughter currently resided. I could hear the cries of babies coming from some of the rooms. Jealous knots twisted in my stomach as I pictured mothers holding their newborns and family members oohing and awing over tiny wrapped bundles.

On the outside of some of the doors, I noticed signs announcing, "It's a boy!" in all blue or "It's a girl!" in all pink. I hadn't thought about it yet, but it had been two days, and we hadn't even gotten a card. I guess our families were being conservative, just in case. I couldn't think about just in case.

"Have you called your parents?"

"Yes, they were here yesterday and this morning. Janie's been here, too."

How had I missed them? I wondered silently.

He cleared his throat. "I told them to give you some space."

"Did they meet her?"

"No, I don't think they're allowed, but even if they are, I want you to meet her first. I have to give you that."

When we reached the NICU, I was struck by how dark it was. Blake, ever so intuitive, began to explain.

"They keep it dark in there. It's better for the babies. Her eyes are still fused shut, so it will help her when she opens them for it not to be too bright."

We washed our hands carefully with a brush under scalding hot water, following the rules, rinsing away as many germs as we could to protect our baby. B pushed open the door and wheeled me over to the incubator where my tiny daughter lay struggling for her life.

She had tubes coming out of every part of her. They had to ventilate her because under developed lungs couldn't sustain her yet. She was fed through a feeding tube in her nose. Her eyes were covered in what I can best describe as a miniature sleeping mask that was taped to her skin, and her skin ... her skin was almost translucent. I could see her rib cage with every breath the ventilator forced her to take. She had fuzzy little hair covering her body, which was camouflaged in bruises that B explained were from both her birth and all of the poking and prodding she was forced to endure. Fragile ... no, not even close.

Ethereal.

I wanted to pick her up and put her back in my womb just to cook her a little longer.

"You can touch her if you want." B showed me how to put my hand through the hole, already so comfortable with her. "Hi, Small." She turned her head to his voice. I stifled a sob. Her little fingers wrapped around his pinky as if she had been holding onto it for months.

"Mommy's here," he said softly. He looked over at me, leaning down so that his face was close to the tiny clear box and said, "I've been thinking." He smiled, looking down at her and then back up at me, "Well, we've been thinking" He cocked his head toward the incubator implying it was a joint decision. "... about her name." Her tiny fingers grasped onto his large one. The light over her incubator framed his face in gold. "We like Scout, Mommy." He looked at me, his eyes somewhat shaded by his dark lashes. I half smiled and nodded my consent.

Scout. Perfect.

I swallowed the lump in my throat. "Scout," I whispered to my daughter. Blake pulled his hand out and placed it around my waist. Scout jerked. "Put it back in. You're upsetting her." I whisper-yelled at him.

"No, it's your turn." He stepped aside and pushed me closer to give me more of a front seat. I hesitantly put my hand into the hole. I grazed my finger over her miniature arm absorbing her diminutive frame. She's the length of a banana with a head the size of a lime.

"She doesn't like it when you touch her too gently. Her nerves are too close to her skin." I jerked my hand back. "No," Blake said patiently, holding my arm and gently guiding it back into the hole. "Let her hold your finger. She likes that the best." How did he know her so well? Why did I wait so long to meet her? She immediately grasped onto my finger.

"She's strong," I heard a voice say from behind me. Not wanting to take my eyes from my daughter, I listened to the voice tell me about her. "She has spunk, a lot of fight." This person had hope for my daughter. I made a mental note to get to know the person behind the voice and find out everything she knew about Scout, but first I had to get acquainted with the tiny fighter.

She left us to marvel at our miracle baby jerking uncontrollably like a little bantam hen in her clear box, and marvel I did. For someone so tiny and covered in so many wires and tubes, she really is beautiful. My heart clenched at the sight of her, and I knew immediately the definition of love.

Waves

Dear Stephanie,

My doctor released me two days ago from the hospital with strict instructions to pump, pump, pump, and pump some more. Leaving the hospital might have been the hardest thing I've had to do so far. It meant leaving my baby behind, which meant leaving my heart behind. The night before they released me, I left the solitude of my quiet room and crept down to the NICU in my slippers and robe.

I pulled the wooden rocker to her little incubator and stayed there for the entire night, ignoring everyone's protests to go get rest. I placed my hand in the porthole, whispering promises to my daughter as she grasped onto my index finger with all of the strength in her tiny body.

"You soothe her," Emma Lee, her nurse, said to me as I sat there. She was the same nurse who spoke of my daughter as a fighter. Emma, a petite little woman, maybe weighs one hundred pounds and doesn't stand taller than five feet on her tippy toes. She has short black hair cut into a simple bob and wears black plastic framed glasses that cover her slightly slanted eyes. She speaks with a hint of an Asian accent, which Blake swears is Japanese, but we have yet to ask. What I do know about her is that she takes excellent care of my baby, and Scout seems to love her.

"You should be able to hold her soon." She was only four days old, and I had yet to hold her. I smiled at Emma. She took the hint and left me alone with my baby.

"Hi, sweet baby," I whispered to her. She had started turning her head to my voice. I know she knows who I am, and all I ever want to do is comfort her, so that night, that's what I did. I quietly begged her to keep fighting, to stay strong, to fight through the pain her body did not deserve to feel, and I pleaded with her to hold on so that I could one day take her home.

I told her all about Blake, how perfect he is, and how much I love him. I had no problem saying it to her. The word "love" just dropped right from my mouth without hesitation. I told her about the house we bought for her. I promised her a puppy when she turned two and a big pink birthday party for her first birthday.

I swore to her that she would never have to want for anything, that I would wipe away every single tear and mend her heart when someone tried to break it, that I would never leave her, that she would never know loneliness as long as I could breathe. I promised her to be present and alive to stop selfishly taking drugs, and to cherish the life that now seemed so very precious to me. All thoughts of suicide vanished the minute I met her.

They had removed the mask over her eyes that day, and as I poured out my promises, her little eyelids opened, and I swear to God, she looked right at me with tiny blue eyes. She quickly closed them back, but I knew in her eyes was a promise from mother to daughter and from daughter to mother. Keep fighting.

We've had to make a lot of decisions in such a short amount of time. So far, nothing in Scout's body is working perfectly. She has severe anemia. Her potassium levels are low and unstable. Her lungs are underdeveloped and can't maintain her. She has a blood clot in her heart. Sometimes they dissipate on their own. Sometimes they get dislodged and travel through the blood to the lungs or the brain, which either way, could kill Scout. They don't want to operate on it though because that too could kill her, and the risk of surgery is much higher than the risk of leaving it.

She has a grade two brain bleed, something apparently very common in preemies, but it's her brain, so it freaks me out. They grade them one through four, so relatively speaking, a two is good, right? But, bleeding in the brain? What does that mean for her future? Will she be blind? Possibly. Will she walk? There's no way to tell yet.

There are so many terrifying possibilities that I can't even think about them. B made me promise to quit doing internet research, but what else do I have? Part of me wonders if we are putting her through too much, if we should maybe just let life happen for her. That's definitely an option, one the physicians discussed with us before she was ever here, but then I see the way people like Emma are with her, and I feel hopeful. I'm scared to trust it, but I have to. She's my baby.

Emma never lies to me, never candy coats anything. She's been taking care of babies for thirty-six years, and she says she can't imagine a day without a preemie. She keeps Scout snuggled in a bunch of blankets to try and simulate the womb, which makes my heart melt every time I see it.

She answers my questions honestly but kindly. Some of the doctors could learn a thing or two from her. She is my child's biggest advocate next to me and will gladly put a doctor in his place if she needs to. I admire her spunk as she calls it. She talks to Scout like a person, not a thing, and she shows her respect in every way. They're constantly putting in and taking out one wire or tube or another, and it tortures me to watch, but Emma does it with so much tenderness and grace that if I had it my way, she would be the only one allowed to touch my baby.

Blake and I take turns with Scout at night, but neither of us is ever far away. Blake's job has been very understanding. He's taken a leave of absence. He can't stand to leave her either.

On the way home from the hospital that first night, we cried for the emptiness in the backseat, the seat that should hold a pink baby seat, with a crying baby in it. He held my hand and kissed my knuckles, and tried to quietly sooth my heavy heart as he drove us back to our apartment building.

Neither of us could even consider moving into the house until we knew we could take Scout there. We bought the house for her, not for us. Somehow, moving into it without her seemed unfair. We agreed to wait until we brought her home and all three move in together.

We both still have our apartments. I haven't even put mine on the market, and B, not yet receiving an offer on his, just took it off for a while until we get Scout well. The downside in that is that I had to put my plans for my own mother on the back burner. At least, I know she won't hold it against me.

Tonight, my heart aches because I again had to leave my too small baby at the too large hospital, leaving her in the care of the fabulous nurses who are wonderful but who are not her mother. I've retreated to my own place for a bit to spend some time alone and gather a few of my clothes. I thought I might find some peace if I poured out some of my thoughts.

I'm so sick of everyone telling me what a long road she has ahead of her, but it's true. We have miles of uncharted terrain, and I'm scared. I'm terrified, and I wonder if I can handle this fight. Dr. Morea prescribed me some medicine, but I haven't taken any of it. I need my breast milk to be untainted. Lord knows I've contaminated my daughter enough, and don't think for a moment that I don't blame myself every minute of every day that she fights for her life.

I want to walk back in time and never touch a drug, prescription or fun. I want to erase the need for medication from my make-up. Remember those side effects that Dr. Morea was so afraid of? Well, one of them was premature birth. Guess we can add my baby to those statistics.

Breath

Breath, we take it for granted. The fact that our lungs move involuntarily to bring air into and out of them often gets forgotten. I can't stop thinking about breathing because my baby can't seem to figure out how to do it. She's a day shy of being two weeks old, which would make her gestation age twenty-five weeks. I got an e-mail, something B set up for me, telling me that my baby is the size of a cauliflower. A cauliflower. My cauliflower is lying in an incubator having air forced into her lungs with every little breath she takes. My cauliflower is no longer in my belly, being fed through me, warm and safe, comfortably kicking me in the ribs. I only got to feel my cauliflower kick for five weeks. Blake never felt her.

There's a number running through my head that I wish I could unread, but I can't. It's there, screaming at me every time one of her monitors goes off while I'm visiting with her. It screams at me every time I gaze at my tender little Scout. It screams at me in my dreams, when I'm actually able to fall asleep. It screams at me in the shower, in the car, in the elevator, in the bathroom. It screams at me constantly, and it will not SHUT THE FUCK UP. It screams that only 25% of babies born at twenty-three weeks live. That means that three out of four babies born at twenty-three weeks die.

Three out of four.

When a baby dies in NICU, we all know about it, but nobody talks about it. The family comes in. They close the curtain. They send all of us away, and when we return, the empty clear box remains, and we are forced to try not to look at it.

We're all sort of a family in the NICU, constantly forced to make small talk, which usually revolves around our babies and their stats. We cheer for each other when one of the babies gets good news, and when bad news is given, empathy doesn't even come close because we all know that it could be our baby, my baby, so we cherish every breath that's taken without a ventilator, every ounce that's gained, every successful swallow. Little things that should come naturally are given extra applause here in the NICU.

But death happens all too frequently, and it happened last night. They were just about to let me hold Scout when I heard monitors going off from little Gavin's incubator. I've gotten to know Gavin a bit. He was born early, too, twenty-nine weeks. He had tons of complications, and a severe defect in his spinal cord. He had been in the hospital for just over three weeks, too, and already undergone four surgeries.

They took him off the ventilator for a bit, but he couldn't handle it. After that, everything went downhill, and we all knew it was coming. When his monitors started to sound, I frantically searched the room for his mom. She rarely left his side. His father wasn't around. I could see on the nurses' faces that things were grim.

"Where's Amy?" I asked Emma.

"She left to get something to eat. They've called her cell, but they can't reach her."

I ran out of the room and knew that I could find her in the cafeteria. I was growing accustomed to the hospital and didn't have quite the fear of germs that I once had, but I still didn't like to touch anything. I got to the elevator and waited for someone else to come by to hit the down arrow. I nervously chewed on my fingernail impatiently.

Then I said aloud, "fuck it," and kicked the down arrow with my shoe. The cafeteria of the hospital is on the first floor. Once the elevator doors closed, I looked at the numbers trying to figure out how to press one without touching it. I used the bottom of my shirt to shield my finger and hit the number. As soon as the doors opened, I ran to the cafeteria. I kicked open the doors and screamed, "Amy! Amy! Amy!" She looked up at me, and time stood still for a minute as she registered my panic.

Then she scooted her chair back, wiped her mouth with a crumpled paper napkin, not giving her scarcely touched food a second look and calmly walked toward me. I wanted to scream at her for taking so long, but I couldn't. We walked to the elevator, my heart pounding in my chest. I waited for her to press the up button. When the doors closed, and we were alone in the elevator, she turned to me and wrapped her arms around me and sobbed into my shoulder. I stood there, not knowing what to do. Then I just gave in and held her until we reached our babies' floor.

"Oh God," she said and leaned against the wall outside of NICU.

"Amy, we have to hurry."

"I can't," she said, "I can't tell him good-bye. I can't do it."

"Amy, you have to."

"I don't have anyone, Paige. He's it. He's all I have." I suddenly felt a sense of relief for having Blake and knowing that his strength through all of this mess has been my saving grace.

I couldn't hold it back anymore. My tears streamed down my cheeks.

"Will you come with me," she pleaded.

How could I say no? I nodded to her and held my hand out, purposely offering my right hand.

We cleansed in the washing area, and walked toward Gavin's box where three nurses and a doctor hovered over him. The doctor said something about it being time, and slowly, they started unplugging all of his monitors, pulling out all of his wires, removing his feeding tube, and finally, they pulled the tube from his throat.

They wrapped him in a blanket and handed him to Amy. It wasn't her first time to hold him, but it was her last. Uncomfortable silence fell between us. The nurses and the doctor left us there as I watched a mother say good-bye to her son.

Amy was stoic. Her tears disappeared, and the panic that we felt rushing into the NICU vanished with them. She sat in the wooden rocker and held her baby to her chest saying, "Shhhhh. Shhhh. Shhhh," as the tiny blanketed form squeaked back at her. At first they were frequent little squeaks, like a mouse, but as I watched in awe at Amy, the squeaks dwindled into almost silent hiccups. I stood there wanting so badly to help her but not knowing how.

Then she looked up at me and said, "I think I want to be alone with him for a while."

I nodded and pushed the curtain aside and walked away. I knew I was supposed to leave the room, but before I did, I walked over to Scout's incubator and stuck my hand in the porthole. "Keep fighting, Scout," I whispered to her. Then I tiptoed out of the room and went straight to the chapel. I grabbed some rubber gloves from the nurse's station and put them on to ensure I wouldn't have to touch anything with my naked fingers. I also made a mental note to keep some with me at all times.

When I arrived at the chapel, it was empty. I walked up to the front and looked at the sculpture of Jesus Christ hanging on the cross. I stared up at him. I've never really prayed, but it seemed necessary. I prayed for Scout, of course. I prayed for Amy, and I prayed for Gavin. I had never really believed in God or heaven or anything like that. The bitterness I felt toward my father and his passion for it pushed me far away from religion, but at this moment, I knew I had to believe in something.

I begged God to be good to Gavin, to give him a home in heaven with healthy lungs and a straight spine and a brain that functioned perfectly. I begged him not to take

Scout. I asked him to comfort Amy, and I challenged him to forgive me for all of the harm that I have caused. I know it's weird, but as I stood there alone in the chapel, pleading to a sculpture, I felt a sense of peace. I sat down on the carpet in front of the sculptured man with his outstretched hands. I stayed on the floor and let the comfort and the tranquility of the chapel seep into me and calm my frazzled nerves.

When I went back to the NICU, Blake and Emma were standing next to Scout's little clear box. As I walked over to Scout's incubator, I tried not to look at the empty one that once held Gavin. "I think you need to hold your daughter," Emma said as I approached them. She and Blake had already discussed it, and they thought I should be the first to hold Scout.

I sat in the wooden rocker and watched Emma move the wires and tubes so that they wouldn't get tangled. Then she handed me my miniature baby. I felt the slight weight of her as Emma removed her hands and left Scout in my arms. Blake squatted down to where he was eye level with Scout.

I held my breath.

Nothing in my life had ever felt so good, so warm, so fulfilling. I kissed her tiny fuzzy head and closed my eyes, allowing myself to memorize everything about the moment. I opened my eyes and looked over at Blake. I watched as tears pooled in his grassy eyes and fell down his face.

I knew that I would not be allowed to hold her for too long, so I relished every second if it. When Emma came back, I knew why she was there. I kissed Scout's head again and let Emma remove her from my arms. I fought between feeling happy and sad and decided that I had felt enough sadness for one night with everything that had happened with Gavin, so I chose to be happy.

Blake and I each had our cars at the hospital, so we drove home separately. I had a hard time focusing on the road. All I could think about was my sweet Scout and how she felt in my arms. I decided that when I bring her home, I'm never putting her down, and now I understand the whole fascination with being a mom. I'm a mom. Gulp.

Socks

Dear Stephanie,

Remember the tiny socks that B got me when we decided to ... wow. I can't even believe there was ever a decision about Scout. Anyway, the socks. B brought them up to the hospital yesterday. Scout is two and a half weeks old. She's gained eight ounces, half a pound. Thank you very much to my overly ample breasts and all of the glorious milk that they spill every two hours. No kidding, Steph, whoot whoop and I are BFF's.

I spend more time with her than I have ever spent with anyone ... ever. I don't mind it though. I'm helping my daughter, and that's the most important thing. She has to get bigger, stronger, or she'll never come home, but it's strange. I have no free time anymore. When I'm not at the hospital or talking to Dr. Morea, I'm at home strapped to the pump, or B is forcing food down my throat. I swear to God, I think he's trying to keep me fat.

Actually, I'm not fat at all. I barely even have a belly. That's what happens when you have your baby seventeen weeks early. I never got a chance to get huge, so the baby weight is pretty minimal. I know it's not right, but I can't help but appreciate that. Let's face it. I'm vain if I'm anything, and I was wigging out when I first found out I was pregnant and expected to gain at least thirty-five pounds. By the time I bring my baby home, I should be back to normal, whenever that is.

B brought the socks to the hospital hoping that Scout could wear them. Even though she's gained half a pound, she is still, as the nurses call her, itty-bitty. Actually, it's not just Scout. They call all of the babies, itty-bitties.

He brought them in and handed them to Emma, telling her that he had washed them in some sort of baby detergent (I know, my B, always thinks of everything) and asked if Scout could wear them. Emma smiled at him and said that she would try. I knew before she even got to the box that the socks were way too big, but I guess even Emma can't tell Blake no.

It was almost ridiculous. We all laughed. Next to Scout, the socks looked like they belonged to a large toddler.

It's so sweet, the way B is with her. I mean, I thought he loved *me*. You should see how he is with Scout. The first time he got to hold her, well, it might be the sweetest thing I've ever seen. He sat in the wooden rocker, let Emma place Scout in his arms, and silently cried, huge tears dripping down his face. I stood leaning against the wall completely awestruck at Scout with her father.

She knows him. She opens her eyes now, and when Blake holds her, she gazes up at him, so content to be cradled in his big arms. He can't get enough of her. The old me might have been jealous by this, but the new me, the mommy, sees how wonderful it is that my daughter has a father who adores her in every way, and all I want is to offer her every wonderful thing that life has. What's more wonderful than Blake?

He is always so calm and at ease with her where I'm usually a nervous wreck. I worry so much every time I hold her that I'm going to pull a wire from her or something, but B doesn't even seem to notice them.

They often let us take part in her daily care. We help with diaper changes, baths, and one day, they'll remove her feeding tube, and we'll get to feed her a bottle. I can't even believe this, but I can't wait until I can feed her from my breast. It's so strange, this heart swelling love that I feel for her. And then I see her with Blake, and I can see it. The three of us. A family. I watch him with her, and that's all I want.

He sings to her. Blanche and Joclyn were right. B can sing. I mean, I've heard him sing, at night clubs and bars when we're singing along to the song playing, but to hear him sing to Scout. He is just absolutely perfect in every way imaginable.

I'm telling you, Steph, I love this man. No, I haven't told him that because I'm afraid to say it, but I do, with every part of my being, I love him, and when this whole nightmare ends, I am going to say yes and marry him, never letting him and Scout go again.

Scout had a really hard night last night. It was strange. She was doing so well that Emma convinced me and Blake to leave for the night earlier than we usually leave. She practically shooed us out of the room. Blake held my hand as we walked out of the hospital. When we got to his Tahoe, after opening my door, he leaned in and kissed me, I mean kissed me. Open mouth, tongue, sexy. It felt so good. We haven't been intimate since before I was admitted to the hospital. It's been over six weeks since he's touched me. I felt my stomach drop in anticipation.

We got to our building and made our way up to Blake's place. When we got inside, he pulled me into him again and gave me another one of his expert kisses.

"God, I've missed you, Paige."

"I know, B, I've missed you too. So much," I said curling my fingers around the loops of his jeans.

We held each other in the entryway for a while. Then he let go and started to the kitchen. "What do you want to eat?"

"Blake, do you ever think of anything else?"

"Actually, I want to cook for you to distract me from what I want to do *to* you."

"Oh, yeah?" I said, playing with my hair, which I wore in a ponytail, "What do you want to do to me?"

"Stop, Paige. We can't." I walked toward him and rubbed my breasts on his back.

"Why can't we?" He turned around, placing his hands on my hipbones pushing me away.

"Because, I don't know. It just doesn't seem right."

"She's not here. She's doing great. Why can't we?"

"Can you even? I mean, are you okay ... um ... down there?"

"I think so. I'm not sure. It doesn't hurt anymore. Fuck, Blake. Quit talking about my vagina. It's weird."

"Your vagina has never been weird," he said with a laugh.

"Okay, just make dinner. All of this talk is taking the fun out of it."

I went into his room and straightened it up, made the bed, picked up some of his clothes off the floor, thinking to myself that I really needed to find him a maid. Then I went into his bathroom and cleaned it while he cooked. As I was putting some things in his cabinet, I looked over at his shower and remembered a very sultry evening spent there. "Holy shit," I said to my reflection in the mirror, "I'm horny."

I went back into the living room and retrieved my iP-hone from my purse. I googled, "when are you allowed to have sex after having a baby?" Okay, I knew I was supposed to wait six weeks until after I had a follow-up appointment from my birth, but my baby was only one pound, no episiotomy necessary. Shouldn't I get a reprieve?

There were a lot of people asking the same thing, which made me feel less like a whore. I read one entry that said she had sex two days after going home because her husband pressured her. It made me want to punch him. Stupid men. Several said that they had sex sooner with second children than with first, and I read a bunch of comments saying, "If your vagina no longer hurts, you're probably okay."

I went into the kitchen, secretly holding onto my new bit of knowledge. We ate a quiet dinner at B's bar. Then he suggested we go watch TV. Oh boy. We watched *River Monsters*. I kept wondering if the monsters were ever anything other than catfish. I could hardly contain my boredom. I finally fell asleep, curled up on the couch, my head in his lap.

He woke me with a kiss on the head. "Come on, sleeping beauty. Let's go to bed," he said, pulling me off the couch. After I brushed my teeth, I slipped out of my jeans, fitted tee, and bra and got into bed in just my panties.

B came in a little later. He had taken a shower, and he smelled delicious. I wanted to eat him, literally. He turned off the light and slipped under the covers next to me. He reached over and pulled me into him the way he does every time when he noticed my lack of clothing. I could feel him grow hard with anticipation.

"Mmmmmm, baby. What are you doing?"

I pushed my ass into his straining hard on. "Ummmm. Nothing," I said playfully.

He rolled me over and kissed me holding my naked chest against his. I loved the feeling of him next to me. I rolled on my back inviting him to get on top of me. He followed my lead, and finally, finally, I felt all of his weight. On me. I was in heaven, and we hadn't even taken off our underwear. He shifted himself, grinding himself into my panties.

"Are you sure you can do this, baby?"

"Yes," I panted. "Please, B, please. I need this."

He pulled my panties down my legs and then removed his boxers. He slowly slid back up to me letting a loose curl tickle my nose. He brushed it out of my face and eased himself into me, and then he gently rocked me, taking such caution not to cause me pain. I winced and sucked in air a few times. It felt like losing my virginity all over again, but it was worth it. I had longed for this.

We connected, physically and emotionally, and we needed it, we needed to become one again, to be us even if it was just for a moment. It was quick. Clearly it had been a while, and Blake apologized at his sudden release.

"Shit, Paige. I'm sorry. You didn't even," I placed my finger over his lips.

"Shhh, B, it's fine. I needed you. That's all. It was perfect. I'll let you repay me later," I smiled at him in the dark.

He leaned down and kissed my nose then turned me onto my side so that he could spoon me. "I love you, Paige."

"I know," I whispered. He pulled me closer, and we drifted into a very restful sleep.

At 3:42 a.m., our phones buzzed. We both shot up, jumping toward the buzzing. "It's the hospital," B said in his sleepy voice.

It was Scout. She had made a turn and was not doing well. Her blood pressure had dropped dangerously low, and they needed us at the hospital immediately. The doctor thought the clot might be moving, and he wanted to try to stop it before it did. We rushed to get dressed and sped all the way to the hospital, neither of us saying a word.

Blake gritted his teeth as he drove one handed, his other hand squeezing my leg. I stared out the window, trying to prepare myself for the worst and hope for the best, as Dr. Morea suggested.

When we got to the hospital, it was eerie quiet. We carefully scrubbed our hands and headed to Scout. I let out a hefty sigh to see her still in her box. The night nurse, Erin, headed over to us quickly. "Dr. Elliot seems very optimistic. He wants to operate right away."

"Okay," Blake said, "Then what are we waiting for?" he asked in a hushed yell.

She handed Blake the paperwork. He didn't read, just signed. I couldn't just sign. I had to read. What if I were signing over her lungs or something? I read every word, as B paced back and forth and rubbed the back of his head. It was all just legal stuff about risks and liabilities, etc. I signed my name. Then I turned to Scout and reached into her porthole. She didn't grab my finger. She looked pale and bluish. I started to panic.

"Hurry up. She's turning blue."

"They're on their way down to get her," Erin said, calmly, which upset me. Why weren't they running? My daughter's skin was blue, and nobody was running to take her away and save her. Finally, the doors crashed open, and a gowned team came in to get Scout.

B grabbed my hand and pulled me into him. We watched in silence as they wheeled her incubator out of the room. As soon as the door closed, I sunk to the floor and began to wail. B nodded his head, silently shushing me, pulled me up and guided me out of the NICU. We found the empty pediatric surgical waiting room and sat there for two hours and twenty-two minutes. I know. Dr. Elliot walked through the door and over to us. I couldn't look him in the eye. I didn't want to see what I was so afraid was written on his face.

"Say something," Blake ordered.

"She's stable. We were able to get the clot, but her body is weak, and she didn't handle the surgery very well."

Blake fell back into his chair and let his head fall into his hands.

"What does that mean?" He couldn't look at the doctor either.

"It means we wait."

"Wait for what?" I finally spoke.

"Wait to see if she pulls through. She's tough."

"Can we see her?" B asked.

"Yes, she's in recovery. She's the only patient, so you're welcome to go in. You'll need to scrub and get into some gowns first."

Blake thanked him as we made our way out of the waiting room and toward the recovery room. We followed Dr. Elliot's directions and scrubbed, then put on the paper gowns, gloves, the paper booties over our shoes, and paper caps over our hair. The recovery room, unlike the NICU, also required surgical masks. We each carefully placed the blue masks on as quickly as we could. Blake opened the door for me and ushered me in first.

The beep, beep, beep of her heart monitor and the swooshing sound of the ventilator greeted us when we walked into the mostly empty room. We approached slowly, both a little leery of what we would see. They had her lying on her stomach, which was pretty typical. It was also her favorite position. I could see a tiny incision on her upper-left shoulder. How in the world could they operate on something so petite? The incision was no more than an inch long.

Her back jerked with every breath she was forced to breathe. Her little butt was up in the air with her legs tucked underneath. I couldn't help myself, and I reached in and gently, barely touching, patted her little behind to let her know we were there. The beeping and swooshing continued. I timed it. The beeping was consistent. That was good, I thought. Beep—one, two, three. Beep—one, two, three. Beep—one, two, three. Beep—one, two, three and so on.

A nurse came in and changed an IV bag, avoiding eye contact with us. I noticed. I flipped her off in my mind as she walked away then realized she was there for Scout, so I mentally apologized. The beeping continued. The swooshing continued, and pretty much that was that.

Blake and I looked at each other confused. Nobody gave us any instructions. We had no idea what to do. Blake started humming to Scout. A few minutes, which seemed like hours later, another nurse came over and told us that we needed to leave, that the doctor needed to examine her, and we couldn't be in there when he did.

We walked back into the waiting room, pulled off our paper shields, and waited some more, hearts pounding, breath held. When Dr. Elliot reappeared in the waiting room, he seemed less concerned.

"She's doing great, guys," he said with a smile and a small clap of his hands. "She is one tough little girl. Her vitals are good, and her blood pressure is getting better. We're moving her back to the NICU as we speak."

Blake sighed. I sighed. We thanked and thanked and thanked Dr. Elliot. He mentioned that she would be closely watched and that we should stay by our phones in case they needed to reach us. I didn't say it, but I knew neither of us was ever going to leave Scout alone again. I mean, apparently our baby knew how to get our attention.

At this moment, Blake's in the NICU with our princess. We aren't allowed to hold her, too much risk for infection, but he's holding her hand, and that's enough ... for now.

Wish

Dear Stephanie,

I turned thirty yesterday. With everything going on with Scout, I almost forgot about it, but not Blake. Normally on either of our birthdays, we get dressed up and go to a night club with a big group of people, drink all night, dance, and then go home together and do our bump and hump routine.

Blake of course remembered that it was my birthday and suggested that we go to dinner. I hesitated, not wanting to leave Scout alone, but Blake insisted that we had to eat, so we went to a little bistro just a couple of blocks away from the hospital. I picked at my food mostly just moving it around on my plate. B devoured his and then finished mine. I got up to go to the restroom, and when I returned there was a piece of chocolate cake waiting for me with a lone flickering candle.

"Happy birthday," Blake smiled as I pulled out my chair and sat down.

"You know I don't eat dessert," I smiled back at him.

"I know. The dessert's for me, but I can't put a candle in a martini, so the candle is for you. Make a wish."

I've always thought that was ludicrous. "Make a wish" as if blowing out a candle makes any difference in what life has planned for you, but I humored him, closed my eyes, and for the first time in my adult life, I summoned up an image, leaned over, blew out the candle, and actually made a wish.

He finished the cake, paid the bill, and we headed back to the hospital. When we arrived in the NICU, something was clearly wrong. People in scrubs and white coats surrounded Scout's box, all working with a hurried sense of urgency. "What's going on?" Blake asked. Emma rushed to Blake and grabbed one hand from each of us.

"She's not doing well. She's gone into cardiac arrest. We're doing everything we can. We need you to wait outside."

"When?" I asked already feeling the guilt of leaving.

"Just now. Please, Paige. Let us do our jobs."

Blake squeezed my hand as we zombie walked out into the hall. My heart raced with uncertainty. We sat on some plastic leather chairs in the waiting room and waited, again holding our breath. Blake kept whispering into my ear, "She'll be okay. She'll be okay."

Minutes felt like hours until finally Dr. Elliot, her heart surgeon, walked into the waiting room, looking down at the floor. Blake stood up immediately. It took me a little bit longer to make my legs work. Dr. Elliot took a deep breath, "We did all that we could. I'm sorry. I'm so very sorry." He stretched out the last sentence. "I'm ... so ... very ... sorry." As if saying it slowly made it less painful to hear.

Blake took a deep breath. I looked up at him and watched him swallow hard, "So she's ... gone?" he whispered.

"Yes, Blake. She didn't make it."

"No," he said frantically, "Oh God, no."

Blake crumpled into me. I held him. Shaking. Quivering. Feeling the weight of an actual broken heart.

"Would you like to see her?"

Blake nodded as his eyes filled with tears. He held my hand and led me back into the NICU to Scout's incubator where she lay quietly still on her tummy in just a tiny white diaper surrounded by her pseudo womb blankets. It was our first time to see her without any wires or tubes. I reached into the porthole and patted her tiny bottom.

Blake opened up the incubator and took her out and held her to his chest. He pulled me into him with his free arm, and the three of us stood together, my head resting on his shoulder. I wrapped one of my arms around B's waist and put my other around Scout. She was still warm. And together the three of us became one as we held each other and wept.

I usually know what time it is. I always have a watch or know where the nearest clock is. It's a crutch. I always need to know the time. But during this moment, all I wanted was for time to stop because the more minutes that ticked on, the longer she was gone, and the sooner we would have to leave her for the last time.

Blake finally broke our connection by handing her to me. He walked over and got the wooden rocking chair and sat down in it then pulled me onto his lap. And we rocked and held our baby in silence for a while. Not long enough.

"Good-bye, baby girl," Blake whispered and placed her tiny fisted hand next to his lips, kissing gently. "Come on, Paige, we should go." I argued with him, wordless, begging him not to make me leave her, but he nodded and his expression told me it was time.

"Good-bye, Scout," I said as I gave her sweet fuzzy head one last kiss. I wrapped one of her blankets around her and laid her swaddled lifeless body in her incubator. I pressed my hand to her chest and gave her a silent promise. Then I turned and ran out of the room. Blake met me shortly after in the hall where we were greeted by a grief counselor.

"Sorry, sir. I think we need to be alone right now," Blake said to him as he hustled me toward the elevator. My hero, always.

When we got into the elevator, he said, "Let's not tell anyone tonight."

"Tell who?"

"We'll have to make some phone calls eventually, but tonight, can we just go home?"

"Yes, of course."

We silently drove home. When we walked into B's apartment, he didn't turn on any lights. He dropped my hand and went into his bathroom. I heard him turn on the shower. I looked over at his unmade bed and realized how exhausted I was. I laid down in all of my clothes, including my shoes, and curled into a ball. I heard the water from the shower turn off, and then Blake's electric toothbrush, and then it was quiet. I pretended to sleep. A few minutes later, he got into bed and pulled me into him like he always does.

Then he began to shake, not tremble, but shake with fierce violent silent sobs. I silently cried, too, my big tears soaking the pillow.

"Ask me what I wished for, B."

"Why?"

"Just ask me." He didn't say anything for a long time, just sniffled and cleared his throat several times.

He finally asked, "What did you wish for?"

"That she would no longer be in pain."

He didn't respond but continued to hold me. A few minutes later, he broke the silence and said, "It's not your fault, Paige."

"Of course it is, B."

Of course it is.

Box

Dear Stephanie,

Today we buried our baby. I have no words to describe it. We put her in a little white box lined in pink silk, closed it up, and left her in a hole in the ground. She lived her entire short life in a box, and now she'll turn to dust in another box.

I cannot grasp the heartbreak that I feel. I thought I knew sadness. I knew the depth of darkness and despair. I allowed it to swallow me multiple times. I look back at those moments and laugh. I thought I was sad, depressed, alone. But today, when I dropped a handful of dirt on a tiny white box, my heart felt a permanent gaping wide hole that will remain with me forever.

I held on to Blake, stabilizing him. Holding *him* up. Because at any moment, I knew *he* might crumble. We leaned on each other as the minister talked about promises of tomorrow. Janie sat next to me, holding my hand. Blake's brother read a scripture about walking through the valley of the shadow of death. I rolled my eyes. Scout will never walk ... period.

We walked through the cemetery to the limousine waiting to return us to his parents' house. We passed Dr. Morea and who I can only assume was his wife. He made eye contact with me and held my gaze. I just stared back. He knows. There's nothing he can say.

Blake's family has tried to be supportive. His mother pretty much planned the entire funeral. We couldn't. We simply couldn't do it. How do you pick out a casket for your own baby? How do you choose a plot of land where a part of your soul will be buried? How do you decide what day will be the last day you're in the same room with her? I did none of it. Neither did Blake.

We stayed in his apartment for two days after we left the hospital. We rarely left the bed. We stayed locked up in his dark bedroom and didn't speak to each other. After the first night, we couldn't even cry anymore. We just laid there, wide awake, staring at his spinning fan. We held hands but didn't touch otherwise.

I can't tell you what Blake thinks or where his mind is, but I can tell you that I don't even recognize him. He's hollow and broken. She took him with her. His heart is buried in that little white box.

After our two-day seclusion, Blake decided that we needed to call his family. Thank God for the Greeks. They handled it all from there. His mother came to his apartment and rallied us out. She insisted that we go stay at their place until all of the plans were made and everything was "taken care of," meaning my kid was in a hole in the ground.

Last night, she came into Blake's room (she actually let me stay in the room with him this time), and settled herself on the end of his bed. She smoothed his plaid comforter when she sat and motioned for me to join her. I languidly walked toward her and sat down. She was quiet for a long time. She kept taking deep breaths trying to summon the right words and stopping before anything came out of her mouth.

"Claire, there's nothing you can say that will make this better."

"I know, Paige. I'm a mother, too."

"I'm not a mother anymore," I interrupted.

"You are, Paige. You will always be her mother."

I didn't respond. I sat on the end of the bed, twiddling my thumbs in my lap trying to keep the vicious words in my head from spewing from my mouth at a woman who was only trying to help.

"Listen, Paige," Claire reached out and grabbed my hand interrupting my thoughts, "Blake told me about ..." She cleared her throat. "Blake told me about your ... er ... problem with ... um ... sui ... um ... depression." I didn't have it in me to put her in her place, so I just stone-face listened to her. "He's really worried about you. He loves you, Paige. He needs you." She let go of my hand. "I'm getting ahead of myself." Another sigh. Another deep breath. "Paige, I have to take medication, too."

What? I continued to stare down at my hands while she talked.

"I've suffered from depression for years. When Blake was nine, he found me."

I turned toward her finally allowing a connection with our eyes and listened to her story. Apparently, Claire struggled with depression as far back as adolescence. She always knew that she had a problem, but she never said anything to anyone because mental illness was something people just didn't discuss. I can relate.

When she met Robert in college, he had a light around him, and his energy was contagious. That sounded familiar. They fell in love instantly, and for a while, she felt normal, happy even. They got engaged three weeks after meeting and were married within six months. Immediately, she got pregnant. Bob was elated. She said when she told him, he picked her up off of the floor, spinning her around until she almost vomited on him. She dropped out of college and decided she wanted to be a mom full time. Three months into her pregnancy, she had a miscarriage.

They were devastated, but Bob never got too down. Claire, on the other hand, felt like her body was broken and that her one hope was shattered. Bob could tell something was going on, but he ignored it. He always told her that it would happen, and they would end up having a giant noisy family. She hid her depression again.

After celebrating their first anniversary, she got pregnant. She gave birth to Blake's oldest brother nine months later, and then the other three boys came. After each pregnancy she said she had the typical baby blues but nothing that ever felt like the depression from her teenage years.

"I think I may have been too busy. I don't know. The boys kept me running most of the time, and they really brought so much joy to my life. Then out of nowhere, I fell, hard and deep into a depression, worse than it ever was in my teenage years."

She said she drank constantly and hid in her room most of the time. The boys didn't understand why all of a sudden she was so tired, but most days, all she could do was get out of bed long enough to get them off to school. On days when she couldn't get out of bed, Robert took over and handled the boys.

"It was horrible, Paige. The sickness of fear and hurt, the feeling that they would all be better off without me. I finally realized that was my answer. Robert could handle the boys on his own, and they didn't need a mother who couldn't get out of bed. I was hurting them, Paige, all of them. I sunk, further and further, and finally convinced myself to end it."

"Had you ever tried before?" I asked her.

"Oh, yes, a few times when I was a teenager. My parents even put me in a hospital for a while when I was sixteen. Nothing ever helped though. I would think I was done with it, happy even, and then it always came back, until the last time."

She made plans for all of the boys. Blake's two older brothers and younger brother were with Robert at a basketball game. Blake had baseball practice, so she arranged that he ride with a teammate and then go to his house after practice and spend the night. She waited until they pulled out of the driveway and went straight into her bedroom where she took out a bottle of pills and swallowed what was left. She fell asleep almost immediately. She woke up in a hospital bed.

Blake forgot his baseball glove and came back home to get it. He walked through the door and yelled for his mom. When she didn't answer, he went up to her room and found her on the bed unconscious.

He called for the ambulance that rushed her to the emergency room where they pumped her stomach and saved her life. Her heart stopped beating before they got her into the ambulance, and Blake watched as they revived her with CPR. Echoes of Blake's saying, "I've witnessed it ..." bounced around in my head. Now I knew what he meant.

She looked down at her hands as she continued to tell me that she was so ashamed. She never expected one of her boys to find her. She figured that the three boys and Bob would return that night and that he would be the one to discover her in bed.

"I can't imagine what it must have been like for him to find me that way." She got up and walked into the bathroom and came back with a tissue. She blotted the tears from her eyes and finished the story.

Blake didn't speak to her for months. He was so angry and sad and disappointed. She said the one thing that he did say to her was, "How could you do that?" She decided then that she needed to get help that she never wanted to see that disappointment on his face again. She checked herself into a treatment center where they assigned her a psychiatrist who in turn prescribed her an antidepressant.

"Every morning, I drop that pill into my palm, and I thank God for my life, my boys, and for the pill, and I ask for His forgiveness and for Blake's. Every single morning. Depression will always lurk in the back of my mind, but with therapy and medication, I try to manage it. There are still moments though," she paused, "Well, you know what I mean."

I looked up at her with tears in my eyes and nodded. She reached over and patted my hand and then held it loosely.

"Paige, the pain that you feel, I will never know. I will never understand it. I know your heart must be broken. Mine is broken for you ... and for Blake. Just know that you are not alone, honey. I am here, and I understand. I just wanted you to know that." She squeezed my hand three times and stood up. She leaned down and kissed my forehead. Then she smoothed her skirt and cleared her throat.

"Can I get you something to eat, Paige?" What is it with food and these people?

"No, Claire, thank you though."

"Of course. Well, if you change your mind," she said as she started toward the door.

"No, I mean, thank you for telling me that. I didn't know. I would have never guessed."

"Oh, well, we hide it well. Don't we?" She winked at me.

Blake joined me in his room shortly after his mother left. We laid down in bed and listened to the crickets, oblivious to our pain, sing outside the window. B kissed the back of my neck and said he loved me. In the darkness of his childhood room, he said, "I couldn't get through this without you, Paige." I squeezed his hand three times and kissed his knuckle, pulling it to my heart, and I fell asleep actually thinking that I, that we, had some hope.

Then we put our baby in a box in a hole in the ground, and nothing else matters anymore.

Redemption

Dear Stephanie,

It's been two weeks. Two weeks since we put her in the ground. I count the days. I wake up every morning, and I count how many days it's been since I last held her. Eighteen.

I've spent some time with Dr. Morea lately. Of course, his concern is palpable. He insists that I get back on my medication. I lie to him and say that I take them. I also lie to Blake. Blake has his own prescriptions. He obediently takes his. They seem to be working, if making him an emotionless walking corpse is the goal. He hardly speaks. Empty. We're both empty, absent of any feeling. Numb.

Dr. Morea keeps telling me that we need to pick up the pieces and move forward. "Have you ever lost a baby, doc?" I asked him.

He didn't respond, just shook his head. Exactly. He can't relate.

Blake and I have met with a grief counselor a few times. Blake usually does most of the talking. I can't seem to say anything. What is there to say? We have a dead baby. She's not coming back. I was finally beginning to feel like a human, like I was worthy of life and even love, and then just like that, I'm back to where I go, the hole, the dark place where the voices constantly remind me of my pain, that I am toxic, horrible, unworthy.

I know what I have to do. I've made the decision, and I'm so ready to end this pain. My problem is that Blake is broken. I don't want to leave him like this. I do love him. I want him to be happy, to find a normal girl who is whole and who can give him lots of healthy babies like he wants. He will be better off without me. This I know for sure. I am a hurricane of trouble, and I can't spread anymore hurt to him.

Days tend to be more bearable. Blake hasn't gone back to work yet. He's scheduled to start back next week, and I think he's actually ready to have something else to do. He opens books and sits them on his lap. I'm not sure he actually reads them. We watch TV, but we can't handle the commercials. If there's a baby, a hospital, a child, a family, Blake quickly turns the channel or turns it off all together.

But the nights, the nights when everything is quiet, when the world rests, that's when we can't escape the pain. We both cry, silent tears, but I can hear Blake sniffle in the dark. I know his pain, and he knows mine, and there isn't anything either of us can do to help each other. He clings to me in bed, and together we lie and remember her, and feel the giant chasm she left on our world. We will never be the same.

I do try to pull him back, little by little. One of the first nights after the funeral, I suggested to B that we go out and pretend we were who we used to be, get drunk and high. I wondered if feeling high could take the ache away from my chest, but he looked at me ... disgusted. I know what he's thinking. Hell, I think it, too. Every time I think at all. Drugs killed my baby. My drugs. Who knows which ones? The antidepressant? Maybe. The cocaine? Possibly. The downers I took to sleep? It could have been any of them, or the combination. Does it even matter?

He looks at me and sees a murderer. And he's not the only one. Is there anything worse than knowing your baby died because of you? I can tell you the answer. No. There is nothing worse, no matter what people tell me. People keep saying that, "It wasn't your fault, Paige." But I'm the one who did drugs. It was my body who failed her before she was ever even conceived, and I will wake up every morning and know that if I am the reason she is dead, I don't deserve to live. The guilt haunts me more than the pain of her loss.

Speaking of guilt, I had a visitor yesterday. Blake and I sat side by side on his couch. Blake looked like he hadn't shaved in days, full unkempt beard and a mane of frizzy curls. He was wearing an old fraternity shirt and a pair of basketball shorts. I had thrown on one of Blake's white V necks and a pair of his boxers and pulled my hair into a high messy bun on top of my head.

We were a mess, just staring into space, listening to the sound of our building, doors shutting, the air condition-er clicking on and the whooshing sound it makes when it comes through the vents, the ding of the elevator at the end of the hall. Then I heard knocking. I sat up and looked at Blake. He looked back confused. I never get visitors. Ever.

I walked over to Blake's door and opened it just enough to peek through. My stomach dropped. A man stood with his back to me, his left hand in his pocket, wearing a teal polo and khaki pants and loafers. I knew right away who he was.

"Paige, you in there?"

He knocked again. Then he leaned on the wall and pulled out his cell phone. He typed something and started to turn around but then thought better of it and knocked again. Blake had come up behind me, and I could feel his chest press up against my back.

"Who is that?" he whispered.

I didn't answer him, just stood transfixed watching the man standing outside of my door. I didn't even know he knew where I lived.

"Please, Paige. Open the door, babycakes."

I don't know if it was the desperation in his voice or the fact that he used my childhood nickname, but for whatever reason, I opened Blake's door and stepped out.

He turned around, I think to walk away, and stopped suddenly. His face tightened when he saw me, blue eyes wide.

"Oh, Paige," he said reaching out to me and pulled me into his chest.

I fell into him and sobbed into his shirt. He held me, one hand holding the back of my head, the other around my shoulders. Blake must have stepped out at some point because he let go and straightened to his full height, clearing his throat.

He reached out his hand to Blake and said, "I'm Peter. Peter Parnevik."

"Blake Demopolous."

We stood awkwardly for a minute, the three of us in the hallway until Blake looked at me and then at him. He nervously tucked an unruly curl behind his ear and said, "And how do you know Paige?"

"He's my dad, Blake."

"Oh," he said and looked at me confused, and then I realized why. Blake thought my father was dead.

I shrugged at him and sort of motioned with my head for him to go back inside. I would tell him what he needed to know later, but first I needed to have a word with good old Daddy.

"Let me just get my key, and we can talk at my place. I'll be right back."

I walked into Blake's and leaned against the wall letting out the breath I hadn't realized I'd been holding.

"Are you okay, Paige? What's going on? I thought he was ..."

"I know, B," I interrupted, "I lied, kind of. I'm sorry. Let me just deal with him, and then I'll explain everything." I could tell by looking at him that he was pissed. "Please don't be mad. It's such a long story. Just ... please, B. I'll be right back."

I rushed out of Blake's and headed to my door, fumbling with the key, my hands trembling.

I ushered my father into the room and closed the door behind us. Only then did I realize how angry I had become in the last five minutes after the initial shock of seeing him there.

"Have a seat," I said and sat down at my dining room table.

He pulled out the chair across from me and sat down, uneasily.

"What are you doing here?" I asked.

"I heard about your ... um ... baby, and I just thought you might ... need something ... need me?"

"What could I possibly need from you?" I folded my hands together and rested my forearms on the table.

"Paige, you can't still be angry with me." He leaned forward and reached one hand out to try and grab my arm. I quickly pulled back and put my hands under the table.

"You can't tell me who or what I'm allowed to be angry with."

"How many times do I have to apologize to you, Paige?"

"You don't have to apologize to me anymore. I just want you out of my life. Why won't you leave me alone?" I could ignore the letters he sent to my post office box, the emails, the text messages and phone calls, but I couldn't ignore his presence, his sitting right there in front of me in my dining room.

"Paige, listen. Let me be here for you now. I can't imagine what you're going through, that kind of loss ..." he trailed off.

"What I'm going through? What gives you the right to even know what I'm going through? I've been on my own for years, for years, and you pick now to show up at my door and try to make it all okay? Don't you realize?" The words spewed out.

"It's all your fault. Yours. You left me over and over again. I was never more than an ornament in your life, something so easily put aside, when all I wanted was for you to want me, and you left. Every. Single. Time. And you took everyone who ever meant anything to me away."

"What are you talking about, Paige? I never took anyone away from you."

"What about Lucy?"

"Oh, dear God, Paige. Lucy? Really? You were a baby, for Christ's sake. Surely you got over that."

"No, I never got over that. And Mom? It wasn't enough that you took her away from her own family, you had to take her away from me, too? And then you pushed her down the stairs, and now she's never coming back."

"Jesus, Paige. How many times do you have to hear that I did not push her down the stairs? She fell."

"I don't believe you." I couldn't meet his eyes, but I could tell he was staring at me.

"Paige, she fell down the stairs." He sighed heavily and then stood up and started pacing and rubbing his chin. "That day, I was going to leave her. I was in our bedroom, packing some of my clothes. I had the condo already and planned to move in there. She was irate and started drinking early in the day. By the time I was ready to leave, she was drunk.

"She came into the room and started screaming at me. Yelling about all of my affairs." He looked over at me then and shook his head.

"I wasn't a good husband, Paige. I know you know this. God I'm so very sorry for that night, too. But with your mom. She didn't make it easy. She was so," he let out a slow breath, "crazy. It was my fault, mostly. I mean, the women, the traveling. It was too much for her. But the day of her fall, she was out of hand.

"She was throwing things at me and screaming and yelling, so I decided I would send somebody for my things. I tried to be calm. I told her good-bye and started down the stairs. She pulled me, like a child, begging me to stay, but by this time, I was mad too. I won't lie, Paige. I was so angry at her and completely done, fed up. I started to go down the stairs, and she pulled my hand back. When I pulled it away, she lost her balance and fell, Paige."

He looked at me for a reaction, but I gave him nothing.

"I tried to catch her. She hit her head on the banister. I watched her eyes sort of glaze over. Then she closed them. I thought she was dead."

"That probably would have been more convenient, huh?"

"Don't be hateful, Paige. I loved your mother. Love her still. I've never had another woman since. I promise. I didn't push her. But it was my fault. I'll never forgive myself."

He searched me for redemption.

"You're the reason why she's dead," I said in a cool voice.

"She's not dead, Paige."

"Not my mother, idiot, Scout. My daughter."

"Oh, Paige. Please."

He sat back down across from me, resting his head in both of his hands.

"Please don't blame me for this, too."

"Well, I don't. I mostly blame myself, but if it weren't for you and your selfishness, none of this would have happened. I have to wonder why you chose now to come here. What is it that you're looking for? What do you want from me?"

"Paige, I've tried to give you your space. You told me once after the accident with your mother to leave you alone. I have done that, but you shouldn't have to handle this on your own, honey."

"I'm not on my own."

I walked to my door and opened it, motioning for him to follow. He slowly pushed out his chair, and walked toward me looking at the floor.

As he left, he turned around to say one last thing, but before he could say anything, I interrupted. "Don't ever contact me again." As soon as he passed the threshold, I closed the door and sagged against it.

I hadn't expected to see my father, and the initial surprise of his presence shocked me, so much so that I allowed myself to fall into his trap for a minute, but after I basically kicked him out, I felt a sense of peace. I wasn't worried about if I had done the right thing or if he would have been able to help me, if he was telling the truth. I didn't care anymore. I wasn't planning on sticking around much longer anyway.

One less person to grieve for me when I'm gone. He's better off without me, too.

I waited a while before I went back to Blake's place. He was sitting on the couch with a book opened on his lap. When he heard me come in, he jumped up.

"Are you okay?" He set the book down on the end table and walked toward me. I searched his face looking for anger but luckily what I saw earlier had vanished.

I shook my head. He was in front of me then and reached his arms around me. I breathed into his chest holding back the tears that threatened to fall. He rested his chin on top of my head and said, "You need to tell me what's going on, Paige. Why would you not tell me that your dad is alive?"

"Because he's dead to me." He grabbed my hand and guided me back over to the couch.

We sat back down, he at one end, I at the other, and I told him the story of the day my mother fell, of Lucy, of the night that I found him with Janie's sister, of all of the times I sat waiting for my parents to come back to me.

I told him about how special he made me feel when I was younger, how he handled my first suicide attempt, and how I basically eliminated him from my life after my mother's fall. I spilled it all, not leaving out a single detail, and B just sat there, his head slightly cocked to the side listening without interruption, letting me spew out the wicked truth of my childhood.

When I stopped talking, he said, "Jesus, Paige."

"I know."

"So how did you leave it with him then? Today?"

"I told him to never contact me again."

He sat there for a second, nodded and then got up and came over to where I was sitting.

"Let's get out of here. I can't look at these walls anymore today." He grabbed my hand and pulled me up.

"I can't go anywhere. I'm in boxer shorts," I said.

"So throw on some regular shorts. I'll wait."

I quickly pulled on a pair of dirty jean shorts that I found on the floor of his room and slipped on a pair of sandals. He got up when I came back into the room and grabbed my hand.

"Want to go for a walk?" he asked as he opened the door for me.

"Not really. It's a hundred degrees outside."

"Paige, it can't feel any worse outside than it does in here."

He was right. The heaviness of our grief had weighed us down and made us fall into an unhealthy seclusion from the rest of the world. Maybe a little fresh air was what we needed.

We exited the building and walked outside, hand in hand. We passed our favorite dive bar, a café where we used to meet for dinner, and a park that we had never once visited. Blake turned toward the park, and I obediently followed.

He sat down on a metal bench. We watched some people throwing a Frisbee with their dog, some kind of a retriever or something. I thought how strange it was that I never had a pet, a dog especially. My father hated animals and wouldn't tolerate them in the house.

Blake had his arm around me and pulled me closer to him. We were both damp with sweat, but still having him close offered a quiet comfort. I laid my head on his shoulder and closed my eyes.

He leaned down, resting his cheek against my hair and said, "It's just the two of us now."

Soon to be one, I thought.

Sunshine

Dear Stephanie,

Blake went back to work earlier this week. He was ready to get back into his routine. I think he wanted to get away from here, from the memories, and maybe even from me. I can understand that. He needs a distraction. We both do. I hate the days though when he works, and I'm here alone with my thoughts.

It seems strange now. She's been gone for over a month (thirty-three days since I held her last), and yet, it doesn't hurt any less. The first few weeks nearly killed us, which frankly would be a relief. Life flipped for us. Until yesterday, Blake's apartment revealed a storm of pain. Half eaten Chinese food containers littered his counter top in his kitchen.

For weeks, neither of us picked up anything that we touched. We threw trash wherever it landed, clothes wherever they came off. We stopped caring. Blake was never a clean freak by any stretch of the imagination, but his place was always at least sort of neat. We even managed to keep it tidy when she was in the hospital. Then she died, and we ceased to care.

Yesterday, though I couldn't take it anymore. I went on a mad cleaning spree and got Blake's place in shape. I spent the entire day throwing out trash, doing laundry, cleaning his room, his bathroom, his disgusting kitchen, vacuuming, and I started to feel a little more normal. The clutter began to consume me, and I simply couldn't stand it anymore. It was nice to have my own distraction. I cranked up The Strokes and almost forgot about my broken heart. Almost.

Blake came home from work, stripped out of his work clothes and instead of throwing them on the floor, placed them in the hamper. He didn't say anything about the place being cleaned. I think maybe I half hoped he would notice. I don't know, maybe I needed some sort of validation.

We crawled into bed last night, and I mentioned to Blake that I washed the sheets. He took a deep breath into his pillow and sighed then pulled me to him. "Thank you, Paige," he whispered to my back, and believe it or not, I actually slept a little, not much, but more than I have since Scout died. I have no expectations of normal, no thoughts that things will ever be the way they were, but it seems we made a turn somewhere toward that direction anyway.

Then today, Blake smiled for the first time. His real, sincere, crooked, fuck me grin. He smiled, his smile. That smile. At me. My heart stopped. I looked over at him and saw it, for just a brief second, I saw *him*.

We were sitting at his bar, drinking our morning coffee in silence, our new routine. Neither of us had dressed yet. He sat in his pajama bottoms and white V neck T-shirt, reading the *Wall Street Journal* while I tinkered with my Kindle reading reviews of new releases. My hair was pulled loosely in a bun on top of my head, but a stray kept tickling my nose. I must have blown it out of my face a half dozen times until I finally got so frustrated that I reached up, growled, and pulled my band lose letting my hair fall onto my shoulders.

"You're so pretty, Paige," he said to me.

I looked up over my Kindle at him and offered him a semi-smile along with a confused brow.

And that was it. He ran his fingers through his hair, just staring at me as I stared back, and then he smiled. Normal. Like we didn't have a dead baby. For the first time in over a month, he smiled, and I smiled back. It might not seem like much, but Blake went away with Scout. Poof. Disappeared. Present in body but absent in everything else until this morning, when a little bit of my B emerged and let his crooked grin return.

I hopped down from my stool and walked over to him, wrapping my arms around his waist. I whispered thank you into his ear, kissing the skin just behind it. He turned toward me, and I stood between his partially spread legs. He placed his hands on either side of my face and pulled my head to his shoulder. I sagged into his body, and we stayed that way allowing time to move on without us.

His warmth pulsated through me, and for a moment, we gave our grief a break. He broke our embrace and stood in front of me, chest to chest. He lifted my chin with his finger and lightly feather kissed my parted lips, piercing me with his green eyes. Then he stepped back and walked into his bedroom. A few minutes later, I heard the running water from the shower.

I sat back down on the stool paralyzed, my heart racing in my chest. This is a big deal, Steph. A huge deal. He's returning to me.

Once B is back, I can exit. That's the plan, my plan. Once his old self resurfaces, I'm done. I know he will be sad to lose me and that he will probably fall right back into this grief, but it will only be temporary. He is so much better off without me. He can have a rich life, a normal one with a wife and children, and if I stick around, he will never have that. He deserves better, and I'm going to give it to him.

I thought about his smile, the heat that I felt between us just minutes before at his breakfast bar. I wondered if maybe we might be ready for a connection, a way to truly have B back, even if only for a minute. I got up from the stool and headed to B's room where I intended to persuade a little more of him to rejoin me, but before I got to his room, my phone buzzed.

I glanced at the screen, thinking I would decline the call, but I recognized the number and thought better of it. When the Assistant District Attorney calls to discuss a rape case where you're the star witness, you probably should answer, so I did.

The trial starts next week. We've met a couple of times to go over my statement, but he wants to meet with me again and rehearse. He asked that I meet him tomorrow at the court to have a mock trial and see how I do when he asks me the questions on the witness stand in an actual court room.

What else do I have to do tomorrow? I tried to hurry the call, knowing that I had a limited amount of time before B got out of the shower. I said the customary, "uh huh," "yes," and "of course," but the D.A. is nothing if not wordy. I heaved a heavy sigh trying to encourage him to stop talking when finally, he set the time and place. I agreed to the meeting, made the appointment on my calendar, and placed my phone back on the bar.

I rushed into Blake's room too late. He stood in dress pants, buttoning up his shirt, his loose wet curls framing his face. I stared at him silently for a minute, watching him put the finishing touches on his attire and then slowly walked back out of the room.

He breezed past me, grabbed his keys from the tray next to his door, and hurried out to work without saying goodbye.

Having nothing else to do with my day, I decided to go back to bed. I didn't need sleep, but the darkness of B's room, and the smell of him on his sheets beckoned me to his bed. I lied down, pulled the pillow into my chest and closed my eyes. For a minute, he was here. I can bring him back. And I will.

Slut

Dear Stephanie,

Ever wonder what it would be like to sit in a room and have your sexual past displayed before the entire audience of "your peers," your boyfriend, your best friend, your therapist, and a handful of strangers? Well, that was my day. It was awesome.

We're in the midst of this trial. It's been going well. All evidence points to the rapist's being guilty. The picture of the cut on my head, the DNA evidence, etc. But then today happened, and to put it mildly, we just went from drinking champagne in the penthouse suite at the Waldorf Astoria, to licking the bottom of a shoe in front of Crackwhore Inn.

Today I took the stand. Today my attorney asked me to replay the scene of my rape, which I did as accurately as I possibly could remember. Today he asked me question after question, all of which we rehearsed first. I answered confidently, surely, looking him in the eye, ignoring the menacing glare from my rapist on the other side of the room.

I could hear my lawyer's voice from rehearsal: "Don't fidget. Don't bite your fingernails (which I would never do no matter how nervous I was), no stuttering, just the truth, straight forward and to the point." And I nailed it. Nailed it.

"Ms. Preston, do you see the man who you described in this room?"

"Yes, sir." *Always be polite and use manners, especially in a courtroom.*

"Can you please point him out to the jury?"

"Yes, Sir." I stated as I raised my right hand and pointed my index finger at the arrogant prick attempting to stare a hole through me. He smirked at me and leaned back in his chair as if nothing could touch him.

Like I said, I nailed it. Until the cross examination where I got raped for a second time by the same bastard.

It started off simple, just a few questions about me. I answered honestly, confidently, again. The rapist's bitch attorney then walked over to the witness stand and placed her forearm on the wooden partition. She took a deep breath and looked at me, and with a brief upturn of her lip, she asked, "How many sexual partners have you had, Ms. Preston?"

"Objection, irrelevant," my attorney barked (because, frankly, he knows the answer, which is I don't know.)

"It is relevant, Your Honor, to show the character of this witness." She tapped a rounded red fingernail on the wood grain where her forearm had just rested.

I stiffened. The judge took a deep breath and cleared his throat, "I'll allow it."

Stupid bitch attorney started pacing in front of me. Four steps one way, turn, three steps the other turn, and so on. I felt like one of those cat clocks whose eyes move back and forth watching her. "Ms. Preston, the jury is waiting."

I leaned forward toward the microphone. My attorney told me that if I was asked a question that made me uncomfortable to be honest, and so I was. "Honestly, I don't keep a list, ma'am." He didn't say I couldn't be a polite bitch.

"More than ten?"

"Yes."

"More than twenty?"

"Your Honor, my client is not on trial here," the Assistant D.A. said.

"Get to your point, counsel," said the Judge.

"Would you say, Ms. Preston, that you have had sex with a lot of men?"

"Yes, I have."

I could feel the sweat dripping down my cleavage and pooling into my bra. I kept my composure, but inside, I was reeling. She knew details about some of the men I have slept with, very intimate details. I knew my rapist had money, and clearly, he didn't spare it in hiring his attorney. She was good and vicious.

I answered her questions, every single one, and each question dug deeper into my past sexcapades. It was dirty, and low, and she murdered my character in every way. She really conducted her research. She knew about a night when I passed out in the hallway of a hotel in just my underwear. She even had pictures and showed the jury. She specifically asked me which drugs I had tried, how often I had taken them. She even had the nerve to mention Scout.

"Is it true that you recently gave birth to a premature baby?"

Big tears flooded my eyes. I swallowed, and managed a quiet yes.

My attorney quickly objected, and the judge showed me some pity. She continued a myriad of questions all about drugs, sex, partying, bad decisions that I've made. I looked out into the courtroom, to seek safety with my entourage. I watched Dr. Morea begin to fidget the deeper she persecuted me as Blake squirmed in his seat, rubbing the back of his head, unable to sit still, listening to what a whore I am. When she asked about Scout, Janie had to pull him back down in his seat. Janie couldn't even make eye contact with me. She fumbled on her phone, pretending to be distracted. It was awful.

Finally, finally, it was over. Bitch defense attorney chirped, "No further questions."

My attorney stood up and asked to readdress me.

"Ms. Preston, my colleague," he gestured toward bitch lawyer, "has established that you ... er ... enjoy ... um ... sex. You enjoy sex, is that right?"

I looked at him questioning. He nodded slightly assuring me to answer.

"Yes ... sir?"

"So then it's safe to say that if you want to have sex with a man, you will. Is that correct?"

"Yes."

"Consensual sex?"

"Yes."

"Did you want to have sex with the gentleman in question?"

"No," I turned my eyes to the rapist. My turn to stare through him. "And he's not a gentleman."

"Objection," said the bitch.

"Over-ruled," the judge said.

"Ms. Preston, did you tell him that you didn't want to have sex with him?"

"Yes. I said no. More than once. I said no."

"Just to clarify, You said no, and he forced himself on you?"

"Yes."

He came up to the stand, gently patted the top of my hand, and said, "Thank you, Paige." He squeezed my hand briefly, then walked back toward his table and said, "Your Honor, I have no further questions."

I took a deep breath. "Thank God," I said to myself.

We bid farewell to my attorney, Dr. Morea, and even Janie, who stumbled through an excuse to have to run out. Before I could thank her for coming, she scurried through the door leaving her deeply spiced perfume in her wake. I wanted to be mad at her. I wanted to hit someone, and she would have probably let me, but I understood.

Janie knows me better than anyone. She knows how important I hold my privacy, and she saw it get plastered across the courtroom. I knew the reason why she left so quickly was because she had no idea what to say to me. I'm not mad at her for that.

She will call me in a few days, and she isn't going to mention this at all ... until I bring it up. Then she's going to tell me what an asshole the attorney was, how wonderful I handled myself, and that she's proud of me. But right then, as I watched her hurry through the door, I knew she was just as upset as I was, and she needed a minute to cool off.

Blake and I stood alone together after everyone left. We didn't say anything, just stood side by side. I finally started walking toward the door. He opened the door and ushered me to go first. The heat zapped me, wrapping me in a blanket of thick sticky humidity. Sweat dripped down my back. My heart seemed to forget how to beat normally. All of the anger, the shame, the pain of the last few months fell down on top of me at once, and I felt like I might pass out.

Blake grabbed my hand and pulled me into him. He wore a suit, light gray with a white button down shirt. He had loosened his tie and opened his collar, and I could see little droplets of sweat on his neck.

"Want to get a drink? I need a drink," he said to me as he brushed his lips over my knuckles.

"Yes. Would love to get a drink. A big one," I replied.

We quickly found a little bar, ducked in, and each ordered a martini, his dirty, mine with a twist.

And we talked. We talked about the trial, about the way the rapist sat there thinking he was unbreakable the entire time and that look on his face. Blake could only see him from the side, so he got the full description from my point of view in the courtroom.

He listened, and then he told me he was proud of me. I didn't bring up the line of questions surrounding my sexual history, and neither did he. What a relief. After we finished our martinis, we decided to head closer to home for a nightcap at our dive bar where we ended up drinking much more than a nightcap before eventually walking home.

By the time we made it back to B's place, my head was doing breaststrokes. It felt great not to be filled with thoughts of Scout or dread of the trial. We brushed our teeth, laughing, falling all over each other, pulled off our courtroom attire, and tumbled clumsily into bed. If felt like the old us. B immediately fell asleep, his breath slowing into a dull snore. I giggled to myself and rolled over draping my leg over his body. I fell asleep not too long after.

I wake frequently in the night. It's kind of my norm now that I'm not taking medication, so when I begin to drift into the slumber I so desperately need, I try to embrace it. I was there, grasping the edge of the deep sleep I longed for when B stirred beneath my leg.

He didn't speak, just pulled my panties off of me, rolled me onto my other side and then ... well, then he ravaged me. Animal like, raw, rough, unfeeling. He pounded into me, flesh against flesh, savagely, mercilessly.

He grabbed my bicep for support, digging his long fingers into my skin. He then turned me and positioned me on all fours and continued his foray. He pulled my hair, and I jerked my head in the direction he pulled as he bit into the back of my neck. I pushed back into him, begging him to take me, to make me cry out in pain, to use me, and he did. I clawed the sheets as he dug his fingers deeper into my skin, possessing me, claiming me as his to take, to own, to devour. And I let him. I surrendered.

He growled deep in his throat, stiffened, and collapsed on my back, weakly throbbing within me. He took a deep breath and rolled off. Then he turned me onto my back and looked down still panting with his soft green eyes. He brushed my hair off of my sweaty brow and ran a thumb across my bottom lip, and then we stared at each other in the dark, neither of us breaking the silence with unnecessary words.

A few minutes later, he relaxed back onto his pillow, and then shortly, his breath slowed again into his raspy drunk snore.

I smiled at myself in the dark ignoring the pain slowly creeping through my body. Finally, some connection that we so desperately needed. Maybe it was the trial, maybe hearing about my past made him need to mark me, to claim me somehow. To make me his.

And then the evening, the drinking, the laughing. I mean, Blake laughed ... a lot ... we had a little bit of normal in our life ... even if it was just for a little while.

Today was a terrible day, but tonight I had a taste of my old B-Large. Even if it was only for a while, we connected. Finally. I know I cannot bring back Scout. God I would if I could. But maybe I'm a step closer to bringing back Blake, and tonight I saw him in there, my sweet funny Blake. It's not much longer now.

Apologies

Dear Stephanie,

Blake couldn't even look at me the next day after he ravaged me in his bed. Back before Scout, we would lie in bed together in the morning. He would play with my hair and kiss my head and sometimes that would lead to more. Those were the best mornings, but not this time.

He jumped out of the bed, rushed through his shower, didn't shave, and left without a good-bye. I watched him from under the covers, silently begging him to climb back in and warm me again, but he didn't even take a glance in my direction.

After I heard his door close and the sound of the lock turn, I got up to examine the damage his nocturnal intrusion left on my skin. My thighs ached as I walked into his bathroom and turned on the light. I looked at myself in the mirror. Finger shaped bruises muddled my upper arm. I pulled my hair off of my neck and discovered the bite marks he left behind. He set out to mark his territory, and he succeeded. I needed to reach out to him.

I sent him a quick text: *Call me when you get a chance.*

When he didn't respond, I called him. Twice. Both times he sent me to voicemail. I know when I'm being sent to voicemail, and I took the hint. After the second failed attempt to make contact, I decided to head out myself. I went home and as quickly as I could, got ready, grabbed a battered book that I've read a hundred times, and headed for the bar.

I looked at my watch realizing that it was much too early for a drink and strolled mindlessly into the coffee shop at the end of our street. I drank my coffee and tried to read my book, but my mind drifted to Scout and to Blake. She's always there in the corner of my mind even if I try to ignore her.

Finally, at 12:00, I headed to the dive bar where I proceeded to get downright smashed hoping that maybe alcohol could quiet her absence and the pain of Blake's indifference.

It was Saturday, so I knew Blake hadn't gone to work, but he didn't say where he went either. He just left, and I didn't feel like I owed him the courtesy of being there when he returned from wherever he went. So I sat at the bar by myself, and took shots, and drank martinis, and laughed with Kirk the cute new bartender who was viciously flirting, and whom I was picturing naked on top of me. Each drink made me more pissed at Blake, and each shot went straight to my underused libido. By mid-afternoon, I made up my mind that I would be joining Kirk at his place that night.

Then my phone buzzed.

B-Large: *Where are you?*

Me: *What does it matter?*

B-Large: *I'm home. Just wondering where you are.*

Me: *Out.*

B-Large: *Okay? You pissed at me?*

Me: *Yes.*

B-Large: *Okay.*

And the texts ended. I ordered another drink, unbuttoned another button on my blouse, and seductively leaned into Kirk as he placed my martini in front of me. He looked down at me with his blue bedroom eyes as I bit my lip, encouraging his invitation.

"I thought you might be here," said Blake's voice from the chair next to me.

"What are you doing here?" I asked Mr. Selfish Asshole.

"I came to join you for a drink." He looked at Kirk, "Ketel One martini, dirty ... please." Then he looked back at me. "Making new friends?" Kirk looked back and forth between me and Blake and then puffed out some air and walked away.

"What do you care?"

"I don't care. Just wondering if I was interrupting something." I rolled my eyes at his attempt to be coy.

"Maybe."

He took a long drink from his martini and set it down. Then he reached over with his graceful long fingers and squeezed my thigh, whispering in my ear, "Why are you mad at me, Paige? Is it about last night?" I winced when he touched my leg. "I shouldn't have done that. I'm sorry."

"What do you mean you shouldn't have done that? You shouldn't have fucked me? You haven't fucked me in months, Blake. No that's not why I'm mad at you, you idiot. I'm mad at you for not fucking me this morning."

"Lower your voice, Paige. Your boyfriend over here doesn't want to hear about our fucking."

I took a deep cleansing breath and spoke in the lowest voice I could muster considering the amount of tension I felt in my neck and shoulders. "I don't like to be ignored."

"What are you talking about, Paige?"

"This morning. You left. After pounding me like a hooker last night. You got up and left, and you didn't tell me where you were going, and you didn't say good-bye or see ya later or even go fuck yourself. You just left. Then you ignored my calls."

"Paige, Jesus. I did tell you where I was going. I had a tee-time with my dad and brothers this morning. Golf, Paige, remember? I told you about it a while back. They haven't seen me in weeks, and they're worried about me. About you, too. I didn't answer your calls because the country club doesn't allow phones on the golf course. I had mine in my pocket. I sent your calls to voicemail. You didn't leave me one, so I figured it wasn't important."

I rolled my eyes and folded my arms. I'm super mature when I'm drunk.

"Seriously, Paige. You're being ridiculous."

"You left at like 6:30 this morning. It's almost five. Golf doesn't take that long."

He drained the last of his martini in one big gulp and rubbed his eyebrows together. Then he motioned for another drink to Kirk who had taken up residence at the opposite end of the bar avoiding our heated discussion. B reached for my hand which was still folded in a pout and pulled it to him.

"I went to the cemetery after golf. I wasn't going to tell you. I needed to be with her for a little while."

"Oh." I looked up at him, and squeezed his hand, "I'm sorry I'm such an ass." I haven't been to the cemetery since we buried her. I'm not sure I can. It's just so ... final.

He offered me his crooked grin in response, "It's okay. I forgive you ... ass. Have another drink. Then I'll take you home and make up for this morning."

We drank several more drinks and then headed home.

When we walked through his door, Blake pulled me into him and said, "I'm sorry for last night, for being so rough with you. I felt," I watched him swallow, "I had to have you. I don't know ..." I placed my finger over his lips.

"Shhh, B. It's fine. I needed you, too."

He kissed me, soft but deep and guided me back to his room. He laid me down on the bed and slowly started to pull off my clothes.

"It doesn't feel right to try and be normal," he said, as he removed my jeans.

"I know, but being not normal feels so horrible."

He looked at me. Torn. I could tell. His body told him to take me, but his mind fought it. I bit his lip, and rolled over, straddling him. I undressed him first and then finished myself.

"We need this, B." I took him, welcomed him into me. We were gentle, visiting each other's bodies like it was our first time, reacquainting ourselves, cautious of the other but hungry, and together we found what we needed, some comfort, some normal, and we both gave it freely.

When we finished, neither of us said a word. He laid his head on my chest. I ran my fingers through his curls, massaging his scalp until he drifted to sleep. As soon as I heard his breath slow and his body twitch, I leaned down and kissed the top of his head.

"I love you," I whispered to the dark.

Arrangements

Dear Stephanie,

Sometimes things fall into place. Sometimes they have to be manipulated and turned and twisted until they finally take shape. Manipulation comes naturally to me. Another gift, I guess.

We still have this house that's just sitting unoccupied and empty waiting for a family to move in and fill it with laughter and love. I drive by it sometimes and pretend that we can go back.

I imagine the night that we closed. The night Blake proposed. I wonder what the ring looks like. What would Blake have chosen for me? I feel his emotion when he whispered "Marry me" into my ear. I wonder what would have happened if my womb had not chosen that moment to betray me, if he didn't have to rush me to the hospital. Would I have said yes? Would we plan a big wedding with a fluffy white dress and flowers and guests? I've tried to imagine us in it now. Without her. I can't. We can't. There is no future now.

I sit outside of the house sometimes and wonder what it would have been like to bring Scout home. To decorate her nursery. Pink flowers and green and white checkers, a white custom made sleigh crib, an antiqued chandelier hanging from the ceiling, a plush white rocker in the corner, a framed photo of the three of us on her dresser. She looks at the camera with round blue eyes, B and I can't be bothered to take our eyes off of her. She smiles, a big toothless grin, with chubby cheeks, and dimples on her ankles.

I imagine holding her to my chest, rocking her to sleep, soft lullabies playing in the background, shushing her tears away, kissing her tiny fuzzy head, and she smells of powder and baby. Delicious, delectable. Alive.

B and I haven't discussed her. I can't bring her up, and neither can he. But I know ... she haunts his soul the way she does mine. This hole in my heart ... it's permanent. Blake's too. We can try to ignore it, attempt to move on, pretend to not grieve, but she's there in every breath, in every beat of our shattered hearts. Always there. But the reality is, she's gone. She's in her box in the ground, and things must continue without her, which leads me to my plans.

First things first. Meet with my finance guy, Mr. Woods. He's handled my family's finances for years, and once I was an adult and had access to my trust fund, he took over for me too.

There are a lot of loose ends to tie up still. I want to arrange for the house to be paid for in cash ... for Blake. He can sell it, move into it and fill it with a bunch of kids, or give it away. I don't really care. I just don't want him to have to deal with it after ... well after.

Not only do I have my trust fund, but I've managed the money well. I've made good investments and purchased properties. He may have been an idiot emotionally, but my father's business sense was genius, and I paid attention to his advice.

He wanted to pass on the family business to his children. He retired a few years ago and did just that, giving Paul, Patrick, and me equal shares. Paul has been working for my father for years since he graduated college and seamlessly stepped up as my father stepped down. Patrick held his shares so that he could travel and play, which is pretty much all he's done since he graduated college, but I sold my shares almost immediately to my brothers. I didn't want any part of it, and invested much of my earnings into everything Mr. Woods suggested. My own portfolio is nothing to laugh at. In fact, B-Large would be quite impressed, and he will be. It's his when I die.

Second: This time I plan to take something strong. I'm not doing the novice bullshit. I'm going for gold ... crossing the finish line. I want Oxy. I've done my research. This stuff works. I already contacted two of my old guys. I'm waiting to hear back. Tic Toc.

Third: Square things up with my mother. She sits, staring at the ceiling, through her window, still refusing to say a word to me, to Blake, to anyone. I visited once after Scout died ... to tell her. No emotions. I didn't really expect any. I made her a promise that day, one that I intend to keep.

I wanted to wait until the trial ended to find out the fate of the man who raped me, but I don't care about him anymore. I did my part. I confessed my dirty secrets for all that love me to hear as he watched unmoved. I can't be there if they let him go, and after what his attorney did to me, they might. I never want to see him again, and I can make that happen.

Then, of course, there's that precious man who melts me with his crooked grin, and Steph, he's using it more and more. Behind his shadowed eyes, I can see the playful Blake. Blake will be fine. He'll be sad. He'll miss me, but he'll survive. He can. He's not broken. He knows how to heal.

My grief holds him back, even if we never discuss it. I know what I should do. He will be so much better off without me. Part of me thinks I should break up with him, end it badly, make him get over me, but I don't know if I can. I depend on him now for so much. And I'm selfish. I need him to breathe even if I don't plan to do so much longer.

There is a pull, a force that draws me to him, and when we are together, it's not good, but it's better. I hate to leave him, but I'm toxic. He can do so much better. I can't give him the love that he wants, but I can't let him go. Like I said, selfish. Some things never change.

I guess it's time to set the plan in motion.

I meet with Mr. Woods tomorrow. My stomach churns just thinking about it. This is happening. Finally.

Oonvdagohvi

Dear Stephanie,

The rain pelting quietly on my window echoes the tears in my heart. I woke this gray morning early, chilled. Blake had taken the covers in the night, and I lay there naked, the breeze from the ceiling fan leaving goose bumps on my flesh. I rolled over and snuggled next to him trying to soak his warmth into my bones.

I knew what today held, and I was afraid. In the dark morning, I prepared myself for my task. I argued with my mind, telling it that I was doing the right thing and finally convinced myself to get out of bed. I kissed the back of Blake's curly head and then his shoulder. Then I crept out of bed and threw on the clothes I wore the day before and snuck over to my apartment. When I got to my place, I ditched yesterday's dirty clothes for my favorite robe.

Thunderclaps announced the storm that was brewing, and I watched thousands of lightning strikes illuminate the Dallas skyline from my window. What a dramatic way to start this day. I wrapped my big terry cloth robe around my body and stood at my window while drinking a steaming hot cup of coffee. I continued to mentally prepare myself for the day and congratulated myself on a job well done last week. I got the phone call yesterday that everything was settled and in writing.

Making arrangements for my estate went quite well. Mr. Woods made some helpful recommendations regarding my money, or rather Blake's money now. We met with my attorney, updated my living will, and finalized everything under the guise that I just wanted to be prepared.

I left Janie's foundation my typical yearly contribution and even decided to give a very healthy one-time donation to The March of Dimes. Mr. Woods wanted to argue with that, but I had a dead baby on my side, so what could he say? The money is situated.

I smiled to myself, still standing at the window. By this time, the lightning and the clouds had quieted, but the rain continued to pour, and the morning threatened a dark and gloomy day.

I pulled myself away from my thoughts.

I grabbed the bottle of Oxy that I was able to procure thanks to my ever faithful guy and poured out a handful of pills. I closed them in a plastic Ziploc bag and banged them with a mallet to pound them into a white powder. After careful examination, I placed them in my bag and began my morning routine.

I left the apartment about an hour later and headed to my favorite French bistro where I ordered a cup of scalding hot tomato bisque, my mother's favorite. I grabbed the white paper bag and ducked under the canopy outside opening my umbrella.

"Beautiful day?" a gentleman said as he held the door open for me, motioning to the pouring rain outside.

"Yes it is," I replied with a smile and hopped out into the rain, grateful for the umbrella to keep me dry.

When I reached my car, I shook the umbrella and threw it in my backseat. Then I pulled out the soup and sprinkled the contents of the baggie into the soup, stirring it into the creamy contents of the cup. I replaced the lid and drove to the home listening to the squeak of my windshield wipers.

I ran from my car to the door, tightly gripping the white paper bag, heart pounding in my chest. Why was I so nervous? This was part of my plan, something that I made peace with months ago, even before Scout died. It was the right thing to do, but that didn't change the fact that if I loosened my grip on the paper bag and my umbrella, my fingers and their trembling might give me away. I stopped before I reached the door and took three deep breaths trying to calm my timorous hands.

I closed my umbrella and left it in the holder by the door, then strolled past Blanche, trying to blend into the floral wallpaper. No such luck.

"Hi, Ms. Parnevik. How are you and Blake doing?"

That's such a loaded question. How are we doing? Well, I'm going to kill myself so that Blake can have a normal life. I replied with: "Better," because that's kind of the truth.

"I'm really sorry, Paige," she said and grabbed my arm.

I swallowed the cotton that had formed in my mouth and managed a "Thank you, Blanche." Then I quickly made it back to my mother's room where she lay in her bed on her back, stark and beautiful, staring at the ceiling.

I stood in the doorway for a moment soaking her in, noticing how serene she looked, picturing her little painted box, her tiny handgun, and the note that she left me all of those years ago. I tried to imagine her thoughts. I wondered if she thought of me, of Scout, if she even understood what had happened, what was happening to her. I cleared my throat to announce my arrival. She didn't move, just continued to stare. I closed the door behind me and slowly walked to her.

I pulled a chair next to the bed and took her hand in mine. I had practiced my speech in my head over a thousand times. Still, summoning the words seemed impossible. Finally, I spoke.

"Mom," my voice cracked. I cleared my throat. "Mom, I'm sorry this has taken me so long. I didn't plan it this way. I wanted to move you into a house, into our house, with me and Blake ... and Scout." I took a deep breath and sighed as

I let it out. The rehearsed speech no longer seemed necessary. I took out the soup and set it on the table next to her bed. I raised her bed, retrieved a brush from my bag, and brushed her long, dark hair, pulling it forward letting it lay in front of her shoulders. Silver hair framed her face, but the rest of her hair was still shiny and black. I pulled out my powder and applied it gently to her skin and colored in her dry cracked lips with my red lipstick.

I grabbed a spoon and the soup. "It's tomato bisque," I announced to the silent room. It might have been my imagination, but I think the corner of her lip twitched at that. I took a small spoonful and placed it between her now red lips. She opened her mouth, and as she swallowed, she closed her eyes. We repeated this until I scraped off the last bit from the sides of the Styrofoam cup.

I put the cup and the spoon back into the paper bag and placed it next to my purse. Then I reached over and grabbed the remote control and turned on her music. My plan was to leave immediately after, but I couldn't.

At first I held her hand and sat in my chair, listening to the music and the rain quietly pelt on her window in the background. It took longer than I had expected. I felt a sudden urge to get closer to her, to feel her hold me again, like she did when I was a child, so I climbed into her bed and laid my head on her chest. Then I whispered, "Go to sleep, Mom."

I held back the tears that threatened an assault, feeling the steady breathing of my mother, listening to the thumping of her heart in her chest. When her breathing began to slow, I embraced her. Then I climbed out of her bed, kissed each side of her face and her red stained lips, closed her soft eyelids over her dark eyes, and said, "Donvdagohvi." It means until we meet again, and she said it every time she left and followed it with a kiss to my forehead. I pictured her, young, vibrant, stunning, and hoped that her journey to wherever she was going was easy.

I grabbed my purse and the tattered white paper bag and left, closing the door behind me. As I passed Blanche on my way out, I told her that my mother was sleeping, hoping to buy some time before she was discovered. Then I ran out into the rain, forgetting my umbrella, and jumped into my car.

I laid my head on my steering wheel, expecting the flood of tears to fall from my eyes, but instead I smiled. One step closer ...

Peace

Dear Stephanie,

My mother died two days ago. I imagine her young and beautiful, hair swaying as she walks in the sun that she adored so much with a healthy tubeless Scout in her arms. I can dream. I'm not sure if there is a Heaven or a Hell. I battle with my beliefs. I want to believe that they're in this beautiful place with golden streets and pearly gates and angels with big wings, so I go to that place in my head when I think of them, and I convince myself that it exists, this paradise the priests spoke of in Mass.

My mother told me once of the Cherokee belief of afterlife, that there are seven heavens reserved only for those who followed rules and behaved. A pleasant place where the good people spend eternity. I think my mother would be considered good. She was just a victim of my dad's selfishness, and her actions were only reactions to what he did.

I can't blame her anymore, and I don't. If what they believe is true, I can only hope that she and Scout are in one of the heavens. I don't care which one, as long as they're together. I wonder if I will go there. My dad would say that suicide is a morbid sin which will send me to hell where I probably deserve to go anyway, but not Scout. And not my mother.

I knew he would expect it, so once I received the news of my mother's passing from my brother Paul, I visited with Dr. Morea. I already had an appointment, so I dove right into it as soon as I sat on the fluffy purple couch.

"My mom died."

Dr. Morea crossed his foot over his knee and leaned into me from his purple chair. "I'm so sorry, Paige."

"Why do people always say that? 'I'm so sorry.' Do you think your being sorry makes her less dead?"

"Well, no, Paige. It doesn't. Are you mad about something?"

"What's there to be mad at, Doc. Life's just a bowl of cherries right now."

"Death is difficult to accept sometimes, Paige."

"Are you kidding, Doc? Hard to accept? No, I'm not mad about my mom's death. I'm relieved. She has been stuck in hell for a long time, and now at least she is ... wherever she is. I've *accepted* it."

I let out a breath of air.

"Paige, it's okay to be upset. You've had to deal with a lot of loss lately, and I'm really proud of you for how well you've been handling it all."

Little does he know.

"Yeah, I'm peachy."

He leaned in and put his hand on my knee, looking at me through silver specked eyebrows.

"I need to ask you something now, Paige, and I need you to be honest." I nodded. "I know your coping mechanisms, Paige. I have to ask. Have you experienced any suicide ideation lately?"

We've talked about this every session since Scout died. I guess he thinks my mother's death is going to send me over the edge. Suicide ideation is a plan to kill myself.

"No." I lied.

"How do you plan to get through all of this?"

"All of this? I'm here, aren't I? And I have Blake."

"And how is Blake doing?"

"Better. He's sad about my mom, sad for me, but he's getting better. He went back to work."

"Are you mad at him for that?"

"No, I'm not mad at him for that."

I was mad at the world. At Blake for being perfect. At Dr. Morea for caring about me, at Scout for dying, at everyone. And at myself for still being alive, but I couldn't let Dr. Morea know that, or he would see right through me, right through my plan.

Time to put on an Oscar winning performance.

"I'm sad, Doc. I'm sad about my mom. I'm more than sad about Scout. I'm broken."

"Are you taking your medications?"

"Of course, and I'm meditating. I even started back to yoga last week," I lied. "Don't worry. I'm dealing with this the way you've taught me."

"Paige, it's going to get harder before it gets easier. I am proud of you for the way you're handling this, but you need to pay attention and let me know if you start having any of your typical suicidal thoughts."

"Of course, Dr. Morea. I have you on speed dial."

He grinned then, lips framed by his salt and pepper whiskers.

And the Oscar goes to ...

He walked me to the door and said, "Keep it up," forming a grin without showing his teeth.

"Of course, Doc." I started toward the stairs but turned back quickly. I ran up to him and gave him a huge full frontal hug, squeezing my chest into his. He stood rigid. I didn't really expect him to hug me back. He's the real deal, professional and caring, but never ever would cross the line. I've seen a lot of therapists, and he by far is the best one. He deserved a proper good-bye.

"Dr. Morea," I said looking into his dark eyes, "Thank you ... so much." And the first actual tear of the day filled my eye.

He let out a breathy laugh before saying, "Sure, Paige. I'll see you in two days, right?"

I smiled at him and turned to leave. "Paige," he called after me, but I kept walking. "Paige," he said louder. I looked back, smiled, and waved as I turned the corner and took the first step down the stairs.

Sitting in therapy, I figured it out. I can't let Blake and Dr. Morea think that I'm sad. They have to believe that I'm handling everything well, without the lingering thoughts of suicide. I can do this. I'm great at charades. Taking this new found knowledge with me, I fired off a text to Blake when I got into my car.

Me: *Hey, B ... want to meet at the dive after work?*

B-Large: *Sounds great. I'll try to wrap up a little early.*

Me: *I'll save you a seat. Better hurry ... Kirk's working tonight ;)*

I had some time to kill, so I drove to the cemetery and parked my car at the bottom of the hill. This was my first visit since her funeral. As I approached her headstone, I noticed a bouquet of fresh pink tulips in the vase over her grave. Blake. I knelt down and traced her name with my finger on the rose colored stone. Scout Elizabeth Demopoulos.

Blake suggested that we give her my middle name when we filled out her birth certificate. I couldn't make myself look at the dates, so I took a tulip out of the vase and placed it over the numbers. At least I won't have any more birthdays to remind me. At the bottom of the headstone were the words, "Always in our hearts." I thought it was cliché when we picked that phrase, but it seemed perfect at that moment.

I lied down in the grass and rested my head on the cold stone. I closed my eyes and let the sun warm me as I listened to the wind and the birds sing a summer's song. I could almost feel her, and my heart swelled in my chest. I patted the mound where small clusters of fresh grass blew with the breeze and whispered, "always in my heart ... sweet baby." I kissed my fingertips and pressed them into the dirt, leaving four prints behind. Then I gathered myself and walked back to my car.

I drove home and parked in the garage deciding it would be best to walk to the bar. I breathed in the warm afternoon air preparing myself for another performance with Blake. It felt great to walk into the darkness of the bar.

As I hopped up onto the barstool, Kirk came over and asked for my order, a double Ketel One martini with a twist. I had only taken a few sips when I turned to the door to see B coming through it still dressed in his work clothes, tie loose around his neck. His eyes smiled when they met mine.

He walked up behind my stool and wrapped his arms around me, kissing the back of my neck. I could feel his stubble, and shivers ran down my spine. I swiveled my stool around and grabbed him around the waist, wrapping my legs around his thighs and offered him my lips. We kissed briefly. Then he cocked his head to one side and said, "Good day?"

"Great day. Better now," I smiled.

He sat down on the stool next to me and pulled mine closer to his. "Good. I'm glad." He looked around. "This place is dead."

"Yep," I replied sipping my martini.

He leaned into my ear. "Meet me in the bathroom in five." Then he hopped off his stool and headed for the restroom, casually glancing over his shoulder and meeting me with a mischievous moss colored glare. I shooed him away, turning to see if anyone had noticed and then quickly walked back to the unisex restroom.

As soon as I opened the door he grabbed my wrist, pulled me into the bathroom, and shoved me against the wall, locking the door with his free hand, and he kissed me, a long satisfying, scruffy kiss. We pushed clothes out of the way. Then he picked me up and pulled my legs around his waist, and we banged against the wall, breathless and needy and quickly peaked. He gently lowered my feet back to the floor and kissed me, catching his breath. We laughed as we rearranged clothing and pulled ourselves together.

"Where did that come from?" I asked him as I touched up my lipstick in the mirror. He ran a hand through his thick locks.

"I don't know. I just saw you sitting on the stool and had to have you, I guess." He teased me with his crooked grin looking at me in the mirror. I turned around and pulled him into me.

"You can have me again if you want."

He kissed the top of my head. "I plan to. Over and over again tonight. If you're up for it, but let's have a drink first."

We each had two drinks then decided to head back to Blake's where he fulfilled the promise he made me in the bathroom. He opened his door then pulled me into his apartment through his living room, through his bedroom, and into the bathroom where he started the water of his shower.

As the steam filled the room, he slowly peeled off my clothes. He started with my shirt, pulling it up over my head. Then he grasped a loop of my jeans and pulled me into him, kissing me as he unclasped my bra, letting it fall to the floor. He unbuttoned my jeans and slid them down my hips. I stepped out of them and started to reach for his pants, but he shook his head stopping me. He got down on his knees and pulled my panties off. I grabbed his hair and leaned down to breathe in his scent from the top of his head. He looked up at me, resting his scruffy chin on my stomach. "God, I love you, Paige."

"I know," I whispered. He stood up and kissed me again, this time allowing me to undress him. We got into the shower, where he stood behind me and washed my hair and my back. "I know how you are about germs. Sorry I fucked you in a bathroom." I felt his laugh on my back.

"Don't apologize. For some reason, when fucking is involved, I forget all about the germs," I said letting him run his fingertips up and down my skin. When we finished the shower, Blake stopped the water, and wrapped a soft white towel around me. I used a different towel to soak up the dampness from my hair. He ran into his room and plopped down on his bed, wet and naked waiting for me to join, smiling at me. I dropped my towel and skipped to the bed, smiling back.

We spent the evening pretending we didn't miss her, that we were our old selves, unbroken and happy. Around 11:00, we realized we hadn't eaten, so he shuffled through a drawer in his kitchen looking for a decent delivery menu. We settled on sketchy Chinese food and ate it using chopsticks on the floor in his living room. I knew what he wanted to do, and I let him. He wanted to take my mind off of all of the loss, and I wanted to soak in one last night with my sweet B.

I realized something as we sat on the floor in his living room.

"Play for me, B."

"What do you mean, play?"

"Your guitar. I want to hear you."

"No, I only play for strangers," he said with a shy smile.

"You played for my mom."

"I know, but stop. It's different." He got up and started clearing away our trash from dinner.

"Please, B. I want to hear you."

He walked to the coat closet and retrieved his guitar case. He gently pulled out an acoustic guitar and settled himself back on the floor across from me, casually leaning against his couch. I pushed myself up to my knees, eager with anticipation and watched as his fingers curled around the neck.

"What do you want to hear?"

"Anything."

He pushed a stray curl from his eye and cocked his head to one side, then smiled, wrapping me with rays of sunshine in the dark room.

He took a deep breath. I watched his fingers begin to move, listening to the squeak of the strings as he rubbed his fingertips along them. Then he started to sing "More Than Life" one of my all-time favorite songs by Whitley. He sang every word, looking at me, and he meant it. I sat in awe, watching his beautiful fingers move along the strings. When he finished the song, I clapped three slow claps.

"Wow," I said.

"Did you like it?" he asked me. He touched my soul with his voice. Of course I liked it.

"Blake, I loved it. Will you play another?"

I listened to his voice, to the shriek of the guitar when he changed chords, and I watched him. He leaned over the instrument, dropped his head, and closed his eyes. I couldn't breathe. I felt myself wanting one more day with him, more time to absorb just a little bit more of him into me. I moved to sit down next to him, and he stopped for a second, kissing the top of my head. Then he just played, I don't even know if it was a song, without singing. I felt everything and nothing all at once.

We finally made it to bed around 1:00 a.m. and settled into each other to fall asleep. As he pulled me into him, I closed my eyes and smiled. I grabbed his hand and squeezed it three quick times. "I love you, too," he said as he rubbed his whiskered cheek against mine. Then he fell asleep slowly breathing behind me.

I turned over to face him and lightly kissed his parted lips. I traced my fingertip along his thick eyebrow and down the side of his cheek to the dimple on his chin. I ran my fingers through his dark waves, down the back of his neck, over his naked shoulder, down his elbow, then back up to his hand. I kissed his knuckles, each wonderfully talented finger.

I put my hand on his chest feeling his heart beat beneath the coarse curls then drew a line with my finger down his torso between the grooves of his abdomen to his belly button to the patch of hair below it. He jerked in his sleep causing my hand to quickly retreat. I hesitated to touch him again, not wanting to wake him, so I placed my hand under my head. And then I just watched him sleep in the dark for the rest of the night, memorizing every part of his beautiful perfection, wishing it was enough for me.

Epilogue

"Seven," *I say, taking the last pill, smiling as I drain the rest of my martini.*

I walk to the couch and lie down, propping a pillow behind my head and wait. I close my eyes and begin to meditate the way Dr. Morea taught me. I hear his voice in my head, "Imagine a place where you feel safe." I see Blake's face. He smiles at me, a full toothy grin. I smile back. I tell myself to breathe.

I can feel my heart beating rapidly in my chest. I know it will pass, but it scares me. I keep trying the meditation. I beg myself to fall asleep. My hands tremble as my heart continues to pound in my chest. I'm cold, so cold. I try to get up, but I can't move, so I close my eyes again, and count my breaths. One ... two ... three ... four ... five ... six ... seven.

My head feels like it's going to explode. My eyes burn. It's never felt like this before. One ... two ... three ... four. I hear banging. Over and over. I can't seem to open my eyes to see what it is. Banging. Pound, pound, pound.

"Paige!" Blake's voice. "Paige. Open the door." He sounds frantic. My voice won't work to tell him to go away. "Paige, goddammit! Open the fucking door!" He got my message.

I want to shout for him to leave, but my voice fails me. What is he doing here? The pounding continues. I can't figure out if it's my head or the door. Probably both. "Paige! Please," Blake yells.

He argues with someone outside. I can hear him. I try to move. My body stays velcroed to my couch. I want to open my eyes, but they won't work. "Carl, open this door. I don't care what she told you. She could be dead in there." I don't want him to find me like this. Don't do it, Carl, I silently beg my door guy to follow my instructions.

I hear the lock turn and footsteps running toward me. "Goddammit, Paige." It's Janie. She must have gotten my message, too. Why am I not asleep? She's walking around my kitchen. I can hear her heels tapping on my marble floors. "Fucking pills again," she says. "They want to know if she's breathing," I hear her say.

I can smell him. Blake. He picks my head up, holding the back with one hand. I feel his clammy finger on my neck. "She has a pulse. She's breathing. It's slow. Tell them to hurry up." His face is so close to mine. I can feel his breath on my skin. I want to reach up and pull him to me, but my arms won't work.

He takes my hand and squeezes it hard. "Not this, Paige. Not you, too. I am *not* better off without you. I don't care what you said," my voice message, "Don't go, Paige. Please. Please. You can't. I can't." He kisses my hand. It's damp with his tears. I feel his mouth close to my ear. Then he whispers, "Don't die on me, Paige. Don't you dare fucking die," he commands. "You don't want to do this."

I battle in my head. Don't I? Part of me wants to open my eyes. Part of me wants to fall asleep.

"Please wake up, baby." He's frantically shaking me by my shoulders. "Wake up, Paige!" He continues to shake. My head lulls back and forth. Then he lays it back down on the pillow. I beg my eyes to open. He's right. I don't want to do this anymore. I don't want to do this to Blake. He wins.

He squeezes my hand three quick times and lets go. I hear his footsteps walk away. No, don't go, please don't go, Blake.

Then chaos hits. I hear the EMT's. Hands probe me everywhere. My blouse rips. Hands push my chest. They lift me up and put me on a stretcher. I'm flying through a tunnel. I hear the ding of the elevator. My head is heavy but no longer pounds. I try to lift it, but my muscles won't work. I need to wake up. To tell him I love him. To at least give him that. I try to pry my eyes open. "Open!"

The door dings as we reach the ground floor. We roll through the door, and I feel the breeze on my face. Then I feel the stretcher being raised into the ambulance. I don't want them to take me away, not without telling him.

"Wait," it's Blake's voice. "Wait."

I feel a pierce of a needle into my right hand. Then the cold liquid courses through the veins in my hand.

"Sir, you can't ..."

"One minute," Blake interrupts. The ambulance shifts with his weight, and he's there next to me on my left side, holding my hand again as the EMT checks my pulse on the other wrist.

Blake whispers, "Paige, listen to me. I love you. From the minute I saw you in the hallway of our building, I've loved you, and I always will. When you wake up, I'll be there." He takes my left hand and slips something onto my finger, cold, round and heavy. The ring. He kisses my hand again. Then he brushes his lips over mine. "Will you please, please, baby ... just let me love you?"

I imagine his crooked grin, his smile, that smile, and see his green eyes light up as they see me. I remember the feel of his lips brushing over my knuckles. I hear his quiet contagious laugh. I feel him strong against my back in his bed, breathing slowly behind me, loving me. Always, and I want nothing more to be back there in his bed, smothered by his warmth, enveloped by him. Everything comes spinning into my head. Blake, my heart.

And suddenly, I force myself to take a deep breath. My eyes pop open. I see a blurry Blake above me, and I let out a weak, "Yes."

And then I hear nothing but silence.

A NOTE FROM THE AUTHOR

This book is a work of fiction. The characters and places are not real or based on any one in real life. Paige Preston represents a community of people who are afraid to discuss the dark cloud that haunts them.

Depression is not a joke. Mental illness is real. In America alone, somebody dies by suicide every thirteen minutes. *Every thirteen minutes.* If you have those undeniable, unavoidable thoughts, please reach out to someone. To anyone. Our world is not better without you. I promise. You are valuable. You are worthy.

If you know someone who suffers from depression or any other mental illness, don't try to fix them. Learn, research, and try to understand. It's not a matter of cheering them up, it's life and death in some cases. Be supportive, and never be afraid to tell somebody that you love him.

National Suicide Prevention Lifeline
www.suicidepreventionlifeline.org
800-273-8255
American Foundation for Suicide Prevention
http://www.afsp.org
National Institute of Mental Health
www.nimh.nih.gov

ACKNOWLEDGEMENTS

It's taken more than three years to get these pages in your hands, and I didn't do it alone. I had a lot of help from my circle of support, my little team who cheered me through this entire process.

To the people who spent hours with me reading this book multiple times, how can I even begin to thank you?

Kimberly: Six reasons why I owe you a huge shout out. #6. You helped create Paige. Thank you for the hours of conversations where we discussed her like she's a real person. #5. For telling me when things were ridiculous or stupid or unbelievable. #4 . For being straight forward and honest without telling me it was shite, even though the first draft I sent you was exactly that. #3. You helped write this book. I just did the typing. #2. For thirty years, you've held my hand. And the #1 reason why I am eternally grateful to you ... You never let go, my dearest friend.

Nikki, my soulmate, you're such an inspiration. You made me believe that my words were worth writing, and you pushed me to finish, even when I had every excuse in the world to stop. I will never be as brave or as strong (or as beautiful) as you are, but you inspire me to try and even to accessorize. I love you more than you love Yoda.

Beth, my MT, my LAS, my BBB, holy cow, if you didn't talk me off the ledge every time I wanted to throw my computer at the wall, I wouldn't be here. Thank you isn't enough for all that you've done: for dealing with my doubt and my neurosis, for pushing me to do it, for introducing me to such a warm family of bloggers, and for believing in this story. I am more than grateful that our little boys became friends.

Dave, I didn't want to send you my book. I have never been more terrified, but I am so glad you insisted that you read it because you gave me some of the most candid and useful advice I received, even if I didn't want to accept it at first. Thanks for reading so quickly and for sending me the play by play of the process. Those three days were highly entertaining and the beginning of one of my favorite friendships. Thank you for your support, for being a good friend, for believing in this story, and for always making me laugh . All of them.

Cortney and Sara, if we didn't have a constant text thread, I might lose my mind. Thanks for being the two other legs in this wobbly tripod.

Keller and Mallory, my favorite people on Earth, I'm not sure I will ever allow you to read this book, but without you, I would have never written it. Thank you for letting me spend countless hours in my chair with my nose in my laptop, saying, "just a minute," only to finally get you what you asked for an hour later. Thank you for making me laugh constantly, for keeping me grounded, and for making me a mom. You are my heart, both of you, and I breathe for you.

To my husband who never finishes a book, thank you first for reading all of mine and for giving me your honest feedback and for not freaking out when I told you I was secretly writing it. Your ability to remain calm astounds me, and in all of those moments when I was having my epic melt downs, you encouraged me to take breaks and to prioritize and to "take it easy." I couldn't have finished without your support.

Mom and Dad, thanks for being my biggest fans. LYM

To the blogging community, you have become like a second family to me. I'm not sure I know how I existed in life before I had you in my virtual world. Thank you all, my blogging buddies, my SisterWives. You're more than just online people to me now. You are real.

Jeri Walker, editor extraordinaire, where do I begin? Thank you for turning a grain of sand into a pearl. I handed you a mess of words, and you took those words, gave me some stellar advice, and somehow, I think we managed to create a novel from it. Without you, this book could not have come this far. I'm so glad Beth sent me to your website. Let's write some more, shall we?

And then the rest: Laura with LLPix Designs for my beautiful cover, Garrett Robinson for formatting and type-setting, Dave Baker, the best graphics designer on the planet for creating the beautiful Castle Press logo. Dawn with Gabel Photography for taking an actual decent picture of me and for even making it fun. Steven, thank you for giving a girl with zero fashion sense (and the inability to shop) specific examples of what a girl like Paige might wear. You dressed her.

And finally, and probably most importantly, to you. The reader of these words. Thank you for taking your precious time to read my book. I am humbled and so very grateful.